the WELL-LAID *Trap*

A WISHVILLE MYSTERY

kari lee townsend

NATIONAL BESTSELLING AUTHOR

OLIVERHEBER BOOKS

Thank you to the real-life Dream Team, Mike Zaccaria and Lauren Glaub, for helping me reach my full potential as the Bionic Woman. My new hips rock, and Captain America doesn't stand a chance. This one's for you!!

Thank you to Kim Zaccaria for letting me kill your husband off, and for helping get my details right!

And a special thank you to the real-life Lourdes Morales for inspiring me to write such a fun and feisty character as LuLu.

DEEP BENEATH THE WHISPER WOODS, where roots twist like ancient hands and shadows breathe secrets, there is a chamber. It is no ordinary hollow, but a vault—mirrored in Elarion below—that binds together two worlds.

Long ago, when humans and Dwellers still clashed and distrust ran like fractures through the earth, a Dweller Elder sought a power forbidden to both realms. Brilliant, ambitious, and blind to consequence, he crossed into the early human settlement and kidnapped a young villager, intending to fuse Dweller magic with human life and create a vessel strong enough to rule both worlds.

The ritual failed.

It tore the human apart. It destroyed the Elder's body. And in the terrible silence left behind, something unnatural remained— his consciousness, ripped free and burning with the need to reclaim a form.

What rose from that chamber was not a Dweller, nor a ghost, but a predatory echo.

An intelligence without a body. A hunger without a name. A mind that could slip into anyone or anything and twist their thoughts from the inside.

Its possession left only hollow shells behind. Its reach grew with every stolen will.

Left unchecked, it could have severed the realms forever. And so, for the first and only time, humans and Dwellers stood as one. With stone and spell, with oath and blood, they subdued the Elder's echo and sealed it away.

Thus, the Veiled Vault was forged—a prison of magic instead of iron. A spiral chamber where power loops curled endlessly inward, coiling stray energy back into the earth rather than letting it spill across the realms. But such knowledge could never be left in open hands.

The Vault was a wound between worlds, and wounds are easily torn wider. So, the Elders decreed secrecy. Only a chosen few were told where the chamber was hidden—the Enforcers sworn by blood and the Council bound by oath. Calderis, son of Vaerion, inherited the heaviest burden: guard the Vault and keep its truth buried.

Over time, few knew the full story. That was the safest way.

But Serenna, Guardian of the Well and mother of Lyra, knew. She helped reinforce the Vault when it stirred again in later years, giving more of herself than she could afford. Her warning lingered, etched into her daughter's pendant—an echo of sacrifice:

Stay away from the Vault, for its cost is more than you can bear.

CHAPTER
One

THE AIR IN WISHVILLE, our small Vermont mountain town, always smelled different in the summer. Not just the familiar pine-and-river freshness drifting down from the Whisper Woods, but the kind of sweetness that came from the summer solstice itself. By the second week of June, the town all but hummed with it. There were banners strung across Main Street, bakery windows lined with test batches of WishFest cookies, and the Wellies buzzed like honeybees everywhere they went.

Then there was me, trying to wrangle an official sign-up table while Vex pawed at the stack of volunteer clipboards as though they were his personal scratching posts.

You're wasting your time, his voice slipped across my thoughts like silk. *Half of these humans will flake out when they realize "volunteering" means sweating under the sun instead of parading around eating candied almonds.* He was half-cat, half-Whispen—the magical creatures from the enchanted world beneath the wishing well—and my best friend because he was the only one who knew what it was like to be me for the past three-hundred years.

"Not helping," I muttered under my breath, tucking a lock of my long, curly brown hair back into my ponytail, the streaks of gold, green, and burgundy shining in the morning sun.

Everyone thought I had highlights, but everything on me was all natural. I was half-human, half-Dweller, and had been the Guardian of the Well for the last century, tasked with keeping the ancient treaty between our worlds intact. Immortal Dwellers remembered our history, but this generation of mortal humans didn't have a clue other than what they'd read in old folklore stories.

They believed Elarion, Dwellers, and the magical wishing well were simply legend, and our seasonal WishFest festivals honored tradition by handing out wish tokens and encouraging attendees to place a wish in the well. They didn't realize the wish tokens were magical and the well granted one wish to a lucky recipient each season. It was my job as Chair of WishFest to keep the festivals running smoothly and protect the treaty.

Centuries ago, the Elders of Elarion and the town council members of Wishville formed a treaty to end the war between them, stating they would stay out of each other's realms so long as the well granted one wish per season.

And so, WishFest was born.

Betsy Plum from *The Twisted Loaf* bakery waddled up with a plate of sample tarts.

"Oh, Lyra, dear, let me set these out on the corner of the table." She plunked down the tray. "Volunteers work harder with sugar in them."

"They also disappear faster once they crash," I said under my breath then arranged the mini tarts anyway.

Sure enough, two passing teenagers swooped in like magpies.

Across the town square, laughter bubbled as the Wellies—Tilly, Belle, and Dot—unfurled a tangled string of bunting. We always decorated the square where all the businesses were, but the festival itself was up the hill by the well in a clearing in the woods. Tents and shacks would be decorated and filled with festival wares, while games and entertainment would take place across the green.

Shrieks drew my attention back to the Wellies, aptly named

because the elderly women were obsessed with all things related to the well. They considered themselves my self-appointed assistants. As quirky and odd as they were, they were the closest thing to family I had left since my human father died when I was a child and my Dweller mother went missing a century ago.

Somehow, in the five minutes the Wellies had been at it, they'd managed to knot themselves together like a three-person maypole.

"Left! No, my left, Belle!"

"You're choking me with ribbon, Tilly!"

"Don't yank, Dot, you'll pull my—oh, fiddlesticks, I'm falling…"

They went down in a pile of patchwork gingham skirts, sparkly floral hats, and polka dots. The whole crowd burst into applause. Only in Wishville would tripping over decorations qualify as entertainment.

I laughed with everyone else, but the sound felt like a paper boat set afloat on a fast river. Bright, flimsy, and quickly swept away. My mother used to say joy was a craft, not a miracle. *Stitch it while you have the daylight, Lyra.* The memory rose so vivid I could smell the chamomile oil she rubbed into my scalp when I couldn't sleep as a girl.

I blinked hard, and the square snapped back into focus: bunting flapping, sugar glazing the air, and a horn somewhere testing three flat notes. Vex pressed warmth against my calf, a living comma in the long sentence of the day.

You're drifting again, he murmured. *Take shorter memories. The long ones drown you.*

"I know," I whispered. "I'm trying." I pasted on a grin, though my chest still carried the faint ache of memory.

Mom would have loved this chaos. She had always found joy in the way Wishville prepared for its festivals, as if each crooked banner and crookedly frosted cookie was another heartbeat in the town's pulse.

A flicker of something tugged at me, unbidden, like the edge of a memory crystal catching the light. My mother's laughter, faint and silvery, echoing as if from far off. I blinked hard, and it was gone. Just the wind shifting through the bunting.

"Hey, um, hi?"

The voice pulled me back.

I turned to see a woman about my age, or rather, my age as humans saw it, somewhere in her late twenties—one human year equaled ten Dweller years—hovering near the sign-up table. She stood around five-foot-four, average height for human females, to my five-foot-ten, short for Dwellers. She had espresso-dark hair that fell in waves around her shoulders, warm olive skin kissed with summer sun, and an expression that was equally curious and wary.

"Sorry," she said quickly. "I wasn't sure if I should just write my name down or if there's, like, an interview process?"

I stifled a laugh. "This isn't the CIA. All I need is your name and what you'd like to help with. Unless you've got a criminal record involving funnel cakes, in which case we might have to talk."

Her smile bloomed then, wide and genuine. "Good to know. I'm Lourdes Morales, but everyone calls me LuLu. I just rented a cottage, like literally a few days ago, for the summer."

"Oh, nice. Where are you from?"

"Miami."

I blinked. "That's a long way away. I'm surprised you've even heard of our small town. We're quite remote."

"Ernie Maddox and my boss are college buddies. Since Marin left the news station for a bigger news gig in the city, I'm here to fill in for her until Ernie finds a permanent replacement." She shrugged. "I figured volunteering would be a good way to meet people."

I laughed. "You figured right. I'm Lyra Wells." I handed her a pen and gave a short bow. "Guardian of the Well and member of the Historical Society. Welcome to Wishville."

Her brows lifted. "Guardian of the Well?"

Whoops. Sometimes I forgot which realm I was in. "I mean Chair of WishFest. The Guardian part is mostly ceremonial," I said lightly. "It keeps me busy."

Vex hopped onto the table with the smooth arrogance of someone who considered himself mayor of Wishville, his sleek black fur glistening in the sun. He pinned his iridescent eyes on LuLu.

She smells new, he murmured in my head. *Like city dust and trouble.*

I shot him a look. "This is Vex. He thinks he runs the place."

"Oh, honey, you are one handsome fellow." LuLu reached out without hesitation, and to my surprise, Vex let her scratch behind his ears without so much as a disdainful flick. In fact, I was pretty sure he was purring.

That was new.

Then again, Vex had always liked trouble.

I narrowed my eyes as he purred so loudly the clipboards vibrated. He rarely gave humans more than a passing sniff. I wasn't sure what to make of the exception. His whiskers twitched against LuLu's wrist, and his eyes shifted from lake-glass green to gold, both curious and a little possessive.

She has the look of someone who runs toward a fire, he said. *People like that either rebuild the town...or they light a second match.*

"Comforting," I said dryly.

"I'm sorry, what did you say?" She looked at me quizzically.

I tucked the observation away. In Wishville, instincts mattered, and my verdict on her character was still out. She seemed nice enough, but I got the strangest feeling she was hiding something.

I shook off that crazy thought. "I was just wondering what you might want to help with?"

"Anything, really." She scanned the list. "Set-up, ticket booth, cleanup crew. Whatever you need."

"Careful," I warned her. "Say that too loud and Dot will rope you into manning the dunk tank."

LuLu laughed, and it was easy and bright. "I'm not afraid of a little water."

That, of course, earned another telekinetic comment from Vex. *She would say that. Humans always underestimate what water can hide, but I like her. She thinks I'm handsome, so she must have good taste.*

I ignored him and watched as LuLu neatly wrote her name on three separate slots. I arched an eyebrow. Enthusiastic? Brave? Maybe even desperate to belong. I knew that feeling well.

Behind us, the Wellies managed to right themselves, their ribbons streaming like battle flags. They immediately made a beeline for my table, obviously spotting fresh prey.

"New face!" Belle declared, her glittery sunhat askew. As a former opera singer, she was all about the sparkle. She grabbed the sign-up sheet and scanned the page. "Oh, you're lovely. LuLu? What an interesting name. You'll be perfect for the pie-eating contest. Just perfect."

"Or the fortune booth!" Dot countered, grabbing LuLu's hand. "She's got the eyes for it, doesn't she, Lyra? Dark. Mysterious. Magnetic." Dot blinked her own owl eyes behind her massive polka dot glasses. She owned *The Quench & Snoop Tea House*, selling wildly inaccurate fortunes in tea leaves.

"I was thinking ticket sales," LuLu said carefully, but they bulldozed right over her.

"Pshaw." Tilly scoffed. "No one remembers the ticket seller. Everyone remembers the girl with blueberry filling on her chin." Tilly was a retired herbalist who loved patchwork clothes and now owned a spell jar booth called *Bibbidi, Bottles & Boo*.

I caught LuLu's skeptical glance and rescued her. "How about we let her ease in this summer? Tickets, setup, maybe handing out water bottles. We'll work her up to competitive pie consumption next time if we don't scare her off from visiting again."

The Wellies groaned but relented, moving on to terrorize the next unsuspecting volunteer.

"Thanks," LuLu whispered, staring after them in fascination, "but I'm pretty sure this job is a temporary thing. At least I hope it is. I'm a city girl through and through."

Which made me wonder once again what her real story was.

"Either way, we're happy to have you here. Hopefully, you won't get bored. Not much happens in Wishville." I crossed my fingers that would be true this summer. The last thing we needed was a reporter snooping around, discovering things I was determined to keep hidden.

"Trust me when I say I don't mind being out of the spotlight for a bit." Her eyes clouded briefly. "I've had my fill of being the center of attention."

"Oh, trust me, the Wellies will gladly take over that role."

"The Wellies?" Her sleek brow arched high.

I pointed toward the three elderly women who had just accosted her. "Belle, Tilly, and Dot. Self-proclaimed experts on all things relating to the well." I rolled my eyes.

"Gotcha. They can have all the attention they want."

"They want plenty. Just wait and see."

The Wellies chose that moment to march by once more in a backwards conga line—Belle leading, Dot in the middle misreading the steps, and Tilly attempting to blow a kazoo that turned out to be a thermometer. Dot's teacup sloshed something lavender and alarming onto Belle's shoe.

"It's only a minor blessing," Tilly assured her. "Your ankles will dream of violets now."

LuLu looked at me with wide, delighted eyes. "Is this… normal?"

"Alarmingly so," I said. "They give each season…let's call it texture. Which inevitably involves more paperwork."

We shared a grin, and for the first time all day, something light unfurled in my chest. I was with Vex. I liked her. I normally kept my distance and didn't make friends because I outlived them and it hurt to see them go, but LuLu was only here for the summer. A temporary friend sounded perfect.

Maybe this summer wouldn't be so heavy after all.

The thought hovered in my brain like a shy firefly. I mentally cupped it carefully. Then the whisper from the woods brushed the back of my neck—cool breath and the faintest echo of my mother humming the old Well-song. Hope faltered, but I held it anyway.

If I let go of every bright thing, the dark might become permanent.

But then the wind shifted again, carrying another whisper from the woods. I felt it like fingers trailing down my spine. The same pull I'd felt earlier when I'd passed near the Whisper Woods. The same glimmer of memory that wasn't mine, tugging like a half-remembered dream…

Mother.

The thought sliced sharp, and for a moment, the world blurred. I saw her silhouette, just a shadow slipping between the trees on the night she vanished.

"Lyra?" LuLu's voice cut through the haze.

I blinked. The town square snapped back into focus. The smell of tarts. The chatter of neighbors. Vex's steady, watchful eyes. "Sorry." I forced a smile. "Just…thinking about all the work ahead."

If LuLu noticed the tremor in my voice, she didn't press. She finished signing her name and gave me another warm smile before heading off toward the fountain where Tilly was now trying to measure bunting with her shoe.

I let out a long breath.

The early summer sun pressed warm against my skin, but the chill that lingered beneath it had nothing to do with the weather. WishFest was supposed to be about celebration, tradition, and joy. But somewhere between the preparation and the laughter, something darker stirred, waiting and watching just up the hill beyond the edge of trees. And I had the sinking feeling that this year…no amount of sugar tarts or cheerful volunteers would be enough to keep it at bay.

∼

The lull between volunteer sign-ups was broken by a chorus of barking instead of another Wellie calamity. Or, more accurately, one enormous bark that reverberated across the town square like a brass bell.

Heads turned as Tasker—the Zaccarias' Golden Bernedoodle—came bounding in with his tongue lolling, a mess of fur and enthusiasm. At a hundred and twenty pounds, he was equal parts bear rug and earthquake, dragging sixteen-year-old Joey Zaccaria along by the leash.

"Tasker, slow down!" Joey called, his Hawaiian shirt flapping around him like a sail. He dug in his sneakers, but the dog had spotted Betsy Plum's tarts and was determined to make them his.

Behind them strolled his parents, Mike and Kim Zaccaria, looking every inch the couple everyone in Wishville adored. Mike's dark hair was cut neatly, though one lock always seemed to defy his tidy nature, and his olive complexion glowed under the summer sun. He had the steady build of a man who worked with bodies for a living—fixing knees and hips at his *Zac in Motion* clinic—and he carried himself with a quiet pride, as if everything from his shirt cuffs to the papers in his pocket had been deliberately arranged.

Kim, on the other hand, was his contrast—brown hair falling simply past her shoulders, pale complexion catching every glint of sunlight, and a notebook poking out of her oversized tote like it had been tossed there on a rush out the door. She smiled warmly, her blue eyes soft and intelligent, though a smudge of flour still clung to her sleeve. Knowing her, she'd been baking another elaborate cake between analyzing chemical reports as a toxicologist.

"Lyra," Mike greeted, his smile genuine and handshake firm. "Tell me you still have a few volunteer spots open for us."

I chuckled. "You? I thought I'd have to fight the Wellies for the honor of recruiting the Zaccaria family."

"Please don't," Joey muttered, finally getting Tasker under control with a treat in his pocket. "Dot already tried to sign me up for fortune telling. Something about my shirt making me look 'otherworldly.'"

Kim laughed, shaking her head. "You did volunteer, Joey. You promised Mrs. Green at *Wishville Wags* you'd hand out flyers."

"I said I'd *think* about it," Joey corrected, though the grin peeking out from beneath his wide-brimmed hat suggested he'd already caved.

Tony appeared then with their father's olive skin and athletic build, his lifeguard whistle still looped around his neck. Looking every bit the solid, steady older brother, he took the dog's leash from Joey—until Tasker jerked the leash again and nearly toppled him into a table of lemonade cups.

"Sorry!" Tony caught himself, his cheeks flushing. "He gets excited when he smells food."

"We'll call it enthusiasm." Mike took the leash firmly, and Tasker immediately sat, his tail thumping as if to prove his best-dog credentials.

"Smart dog," Belle observed, fanning herself with a sequined hand.

"Lazy dog," Joey countered. "You should see him when it's time for a walk. Suddenly he remembers his Bernese side and pretends he doesn't have legs. The only time he's crazy is when food is involved."

Laughter rippled through the crowd that had gathered, and Tasker sprawled dramatically in the grass, proving Joey's point.

"So," Mike said, turning back to me, "we wanted to pitch in before we head up to Lake Mistfall. The boys insisted."

Tony perked up. "It's our tradition. We do our part and then go camp by the water. Lake Mistfall is awesome. It's always covered in mist, making it look enchanted."

Joey leaned in. "Last year, I swear I saw a shadow swimming under the surface. Might've been a monster."

"Or a fish," Mike said, amused.

"Or a log," Kim added, pragmatically, "but a monster makes for a better story, I suppose." She winked.

"Exactly." Joey grinned and plucked a tart off Betsy Plum's tray.

"Well, as long as you don't come back cursed," I teased, sliding the clipboard toward them. "Sign up wherever you like."

Mike reached for the pen, his handwriting as neat and orderly as his pressed shirt. Kim leaned over his arm and scribbled her name in a slanted scrawl beside his—messy but heartfelt. The boys jostled to add theirs, Joey doodling a tiny hot pepper next to his, which earned a groan from Tony.

"You still making that hot sauce, Joey?" I asked.

"Of course," he said proudly. "This year's batch is called *Dragon Breath.*"

Mike groaned playfully. "Remind me why I let him use the kitchen?"

"Because he's the only one who can get Tasker to move when he decides to nap across the whole couch in the living room." Kim snickered. "Bribes work on dogs, too."

The crowd chuckled again, and warmth spread across my chest at the sight of them. They were dependable, generous, and always ready to help.

Mike glanced back at me. "How's the house? Did the renovations finally wrap up?"

"They did." I smiled. "Thanks to you. Holden never would've gotten that shoulder moving again without your magic."

Mike's ears colored faintly. "Physical therapy, not magic." He cleared his throat and nodded once. "But I'm glad it helped."

"It helped more than you know." It was true. Without Mike's expertise, Holden might still be sidelined. Fighting a Dweller was no joke. "Oh, and he said to thank you for the free passes to the gym. Brittany is one tough personal trainer. She knew exactly how to build on the exercises you gave him." Brittany Voss was the owner of *Voss Vitality.* A slender blonde who was much tougher than she looked, even with a big guy like Holden.

"Good to hear." Mike's gaze softened, but only for a heartbeat. Then he straightened, businesslike again, shepherding his family toward the fountain. "We'll get out of your way before the Wellies rope us into the three-legged race."

"Too late!" Dot cried, brandishing ribbon like a lasso as she hustled toward them.

Kim laughed, herding the boys along. Tasker trotted after them, his tail wagging, already forgiven for his chaos.

As they left, townsfolk called out warm greetings, their affection following the family like the morning fog that lingered. Vex slid out from under the table and curled around my legs, his eyes now golden as he watched the Zaccarias fade into the bustle.

I watched Kim watch Mike every step of the way, and something in my chest squeezed.

You could choose, Vex said gently.

I'd been spending more and more time with Holden the last few months. Our relationship was easy and because he was here, a future with him seemed so much more clear. But I couldn't quiet that part of my heart that still searched for Calderis whenever we were apart. It had known him my whole life, after all.

"There are consequences to choosing," I answered, my eyes drifting toward the tree line where Elarion pulsed beneath the world like a second heartbeat. "That's the problem."

That's the least of your problems. Vex looked towards the woods.

A chill rippled through me, despite the early summer warm spell. Vex had a habit of talking in riddles and making me figure them out on my own.

"Right. *Problems*," I whispered. "It's WishFest. Every festival has its own set of problems. That's to be expected." But even as I said it, the wind shifted once more, carrying the whisper of the woods.

And deep down, I feared this season's festival might present our biggest problem yet.

CHAPTER

Two

THE TOWN HAD FOUND its rhythm once the noon bell tolled from the massive clock tower Mayor Doug Delaney had insisted on adding to the square after the election that made him our official mayor. Vendors trickled in with crates of bunting and boxes of paper lanterns, Mr. Finch, the new handyman, argued with his tape measure as if it were alive, and the Wellies staged an aggressive campaign against symmetry.

The sun had crept high enough that my shoulders felt toasty, and Vex had already slunk back under the sign-up table.

You should drink water, he murmured, a velvet thread in my mind. *Or the humans will gossip that the Chair of WishFest fainted into the tart tray. I will not be blamed for eating around you.*

"You'd eat the tray," I muttered, taking a swig from my bottle.

"Wells." My name drifted across the square on a deeper voice I knew far too well. A voice that never failed to send butterflies dancing through my stomach from the moment I'd first met him three months ago.

I turned at the same moment a shadow cut across the table.

Chief Holden Thorn stood a few paces away, his tall frame squared beneath his dark gray sport coat over a pale gray button-down shirt. His mouth, framed by his beard, was caught in a half-smile, half-grimace—the expression of a man doing his best not to let any weakness show. His dark hair was a little longer than his normal buzz cut, curling slightly at the nape in a way that would have made the Wellies sigh into their tea. Sunglasses hid his stormy gray eyes, but I felt them on me all the same. Assessing, cataloging my mood and my tells, even the way my fingers hadn't stopped worrying the corner of the volunteer list.

Seeing him was like stepping beneath a storm awning, into the shadows but out of the rain. His presence made me feel safe yet had a way of unsettling me every single time. When his gaze snagged on me, a warm sensation wove through my ribs, making me feel weak. Ridiculous. I had centuries of resilience, while he had one very breakable human life.

You're staring, Vex sang in my head. *If you purr at him, I'll disown you.*

"You look like you're in pain," I said, ignoring Vex. "Is it the shoulder again? Maybe you should see Lauren." When Mike was off, his assistant Lauren Glaub—the other half of the *Zac in Motion* Dream Team—took over.

Holden shook his head and tapped the small of his back with two fingers. "Don't tell Dot; she'll try to 'bless' me with eucalyptus steam."

"She already did. Yesterday, in the post office."

"Of course she did." He ran a hand over his trimmed beard, looking amused.

"How's your back, really?" I asked.

He huffed out a sigh. "I'll live." Then he stepped aside with a conspirator's flourish. "Good thing I brought back-up."

A second figure, even taller at six-foot-ten, strode up beside him. A figure I had been infatuated with my entire life. Instead of his usual black leather jacket, he wore a black blazer paired with a silky, open-collar, ruby red shirt that read "business casual" but whispered "controlled danger." His features were as precise as ever. He had high cheekbones, a strong jaw, and eyes the unsettled blue of a storm-bound lake. His pale blond hair was pulled back neatly in a manbun, though I knew all too well how quickly it could come loose in a fight.

He appeared every inch the human detective he was pretending to be...except for the way the air bent around him, shifting subtly.

"Lyra," he said in a practiced Boston cadence that still sounded far too formal as he extended his hand, "good to see you again."

I slid my hand into his, the contact charged with centuries of familiarity, though he played it off as if we had only crossed paths at the spring festival. His grip was firm, his cover flawless.

"Detective Cal Deris in case you don't remember," he added smoothly for the benefit of any listening ears. But beneath the disguise, he was Calderis, the Chief Enforcer of Elarion. One of The Covenant Three with Holden and me. My ally, my counterpart, and in many ways, my mirror.

If Holden was a storm awning, Calderis was the electricity that charged the air when the tempest passed. The energy changed when he stood near me. I knew the way he moved the same way I knew my own breath. We had trained together until our bones spoke the same language in battle.

I held his hand longer than was necessary. Electricity danced where our fingers met, and memory unfurled: the first time I'd seen him in true armor, the oath he'd spoken in the Old Tongue, and the way he'd looked at me when my mother disappeared.

"I remember who you are," I said softly. *Too softly.*

His lashes flickered.

Before I could say anything more, another voice joined us, bright and inquisitive. "Oh, honey, I don't think anyone could forget you. Detective, huh?"

LuLu Morales slipped through the bustle like she'd been born for it, a small notebook tucked casually in the pocket at her hip. Her espresso-dark hair framed her face in loose waves, and her snappy brown eyes missed nothing. She had the kind of presence that made you want to tell her everything…and regret it the moment you did.

She stopped just short of us, her smile warm but edged with curiosity. "You must be newer in town than even me. I thought I'd met everyone by now."

"This is Lourdes Morales." I quickly introduced her before the Wellies could swoop in again. "She's filling in at the station for Marin until Ernie finds a replacement. She's also volunteering for the festival. LuLu, this is Chief Holden Thorn and his friend, Detective Cal Deris from Boston."

"Boston." She tilted her head. "That explains the yummy accent, though it sounds a little different."

He shrugged smoothly. "I've traveled around a bit."

"Hmmm." She studied him as though fascinated. "What brings you all the way up here? Surely not the sack races."

Holden's voice drew her attention. "Professional curiosity and excellent timing. Cal's helping me make sure things go smoothly with the crowds."

LuLu's gaze shifted back to Calderis, her eyes narrowing slightly as if she were already pulling apart the story. "That's dedicated. Wishville doesn't seem like the kind of town that requires big-city detectives. From what I've observed, they mostly argue about bunting."

Calderis held her look with a steady ease. "Sometimes it's the small towns that surprise you."

Her smile tugged sideways, part tease, part test. "Is that your professional opinion?"

"Call it instinct," he replied, the faintest hint of amusement coloring his words.

And there it was…a spark.

Calderis lingered half a beat longer than necessary, and LuLu noticed. She was too sharp not to.

Vex's voice purred in my mind. *The enforcer and the reporter. This should end well. Should I fetch popcorn?*

I resisted the urge to glare at him, instead, arching a brow at Calderis. He had never shown interest in humans before. Not once. Duty was his religion, the treaty his scripture. But now, standing in the middle of Wishville before this petite dynamo, he was…curious. That was dangerous. And disturbing, if I was being honest.

I frowned, uncomfortable with the feelings flooding me.

"So, Detective," she pressed, tucking her hair behind her ear, "is Boston really so dull you had to chase small-town mysteries up here? Or is there something more interesting going on in Wishville than you're admitting?"

Holden cut in smoothly, clearly trying to redirect. "Don't encourage him, Ms. Morales. He'll write a report on your coffee order and call it surveillance."

"Hey," she said, laughing, "don't knock investigative instincts." Her eyes shot back to Calderis, sharp again. "Speaking of coffee orders, I like lattes. He doesn't strike me as the latte type, though I wouldn't mind letting him buy me one."

"What type do I strike you as?" Calderis asked, his tone polite, but the question held a note of playful curiosity I hadn't heard in over a century and *never* towards a human.

LuLu tilted her head, studying him as if he were a puzzle worth solving. "Straight black coffee. No sugar. No patience for small talk. You probably keep your desk immaculate, but your car's a disaster."

Holden barked out a laugh. "Dead on."

Calderis' lips curved faintly. "Not bad," he said, "except I don't own a car."

Her grin widened. "I read people. It's an occupational hazard. And I don't have a car, either. It's a city thing, I guess."

"I guess." He studied her. "So, you read people, huh? And write about them?"

"Sometimes." She tapped her notebook. "Off the record…for now."

That single pause—*for now*—was enough to make my pulse

skip. LuLu was already sizing him up. And Calderis, instead of deflecting, looked…intrigued.

Jealousy wasn't my color, but it bloomed anyway like a bruise beneath the ribs. It wasn't just that she was quick and pretty and clever; it was the way Calderis' attention slid toward her like a compass needle finding north and refusing to budge. Dwellers didn't do that with humans.

Calderis didn't do that with *anyone.*

Perhaps the compass is rattled, Vex mused. *Perhaps the needle just wants to rest somewhere that isn't a war map.*

I kept my smile pinned in place. "LuLu's off the clock," I said lightly, but my pulse was tired of pretending indifference. I shot her a questioning look, but she shrugged noncommittally. "She's been helping with tickets. She's also very brave around the Wellies, which is more than I can say for most newcomers."

"Survival instinct." She winked. "Besides, they're harmless, and I'm bored." Her gaze traveled back to his. "I'm always ready to explore a new angle."

My heart sank.

Holden snorted. "Harmless? Tell that to my back after Tilly roped me into carrying her glitter crates."

"Big strong man like you? I'm sure you managed," LuLu teased.

Holden muttered something about a slipped disc under his breath, but Calderis wasn't listening. His gaze lingered on the feisty dynamo, measuring and weighing her, as if she were a variable he hadn't anticipated.

As for me? I raised my brow higher and tried not to clench my jaw.

The late afternoon light had shifted toward gold by the time I climbed the hill toward the clearing. Up here, where the wishing well waited in its ring of old stones, the world always felt quieter.

Though tonight the forest hummed with activity.

The festival shacks were half-assembled, their wooden beams rising like skeletons against the sky, and the scent of sawdust mingled with the tang of pine. Fireflies had already begun blinking at the edges of the clearing, their glow soft as candlelight.

Lauren Glaub was crouched over a pile of canvas, her curly dark blonde hair falling below her shoulders as she directed two teenagers on how to stretch the tent fabric over its frame. She had a knack for making hard work feel like art, with every movement graceful and her blue eyes shining in the dimming light.

"Not too tight, or it'll tear when the wind picks up," she said gently, her voice calm but firm. "See this seam? That's your guide. Keep it even."

The boys and girls—clearly her husband Matt's biology students from Wishville High School, judging by their matching red-and-white jackets—nodded obediently, fumbling a little but eager to please. School was out for the summer, but summer school was in full session.

I stepped closer, brushing pine needles from my standard spandex-blend hiking gear. "I see you've got yourself a crew."

Lauren looked up, her face brightening. "Matt recruited them. He promised extra credit if they didn't collapse a tent on me. Victoria has her own set of chemistry students working on the science display."

"That's one way to motivate teenagers." I smiled as I glanced over at the chemistry teacher who had her sandy blonde hair woven in a French braid as she directed the students on how to set up the supplies.

As if summoned, Matt appeared from behind one of the half-built booths, hauling a beam across his shoulder like it weighed nothing. At six-foot-three with lean runner's muscles, he carried himself with the boundless energy of someone who thrived on movement. His green eyes lit when he spotted me.

"Lyra!" he called, grinning. "We're almost done with the game booths. I told the kids whoever finished first got first crack at Deanna's ball."

At the sound of her name, Deanna, an enthusiastic mix of herding dog and lab, came barreling out of the trees, her tail a blur, a ball already clenched triumphantly in her mouth. She dropped it at the feet of the nearest student and barked, demanding attention.

"See?" Matt laughed. "Best motivator there is."

Meanwhile, Sully, their husky-malamute-shepherd mix, lounged at the edge of the clearing like a cat pretending he was above it all. His thick black coat blended with the deepening shadows, his pale eyes half-lidded but watchful.

Lauren shook her head fondly. "Sully thinks manual labor is beneath him."

Smart dog, Vex's voice slid silkily through my mind. *Why sweat when you can supervise? He's clearly superior to the ball-chaser.*

"Don't you dare tell Deanna that," I whispered.

Lauren tilted her head at me, curious, but I waved it off. It wasn't the first time she'd caught me talking to myself, though thankfully, she'd never commented on it.

The students finished securing the tent, and Lauren stood, brushing dirt from her jeans. The glow in her cheeks and the smudge of sawdust on her wrist made her look entirely at home in the clearing, surrounded by half-built shacks and laughing teenagers.

"You two didn't have to come all the way up here tonight," I said.

"Of course we did," Matt replied easily, setting the beam down with a thud. "You need all the hands you can get, and it's good practice for the kids. Better than another night staring at their phones."

"Besides," Lauren added, "we like helping. And being out here." She glanced at the well, her expression softening. "It's peaceful. Almost like it breathes."

Her words tugged something deep in me. She wasn't wrong. The well did breathe, just not in a way she'd ever guess.

"It does seem that way, doesn't it?" I said carefully. "That's why the festivals are so popular. There's something special about a wishing well. It gives people hope. Something the world needs more of these days. Lucky for us, we're the only town I know of to have one this old."

Tasker's bark drifted faintly from down the hill, and I realized the Zaccarias must have lingered nearby with their dog. For a moment, I pictured both families gathered here, their laughter tangling together in the fading light. Wishville's heart, steady and warm.

But warmth wasn't the only thing that lingered.

The forest edge was darkening, shadows pressing closer, the whisper of the woods threading through the leaves. The forest had been calling to me a lot lately, and I wasn't sure why.

Lauren's laugh pulled me back.

She had found a hammer abandoned by one of the boys and was holding it like a violin bow, pretending to play and then conduct the students as they pounded stakes into the ground. "Steady rhythm, boys and girls! This is music too!"

Matt rolled his eyes but smiled, coming up behind her to press a quick kiss to her temple and sing along to the hammer strikes with his own lyrics.

"Matthew," she teased softly, "you're off key."

The students groaned at the display, though they were grinning all the same.

Unable to hide my smile, I said, "Everyone loves you two. Just like the Zaccarias."

Lauren's cheeks colored at the comparison. "They do a lot for the town. We just like being part of it."

"Don't sell yourself short. You're more than just a part of it," I said. "You make it better."

Matt brushed a hand through the top of his thick, dark hair, suddenly modest. "Sitting still doesn't suit us. If Lauren's not treating patients, she's painting or planting something. If I'm not teaching, I'm running."

"Or baking," Lauren teased. "He calls it baking. I call it science experiments with flour."

Matt laughed. "Sixty-forty odds. And the forty percent is really good."

"Your breakfast muffins were *not* forty percent," she shot back.

"They were experimental!" he protested.

The clearing echoed with their laughter, joined by the students, who clearly adored their teacher. Deanna bounded back with the ball, panting happily as if to declare the moment perfect.

And for a moment, it was.

The lanterns flickered on one by one as dusk settled deeper, painting the tents in a golden glow. The wishing well stood at the edge of it all, silent and patient, its stones damp with evening mist drifting down from Lake Mistfall to the north.

Lauren paused to catch her breath, resting her hand on the well's cool edge. She smiled faintly, her curls lit by firefly glow. "I can see why you're so passionate about these festivals and the well, Lyra. They're so important to our town."

My chest tightened. If only she knew.

When Lauren moved her hand across the old stones, the well answered with a breath I could feel against my cheek. *Careful,* I warned it silently, the way you warn a sleeping dog not to dream of running.

"It gives people hope," I told her, because that was a truth I was allowed to say. The other truths lived beneath the earth like uncut gems.

Deanna trotted over and leaned her warm shoulder against my leg. The sudden weight startled me into laughter. The sound cracked, then steadied, sending her bounding off after a group of kids.

On the far edge of the green, fireflies stitched bright errant commas into the dusk. The scene was postcard-perfect, the sort you'd hang on a kitchen corkboard with a grocery list tacked beneath. But the woods kept tugging at my bones, a low drumbeat saying, *You're not done and not safe, not yet.*

Vex brushed against my ankles, his fur prickling with unease. *Careful,* he whispered in my mind. *The ones who love the well too much are often the first to lose it.*

I shivered, though the clearing was warm.

Lauren didn't notice. She had already moved on, calling to Matt that one of his students was trying to race Deanna and losing badly. The laughter rose again, rich and bright, threading through the trees. And still, under it all, the well waited…for what?

Only time would tell.

CHAPTER
Three

THE FIRST DAY of summer arrived with a blaze of sunlight on Monday morning, as though the Green Mountains themselves had pulled back their curtains to reveal June in all her golden glory. I stood at the edge of the festival clearing at the top of the hill, watching as vendors manned their booths, streamers fluttered in the breeze, and the air thickened with scents both sweet and savory.

And of course, maple everything.

Wind plucked the banners into little waves. Children's laughter skipped like stones across the green and sank in the shadows near the trees. Every booth had its own weather: cinnamon drafts by the fryers; a cool tea breeze by Dot; a hot anvil haze near Gus's caramel kettle. The well, set back like a quiet old aunt at a wedding, watched everything and gave away nothing.

After a week of planning, Summer WishFest had officially begun.

I tugged at the strap of my crossbody bag, my heart swelling. As Guardian of the Well and chair of WishFest, I'd spent the past week worrying over every detail: permits, performers, food trucks, and the stubborn string of lights that refused to cooperate until yesterday. But now, with the morning sun glinting off the well at the edge of the clearing and laughter bubbling from every direction, I allowed myself a small smile.

For once, it looked like everything was going right.

The grounds were packed with so many new faces as tourists of all walks of life flooded our town. After what happened last time, we'd all been in agreement. We all had our own jobs, but came together in times of necessity; and it seemed WishFest was always going to be one of those times.

Children raced across the field, clutching dripping snow cones dyed brilliant shades of cherry and blue raspberry, their parents following with maple soft-serve ice cream.

The Wellies had already crowned themselves with daisy wreaths and were prancing about in the clearing, declaring themselves "Summer Solstice Priestesses." Belle's sequined shawl sparkled so brightly it nearly blinded me, while Dot waved a teacup at strangers and promised fortunes about "unlimited popsicles and romantic entanglements." Tilly jingled a jar of lavender sprigs, insisting they brought luck when tucked behind an ear.

They attempted a solemn blessing and immediately lost the thread.

"May your summer be ripe—" Belle began.

"—with berries and sensible shoes," Dot added, peering severely at a teenager's platforms.

"—and free of bunion-beasts," Tilly concluded, sprinkling dried lavender like confetti.

"Bunion-beasts aren't canon," Belle hissed.

"They are in *my* headcanon," Tilly hissed back, then beamed at a bewildered tourist. "We take tips!"

"Oh my, how awful. You must get quite the headaches, you poor thing." Dot tsked.

"I wouldn't trust the things in her head," Belle grumbled. "No tellin' what's crawled through there."

"You two nitwits need to get with the times," Tilly said dryly.

Vex snorted inside my head. *Priestesses? They are feral pigeons in hats.*

Most people humored them with fond smiles.

A few actually did as they were told.

Festival food is almost better than granted wishes, Vex purred, his tail flicking as he slunk past a booth where Tasha Frimble sold mini strawberry-rhubarb pies alongside raspberry, blueberry, and blackberry ones.

"Don't even think about it," I murmured aloud.

He shot me a look that could only be described as offended, then darted toward *The Twisted Loaf* stand, eyeing the maple glazed donuts. Betsy Plum spotted him and wagged a flour dusted finger, but by the time she bent to shoo him off, he had already filched a stray chunk.

Everywhere I turned, there was something new to savor. Fiona Fitzwhistle had a table outside *Once Upon a Time* bookstore stand stacked with gently used paperbacks tied in ribbon bundles she called, "Summer Mystery Grab Bags."

Gus Grimly, his handlebar mustache freshly waxed, handed out striped bags of popcorn beside *The Dapper Den* shack.

Willa Hartman leaned out of *The Wishbone Café's* food truck window, calling, "Strawberry basil iced tea—two for one!" Her voice was drowned out by the hiss of grills where skewers of lamb and vegetables sizzled beside corn on the cob brushed with lime butter.

I sampled a paper cone of fried zucchini blossoms from Maisie Flint's *General Store* booth. She barked, "Don't drip oil on my charms!" and pointed at her table lined with glow-in-the-dark trinkets shaped like duck feet and skeleton keys. Maisie wore oversized sunglasses to protect her precious eyes and photographic memory.

Across the green, *Blooms of Glory's* Magnolia McHoggin staged an overly dramatic "farewell ceremony" for a wilted sunflower bouquet, complete with a black veil and a hymn off-key enough to send pigeons scattering.

Boar's Board & Brisket's Bart Gildersnipe, never one to miss a spectacle, had Trotter the pig wearing a flower crown while he carved samples of brisket for festivalgoers.

I moved through it all with my usual mixture of pride and nerves. The treaty depended on the smooth running of each Wish-Fest. If the festival faltered—or worse, if no wish was granted—peace itself could be at risk. I shook off the thought, letting the noise and color wash over me.

On the makeshift stage, Mayor Doug Delaney stood beside his new assistant, Laisira. The serious sort, she wore her dark-blonde hair with golden highlights in a twist, her clear gray-blue eyes sharp and eager to please. He adjusted his tie and tapped the microphone. His comb-over was plastered so firmly to his scalp it looked carved.

"Welcome, friends!" he boomed, sweat already beading at his temples. "Welcome to another glorious Summer WishFest! May your wishes be plentiful and your funnel cakes even more so!"

Applause rippled across the clearing. Firecrackers popped. Children shrieked and clapped, their laughter carried on the warm breeze. Trip Danderly, self-appointed wish sheriff, stood watch with his wand flashlight. For a brief moment, Wishville felt timeless, aglow with the same magic it had clung to for centuries.

I spotted Holden Thorn at the dunk tank, his arms crossed and storm-gray eyes crinkled in reluctant amusement as he watched a teenager hurl a baseball. The ball struck its target with a satisfying smack, and the volunteer splashed into the water. Holden shook his head, his lips twitching as if fighting a smile. His shoulder was better, and his recent achy back was mostly healed, though I caught the way he shifted carefully, still testing his strength.

He caught me looking and tilted his chin in that way that meant *I see you, Lyra. I'm fine. You don't need to fuss over me.* Affection and exasperation twisted together until I couldn't tell them apart. Another splash sounded and a teenager whooped. Holden's mouth bent toward a smile and then away from it like he didn't quite trust the shape.

Stand closer, Vex suggested. *He smiles longer when you're orbiting.*

I rolled my eyes. Nothing got by my cat.

I considered walking over, maybe even teasing Holden about enjoying himself, but before I could take a step, a tingly sensation swept over me. A cry cut through the noise. The clearing hushed, laughter dimming as heads turned toward the tree-lined path through the woods.

A woman hurried into view, her sandals slapping the earth, her hair clinging damply to her cheeks. Kim Zaccaria. I had only ever seen her laughing and happy. She was always gracious and warm and smiling. But there was no smile now. Her face was paler than normal, her eyes wide with terror.

She shoved through the gathering crowd, alone. "Chief Thorn!" she called, her voice cracking as it carried over the festival hush. "Chief—please—it's Mike. He's missing!" The words landed like a stone in the well, sending shockwaves outward.

Gasps rippled through the crowd.

Betsy dropped her tongs.

Fiona clutched a book bundle to her chest.

Even the Wellies stopped mid-blessing, their flower crowns slipping askew.

The crowd pulled tight around the sentence like a drawstring on a bag. My body went cold-hot the way it did before battle, the way it had the night my mother vanished and the world tilted. Kim's eyes were wide with the terrible hope people get when they say *missing* and mean *please let me be wrong.* I knew that hope. It had lived in me for a hundred years like a tenant who wouldn't pay rent or move out.

Holden was already moving, steady and calm. "Slow down, Kim. What happened?"

She swallowed hard, her eyes darting wildly. "We were camping at Lake Mistfall. Early this morning, Mike went for a solo hike with Tasker. That's not unusual, so I didn't think anything of it. But after hours of being gone, Tasker came back alone. That never happens. The boys and I searched. We shouted his name for hours, but…he's gone." Her voice broke.

The clearing erupted into murmurs.

Mike Zaccaria, the man who cheered kids through physical therapy like they were athletes at the Olympics, who always carried granola bars in his pockets "just in case."

I felt my chest tighten, the early summer sun suddenly feeling oppressive.

Vex pressed against my ankle, his thought brushing mine with cool certainty. *This is no accident.*

Holden's jaw flexed. He rested a firm hand on Kim's shoulder. "We'll find him," he said, his voice steady though his storm-gray eyes flickered with unease. Then he raised his head toward the crowd. "Show's over, folks. Enjoy the festival and let us get to work."

But I knew, deep in my bones, that this wasn't a simple disappearance. Lake Mistfall was deep in the Whisper Woods, and the woods were still calling me. Maybe now I would find out why. The first day of summer had begun with light and laughter.

Now it hung heavy with dread.

Holden's office smelled faintly of stale coffee grounds and office supplies, the kind of scent that clung to small-town police stations everywhere. The blinds rattled softly in the breeze from the oscillating fan, its steady hum the only sound until Kim Zaccaria lowered herself into the chair across from his desk.

Her hands trembled as she laced them together. She was still damp from her hurried walk from Lake Mistfall, her hair sticking to her temples and face still pale. Vex had claimed a corner near the file cabinet, his tail wrapped neatly around his paws and green/blue eyes never leaving her.

Holden leaned forward, his pen poised over his notepad. His

storm-gray eyes were sharp but his voice gentled. "All right, Kim. Let's start from the beginning."

She nodded shakily, her gaze darting between us. "Mike woke early this morning. He always does when we camp. He said he wanted to get a hike in before breakfast, just him and Tasker."

"And you said he brought the dog, correct?" Holden confirmed.

"Yes. Tasker loves that ridge trail." Her voice faltered. "But a couple hours later...only Tasker came back. His leash was dragging in the dirt."

I couldn't stop picturing the leash dragging—a punctuation mark at the end of a sentence Mike hadn't meant to finish. "Does Tasker ever...bolt?" I asked gently.

"Only for squirrels," she whispered, "and, even then, he checks back."

Vex's tail curled over his paws. *The woods took something it shouldn't have.*

I swallowed. The pendant against my skin warmed as if remembering a different leash, a different loss. I wasn't sure if memory made a good compass or a bad one. I only knew it kept pointing me to the trees.

A shiver moved through me. I pictured Mike's easy smile, the way he could talk even the most stubborn patients through pain with patience and humor. To imagine him simply vanishing in those woods...it felt wrong.

Holden kept his tone even. "What time did he leave?"

"Before sunrise," Kim said.

"And Tasker returned when?"

"A couple hours later. I wasn't watching the clock. I knew something was wrong the moment I saw him without Mike." Tears welled in her eyes, but she blinked them back. "The boys and I searched. We called until our throats were raw, but there was nothing. No tracks, no sound, nothing. I panicked and rushed here. Tony and Joey stayed at camp with Tasker in case Mike comes back."

I stepped closer, my voice softer than Holden's. "Did Mike ever mention meeting anyone out there? A patient, or a friend, maybe?"

She shook her head. "No. He just…he loved those morning hikes. Said the trail cleared his head."

"Maybe he took a different trail," I suggested.

Her brow puckered and she shrugged. "It's possible."

Holden wrote quickly, then set his pen down with purpose. "Lake Mistfall's not too far of a hike from here. That means anyone from Wishville could've been there. We won't wait on this. I'll organize a search party immediately."

Kim let out a breath that sounded like it had been lodged in her chest. "Thank you."

Holden pushed back from his desk, already in motion. "Lyra, stay with her for a moment."

I nodded.

Kim rubbed her arms as though warding off a chill.

The fan hummed. Vex's thought brushed against my mind. *She speaks the truth, but fear has a scent—and it's not all for her husband.*

Before I could puzzle over that, Holden's voice boomed from the squad room. "Listen up! Mike Zaccaria is missing. Last seen this morning on the ridge trail at Lake Mistfall. We move out shortly. Deputies, volunteers, anyone with search-and-rescue experience—gear up. Bring flashlights, radios, and dogs if you've got them. Spread the word."

The building came alive at once. Phones rang, boots thudded across linoleum, and voices rose with purpose. The weight of celebration that had filled Wishville only an hour ago was gone, replaced by something heavier…grim determination.

Holden returned with his jaw set, and his eyes slid briefly to mine. "We leave now."

It wasn't long before the search party wound its way up the mountain roads, pines hemming us in on either side. By the time we reached the lake clearing, the air had cooled, heavy with the scent of pine and water.

Kim's boys bolted from the campsite when they saw her, two lanky teenagers with worry written in every line of their faces. Tasker bounded beside them, his leash trailing, his coat muddy and tongue lolling. He ran straight to Kim, whining, as if apologizing for failing his job.

She fell to her knees, burying her face in Tasker's fur. "It's okay," she whispered, though her voice cracked as she looked up at her boys. "It's okay, we'll find him."

Holden gave them a moment, then crouched beside the fire pit where embers still glowed faintly. "Which way did he go?"

"The ridge trail." Kim pointed toward a path that snaked into the woods. "He said the view cleared his head."

Holden studied the ground, scanning for prints, then straightened and called out to the volunteers. "All right, listen up. We split into three teams. One up the ridge trail, one along the lake, and one circling through the lower woods. Stay in radio contact. If you see anything, you call it in. No wandering alone."

A chorus of agreement followed. Flashlights clicked on even though daylight lingered, radios buzzed, and dogs barked eagerly, picking up the tension in the air.

I moved to Kim's side. "Do you want me to stay with you?"

She shook her head, her eyes brimming but resolute. "No. Please, Lyra. Find him."

Vex brushed against my calf, his thought slipping into my mind like a whisper. *The woods will answer if we listen closely enough.*

As we stepped onto the trail, the celebration of the morning felt like another world left behind with the scent of fried dough and laughter. Here, the air was damp and hushed, the silence broken only by the crunch of boots and the occasional distant bark.

Spring WishFest had a murder happen before the festival had even started. Now, Summer WishFest had begun in Wishville with joy and light. But here, beneath the shadow of the ridge, the season had opened with a mystery darker than any festival could mask...again.

The lake breathed like a sleeping animal.

Mist crawled in slow patient coils over the skin of the water, and the pines held their arms up as if waiting for rain. I slid my palm along the dirt and opened my Seismic Sense a fraction. Footfalls trembled in the ground—old deer tracks, a scattering of raccoon prints, something heavier pacing the shore at dawn. And then—an absence where there should have been a weight, as though the earth had flinched around the shape of a man.

There's a hollow in the woods where Mike should be, Vex said, uncharacteristically solemn. *Find the edge of it, and you'll find him.*

Four

THE WHISPER WOODS had a way of swallowing sound.

The moment our boots crunched past the tree line, it was like stepping out of summer and into a cathedral of shadows. Fog coiled low to the ground, twining around grassy roots and broken branches, muting the sunlight into fractured beams. The sharp scent of pine needles mixed with the damp earth, cool and metallic.

Holden's voice carried steady authority as he split the search party into sections. "Fan out and stay within shouting distance. Keep your radios on. Nobody goes alone." His words echoed briefly, then vanished into the hush.

The deputies snapped into motion, with volunteers following their lead. Leashes tugged taut as dogs whined, eager to catch a scent. Radios crackled. People shuffled nervously, having no clue that even their footsteps might wake something ancient slumbering beneath the ground.

I nodded along with the rest, but even as the group shifted into pairs, I felt the tug in my chest. It was subtle at first, then became insistent. It wasn't panic or grief. It was something older, deeper. The woods wanted me elsewhere.

It's pulling you, Vex murmured in my mind, his tail flicking as he padded at my side. *Not this trail, but somewhere deeper in the woods.*

I hesitated, the weight of Holden's warning pressing against my conscience. Then I angled off from the main group. "I'll take the lower path," I called, pitching my voice casually as if I were just being strategic.

Holden's eyes caught mine from across the clearing. He studied me, but after a pause, he gave the smallest nod.

The moment the other voices thinned behind me, I let go of the surface hum of noise and reached for the rhythm beneath my boots. My Seismic Sense stirred, the way it always did when I opened myself to the earth. Vibrations rose through the damp soles of my boots and into my bones. The faint scurry of chipmunks resonated, then the uneven drumming of a deer bounding away, followed by the shifting of stones somewhere nearby.

Suddenly there was silence, like the land itself had sucked in a breath and refused to release it.

I slowed, then crouched, pressing my palm flat to the ground. The vibrations sharpened, drawing me like a compass toward the east. Roots reached like gnarled fingers across the path, warning me to turn back, but I stepped over them with a pounding heart.

I was focused on finding Mike, but a nagging sensation told me what I might find would be something bigger than just a missing person.

Lyra, Vex warned, his thought edged with unease. *Be careful. What hides this long often wishes to stay hidden.*

Still, I followed the pull until the forest thinned into a hollow I didn't recognize. The air here felt denser as if I were breathing through a wet cloth. A spiral lay etched faintly in the clearing, its pattern barely visible beneath moved dirt and loss of vegetation. Someone had been digging deep into the ground right at its center. Beneath its faded lines, I felt power thrumming, restrained and patient. My chest tightened. Could this be what my mother had told me about centuries ago?

The Veiled Vault.

I drew closer, searching the area, and then gasped. Lying against the base of a nearby oak was Mike Zaccaria.

My breath caught. "Mike!" What on earth was he doing here of all places?

I sprinted across the clearing, falling to my knees beside him. His head lolled at an unnatural angle, his dark hair matted with blood where it had struck the bark. My shaking fingers pressed desperately to his throat, searching for that steady drum of life.

Nothing. Just silence.

"Please, no…" The words tore out of me, raw.

Mike, who had coaxed half this town back to health with his easy grin and steady hands. Mike, who laughed like everything was fixable. Mike, who was now *gone*.

The earth vibrated beneath me again, stronger this time. The spiral glowed faintly as though the Vault itself had awakened, aware of my presence, eager for me to open it.

"No," I whispered fiercely. "Not now."

Summoning Skycall, I moved the wind into a twister, picking up the piles of dirt and dropping them back into the hole. Then using my Harmony Pulse, I pressed my palm flat to the spiral. Energy rippled outward in concentric waves, bending sound, sight, and memory. The etching blurred, then vanished, cloaked so completely that even the sharpest eye would see only roots and soil. The humming stilled, muffled under my will.

It would hold…for now.

Only then did I sag back, my throat raw and chest tight.

They're coming, Vex warned, his ears swiveling toward the rustle of branches. *You need to call them.*

I forced air into my lungs and steadiness into my voice. "Here!" My cry cracked the silence. "I found him!"

The forest answered with shouts, crashing footsteps, and the static of radios talking about twisters and crazy wind. My Skycall covering the spiral must have been what led them in this direction. I brushed trembling fingers once more against Mike's shoulder, blinking through the sting in my eyes. I couldn't save him, but I could protect the town from what lay beneath him.

And I could make sure his death was not ignored.

Branches snapped as the search party burst into the clearing, breathless and wide-eyed. Holden was the first through, his radio swinging at his side. His face was grim even before his eyes landed on Mike.

He cursed softly, crouching beside me. His fingers checked Mike's throat with practiced precision, though I already knew what he'd find. His eyes lifted up to meet mine after only a moment, then I saw the faintest shake of his head, confirming what I already knew. The clearing filled quickly with volunteers, deputies, and whining dogs. Murmurs rippled like wind through grass, then a sound sharper than all the rest pierced the air.

Kim's wail.

She must have decided to join the search instead of staying back at camp. I couldn't blame her. The waiting was the hardest part. Townsfolk hurried her forward. She fell to her knees beside her husband, clutching his hand as if she could anchor him back to this world by sheer will.

Her sobs tore at the air and broke my heart.

Holden rose, his voice stacking order onto chaos, plank by plank. I let his steadiness be a bridge and moved across it to the only task left to me…to witness. If I couldn't save, I could at least bear witness—and vow to seek justice for what was taken.

"All right, back up! Give us space. Nobody touches anything. This is a crime scene now." Holden's jaw worked. "This is no longer a search. It's an investigation."

The words drew another ripple through the crowd. Wishville wasn't built for pronouncements like that. Gossip, yes. Rumors, certainly. But not death declared in a whispering wood.

Movement caught my eye.

Lourdes Morales, ever the reporter, slid in along the fringe of the clearing, her eyes sharp as a hawk's. She had her phone out, her thumb hovering over the record button, and her journalist's notebook already open in the other hand. She bent low, angling for a shot of Mike and of Holden braced in command.

My stomach tightened. "LuLu, not now," I snapped, the words sharper than I intended.

She blinked, feigning innocence. "I'm just…documenting. Trying to help. People are going to want to know what happened."

"People," I repeated, my voice flat. "Or Ernie?"

Her smile faltered but only for a heartbeat. "I'm off the clock. This is for the people in town who loved Mike."

Dangerous, Vex whispered, his tail lashing. *She's stringing threads together already.*

Holden's eyes cut to her phone. He didn't speak, but the weight of his glare was enough. She lowered the device, though she didn't pocket it.

The deputies shifted uneasily as Holden barked more orders. "Secure the perimeter. Nobody leaves until names are logged. We'll comb every inch."

As the others moved, my hand rose to the pendant at my throat. The silver had grown hot, too hot, as if burning against my skin. A hum shivered through it. Then came the whisper, faint and smoky, curling through my thoughts.

Stay away from the Vault, Lyra. It will cost you everything.

My breath stuttered. My mother. Serenna's voice. A ghost echo locked in the pendant, reaching for me across years.

I staggered back, clutching it tight, the warning coiling in my chest like ice.

Vex pressed against my leg, urgent. *Do not let them see what you've hidden.*

I forced my breathing to steady, smothering the memory of the spiral deeper beneath my Harmony Pulse. To everyone else, this was a tragic clearing with a fallen man. Only I knew the Vault thrummed beneath, but my veil was only temporary. I would have to talk to Calderis about a permanent cover.

Holden straightened, brushing dirt from his knees. His expression had hardened to iron. "We treat this as suspicious. No one leaves until we cover anything you all found. A lethal blow like that doesn't happen by itself. I want to know who else might have been in these woods at the same time as Mike."

Whispers rose. Kim sobbed into Mike's chest. LuLu scribbled furiously, her lips pressed tight as though already shaping her story.

And me? My pendant seared my skin, my mother's warning echoing louder than Holden's orders, Kim's cries, and even louder than my own heartbeat.

The Vault had revealed itself to me at last.

And Mike had died on its doorstep.

By the time we wound our way back to the lakeside camp, it was late afternoon. Kim's boys sat huddled on a log with Tasker pressed against their knees, his ears drooping as if he, too, knew. They looked up as Holden approached with a heavy stride.

Kim walked ahead, her face blotched with tears as she knelt between her sons. They might be teenagers, but they turned into little boys who need their mother. She didn't have to say the words. They read it in her eyes. Joey broke instantly, burying his face on her shoulder. Tony stared hard at the ground, his fists clenched and jaw trembling.

The dog whined, nudging toward the empty space where Mike should have been.

I stood back with the others, my heart aching. The weight of grief was heavier here than in the woods. Here, it wasn't a mystery or whispers. It was raw, unspooled love torn apart by loss.

Holden removed his hat, pressing it briefly to his chest. His voice was low when he finally spoke, but it carried all the same. "We'll find out what happened, Kim. I can promise you that."

The promise hung there, fragile and fierce, as the search party made its way back to town.

$\sim$

The clinic sat on a side street off Main in a low, modern building that always smelled faintly of antiseptic and eucalyptus. Mike had insisted on the scent when he designed the place, wanting it to feel clean but not cold.

The bell over the glass door didn't jingle when I pushed it, because the door was still locked. I tugged the handle twice, then let go.

Lauren was never late.

Zac in Motion always opened at eight sharp, even on blizzard days. Yet here it was, late in the afternoon, and patients were gathered outside looking restless. A man leaned heavily on a cane, rocking on his good leg. Two women in matching yoga pants murmured to each other, one rubbing her neck. Another man with a shoulder sling paced the sidewalk, scowling.

"She's never late like this," the man with the cane grumbled. "Not once. I've been back three times, and she's still not here."

I forced a polite smile, though unease twisted in my gut. "I'm sure she'll be here soon."

The truth was, I wasn't sure about anything anymore.

I still had dirt under my nails, scratches on my forearms, and my shirt smelled faintly of pine needles and mud. There hadn't been time to change. As soon as Holden confirmed Mike's death, I'd left the woods and headed straight here. He needed to stay behind to manage the crime scene, but I couldn't shake the thought of Lauren waiting innocently for him to come back, not knowing he never would.

I was debating whether to leave a note when the sound of tires crunching on gravel drew everyone's attention.

A dusty SUV pulled into the lot, the windows halfway down despite the heat. Two mutts crowded the back seat, one barking sharply, and the other pawing at the glass.

Lauren climbed out, her curls in disarray and cheeks flushed. She juggled her keys and phone, calling out, "Sorry, everyone. Sorry, Nancy. I know I'm so late! Sully got lost in the woods, and I didn't have any reception." Her laugh was high and brittle, not like the calm, professional woman I knew.

The patients muttered. Some sounded relieved, while others grew impatient.

Lauren hurried to the door, unlocking it with fumbling fingers. "Come on in. Nancy will get everyone squared away."

The front desk receptionist led the way as the others shuffled inside behind her. Lauren opened the hatch, and the dogs bounded out, their leashes tangled. "In you go," she ordered, ushering them into her office with a practiced sweep of her arm.

When she turned back, her eyes met mine. Whatever smile she'd been wearing dropped away. "Lyra. What's wrong?"

I hadn't said a word yet, but she saw it all over me. The mud, my pallor, the raw edge in my gaze. It was clear she hadn't heard the news.

"Can we talk?" I asked softly.

Concern tightened her features. "Of course. My office." She ducked into the waiting room. "Folks, give me just a few minutes. Warm up on the bikes, and I'll be right with you."

Inside, her office smelled of antiseptic and dog hair. Sully flopped against the desk with a huff, while Deanna circled before curling up near the filing cabinet, looking exhausted. Lauren perched on her chair, her face still flushed and damp curls sticking to her forehead.

"You look awful," she said bluntly. "What happened?"

The words stuck in my throat. How did you tell someone their mentor and partner, the man who built this clinic, was gone?

"It's Mike," I said finally. My voice sounded strange in my own ears. "Lauren…he's dead."

Her whole body went still. Then she laughed, her voice sounding short, shocked, and hollow. "That's not funny."

"I wouldn't joke about this."

Her hands gripped the edge of her desk. "No. No, it's not possible. He was just—he was camping with his family. He texted me before he left. He said he'd be back Tuesday and—"

"We found him this morning," I said gently, though the words burned. "In the Whisper Woods near Lake Mistfall. He had a bad head injury and was already gone by the time we found him. I'm so sorry."

Her face drained of color. She pressed both hands to her mouth, her eyes growing wide. "Oh my God." She turned away, her shoulders hunched as her breath came in ragged bursts.

The dogs whined, sensing her distress. Deanna nosed her knee, and Lauren stroked the dog's fur blindly, still trembling.

"I'm so sorry," I said again, my throat thick. "I know how much he meant to you, and to this clinic. To all of us."

She lowered her hands, and her fingers trembled. "He was my mentor. My idol. He...he gave me everything. This place exists because of him." Her voice broke. "I don't understand. How? He was an experienced hiker and always careful."

"We don't know yet," I admitted. "Holden's treating it as suspicious. It didn't look like an accident."

Her eyes snapped up sharply, glossy with tears.

I hesitated, but I had to ask. "Where were you early this morning?"

For a heartbeat, something unreadable flashed across her face. Defensiveness or fear, maybe. Then she smoothed it away. "I went hiking."

"Okay," I said. That wasn't unusual. She lived on thirty-four acres of fully forested land on the outskirts of town.

"At Lake Mistfall," she added.

The words hit like a stone in my stomach. "You were there?"

"Yes. Mike always said the ridge trail was good for clearing your head. I thought I would try it." She gave a shaky laugh. "Usually I just walk our land, but I was craving different scenery. Matt's at summer school, and we had a couple cancellations here at the clinic. I didn't have anyone scheduled until ten today, so I had the morning free for once. I took Sully and Deanna." She gestured at the dogs. "Only...Sully bolted." She shook her head. "He's never done that. Something distracted him. It took me forever to catch him. By the time I did, it was afternoon. I came straight here. I didn't want to keep my patients waiting any longer than necessary by driving all the way back home."

I studied her closely. Her words tumbled too quickly, filling every silence before I could question them.

"You didn't see Mike?" I pressed. "Or any of us? We had a whole search party out there looking for him for a couple hours."

Her eyes filled again. "No. God, no. If I had seen him, I—" She broke off, covering her mouth. "I would have helped him. Called someone. Anything. But I swear, Lyra, I never saw him or any of you. Maybe because I was chasing Sully through the woods and not on any official trail."

The Veiled Vault wasn't on an official trail, either, I thought. I watched the way her throat worked around the words—small, stubborn swallows, like she could push the morning back down and pretend it hadn't happened.

"The fog can play tricks," I said quietly, and thought, *It turns distance into doubt and doubt into excuses.* I wasn't accusing her; I was accusing the day. The pendant at my collarbone warmed, a pulse of memory—my mother's hands steady on mine as she taught me to listen to the spaces between sounds. *Truth lives in the pauses, little star.*

Deanna's head turned in my direction as if she'd heard the memory.

Vex hopped to the windowsill and fixed Lauren with that unblinking cat-judge stare. *She's hiding something,* he told me, *but not what you think.*

Sully stirred, letting out a sigh as if echoing the heaviness in the room.

"Okay, then." I nodded slowly. "Holden will want to speak with you officially."

"I understand." Her fingers twisted together, white at the knuckles. "But please believe me. I loved working with Mike. I never would have…" Her words trailed into silence.

"I'm not sure who in the waiting room knows yet. Do you want me to help you tell them, or call someone for you?"

She shook her head. "No. I just need a minute, then I'll tell whoever doesn't know. They deserve to hear it from me."

I nodded as I rose, brushing dirt from my palms. "I'll let you get back to your patients, then. But if you need something or remember anything, call me."

She nodded, then cast her eyes down. Deanna had already fallen asleep by the cabinet, and Sully's breathing grew heavy beside her chair. The only sound was their steady rhythm, a fragile anchor in the wreckage of the day.

When I stepped into the waiting room again, the patients looked up, curiosity sharp in their eyes. No one asked, though. Maybe they saw the answer in my face.

Outside, the sun was still bright, but it felt dim. I drew in a lungful of warm summer air, but it didn't wash away the chill spiraling in my chest.

Mike was gone.

Lauren had been at Lake Mistfall too.

And no matter how convincingly she told her story, confusion twisted in her words like Sully's leash in the underbrush.

CHAPTER
Five

MIDNIGHT FOUND us at the well.

The summer air was warm and heavy, laced with the sweet musk of crushed grass and the faint, smoky tang of bonfires dying down after WishFest. The meadow hummed with the lingering echoes of laughter and music—ghosts of joy dissolving into crickets and quiet wind. Fireflies drifted lazily through the dark like bits of restless starlight, but around the old stone well the air was different.

Dense, waiting…alive.

Holden stood beside me, broad-shouldered and steady, though the shifting shadows carved hard lines into his face. He carried no flashlight, trusting my light instead. His robe—folded neatly across his arm—looked strange against his usual sport coat and badge, but he didn't complain. He never did when it came to Elarion, taking his role as a member of The Covenant Three seriously.

"You ready?" he asked, his voice low enough to almost blend with the hum of night. His storm-gray eyes settled on mine, steady but searching.

"As ready as I ever am." I forced a small smile, though my pulse betrayed me.

The well left no room for hesitation. It demanded surrender. I tugged the dusky rose sash of my ceremonial robe tighter around my waist. The moss-green fabric whispered as I moved, its copper threading catching the moonlight like water over stone. My crest —a sapling rooted by a stream, stitched in silver and green— rested over my heart. It pulsed faintly, a reminder of who I was and what I carried.

The balance between two worlds.

Drawing a slow breath, I raised my hand and whispered the ancient words that had lived on my tongue since childhood. My pendant warmed, pulsing once…twice…before the air thickened and glimmered. The well's rim glowed, the stones vibrating with power. Then, with a sound like the tide inhaling, the water parted and the iron grate vanished below.

Holden's jaw tensed, but he didn't hesitate. He stepped beside me, and together we crossed the threshold.

The world dropped away.

The descent was never like falling. It was like drifting through liquid starlight. Cool ribbons of blue and silver wrapped around us, thick as silk, each pulse of magic pressing close like a heartbeat. The pull was neither up nor down, but inward, toward something ancient that recognized us both.

When the light released us, we stood on moss that glowed faintly beneath our feet, soft as memory. The air in Elarion always felt alive, as if breathing in rhythm with us. Holden stumbled, catching himself before his robe finished settling over his shoulders. The fabric shifted color between slate and midnight, adjusting to him, testing him.

In Elarion, everything shimmered.

Holden's beard gleamed faintly, the hairs moving as if under water. My own locks floated around me, their chestnut hue deepened to burnished gold, burgundy, and green under the magic. Dwellers' eyes, normally luminous, burned brighter here. Iridescent like oil on water.

Even the air was heavier, tinged with minerals and melody.

Before us stretched the outer ring of Elarion's forest, the

Dreamroot trees arching overhead in a living cathedral of light. Veins of silver ran through the marble path like quiet lightning, pulsing with the realm's heartbeat.

Holden blew out a breath, slow and reverent. "Still feels like stepping into a fairy tale," he murmured.

"Fairy tales in Elarion end badly," I said.

He glanced sidelong at me. "And this one?"

"This isn't a fairy tale. It's politics, duty…and danger."

As if on cue, a ripple of power moved through the trees. Calderis emerged from the obsidian archway ahead, his tall frame cutting a commanding figure against the glow. His robes were formal—cobalt trimmed with azure, his crest of flowing water around a sunstone glinting faintly. His hair spilled over his shoulders like molten moonlight. Even the air seemed to bow around him.

I'd already filled Holden in on my meeting with Lauren, and on what I'd found near Mike's body. Afterward, I'd messaged Calderis through my crystal orb, telling him it was urgent.

"You're late," Calderis said, his voice smooth but edged, his fake Boston cadence replaced by the natural formal tone of his native tongue. His gaze lingered on me longer than it should have.

Maybe he wasn't as into LuLu as I'd thought. Not that I had room to judge. My heart was still a battlefield, and both men were caught in the crossfire.

"Blame WishFest," I said, shaking off the thought. "We made it through day one—barely."

"Another disruption?" he asked.

"Worse. The Veiled Vault and a possible murder, but the well is fine, so a wish should get chosen and the treaty should stay intact."

A glimmer of tension crossed his face, but then was gone in a breath. He nodded once. "Follow."

Holden fell in step beside me, his robe whispering against the quartz-veined path as Calderis led us deeper. Pools of mirrored water reflected constellations from skies unseen, and vines of living crystal wrapped the arches overhead. The scent of damp stone and ancient power filled the air.

We entered the *Council Chamber* through crystal doors that rippled like water. The vast hall glowed faintly, its acoustics swallowing every sound into solemn silence. Twelve elders sat in their crescent tiers, their robes gleaming in the colors of their domains: ember, obsidian, silver, and seafoam. Orbs floated above them, glowing softly like moons.

And on the highest dais sat Vaerion.

Calderis' father radiated the kind of stillness that made air itself hold its breath. His white hair was braided with twilight threads, his robe a glimmer of whirlpool blue encircling a starburst crest. His eyes—pale, sharp, and unrelenting—pinned us where we stood.

We bowed. Holden stiffly, me fluidly, and Calderis with the cool grace of a man performing a duty he despised.

Vaerion's voice cut through the hall. "Report."

"WishFest proceeds as planned," I began, "but Mike Zaccaria found the Veiled Vault."

A collective murmur rippled through the elders. The orbs flared, then dimmed.

"You know of the Vault?" Vaerion demanded.

"My mother told me," I said evenly, "before she vanished. I knew of a spiral vortex that led to a secret chamber that housed a vault with danger inside, but no details other than that. I never knew its location until now." I met his eyes. "When I found Mike in the Whisper Woods, I saw the spiral. Someone had been digging in its center. I filled the dirt back in and sealed it temporarily with my Harmony Pulse, but that won't hold. Mike was already dead when I found him." My throat tightened. "I was too late."

"Murder," Holden said quietly, his tone stripped of everything but truth.

The orbs dimmed further, their glow softening like grief.

"I could feel an energy," I added.

Vaerion's eyes narrowed. "So. The Vault must be compromised and what lies within has awakened."

"I didn't get any security alerts." Anger laced Calderis' voice. His hands were tight at his sides, his knuckles white.

Holden frowned. "You mean you knew about it?"

"Enough," Vaerion snapped. "You three are a team now. Take them to the Vault from our side, and then seal it."

"Father—"

"Apparently, you need help keeping the Vault secure. You are Chief Enforcer," Vaerion cut him off. "Do your duty."

The tension between them vibrated through the chamber like a struck chord. Calderis bowed stiffly. Neither man looked at the other again.

I swallowed. "And if sealing it fails?"

Vaerion's gaze found mine, ancient and heavy as the deep. "Then the treaty won't matter, and what sleeps will ruin us all."

Silence rippled outward like a wave. The orbs dimmed to near dark. I pressed my hand against my pendant, its warmth pulsing faintly against my skin. My mother's voice echoed again through memory, *Stay away from the Vault, Lyra. It will cost you everything.*

But staying away wasn't an option anymore.

"Come," Calderis said softly. "We go now."

Holden adjusted his robe, muttering, "Midnight fairy tale, and I'm the only one without a sword."

I smiled weakly. "You've got me. I'm not sure if that's better or worse."

He grinned just enough to break the tension. "Depends on the night."

Then we followed Calderis into the glow. He moved fast, his cobalt robe cutting through the light like a blade. Holden's boots echoed faintly behind me while my slippers whispered against the marble. The path wound through Elarion's inner ring where crystal spires jutted skyward like frozen lightning. Warding sigils shimmered faintly, brushing against my skin like static.

Holden murmured, "Feels like walking through a cathedral… yet it's contained like a prison."

"That's because it's both," Calderis said without turning.

The deeper we went, the colder it became. Magic hummed beneath the surface like the thrum of a great heart, but something in the rhythm was off. Even the light dimmed, tinged with faint shadows.

At the cliffs, Calderis finally stopped. His expression was carved from control, but unease swam in his eyes. "The Vault lies between both worlds," he said, "but our entrance has changed." He inspected the entrance and his face hardened. "Someone tampered with my security system."

We followed him silently through an arch of ancient runes. The air turned damp and metallic, tasting faintly of rain on stone. The vibration beneath my feet stuttered, like an irregular sinus rhythm.

When the tunnel opened up, the sight stole my breath.

The spiral path I imagined was once-perfect, that lead to the chamber of the Vault, was half-collapsed. Crystal pillars lay broken, glowing faintly from within. Dust shimmered in the air like ghost light.

Holden let out a low whistle. "That doesn't look natural."

"No," Calderis said grimly. He knelt, tracing a fracture. "Someone forced this."

I pressed my palm to the ground. My Seismic Sense thrummed, revealing jagged, violent vibrations as if the earth had been torn open by will, not time. "Mining," I whispered.

Holden crouched beside me. "Mining for what?"

I reached into the rubble and drew out a shard of pale green crystal. The warmth pulsed through me, soothing muscle and bone. "Healing stones," I said. "Powerful ones."

Calderis' voice hardened. "They're forbidden to leave Elarion. Whoever mined here defied both realms."

Vex padded forward from the shadows, having followed us

through the well, his fur a halo of faint starlight. *Not just stones,* his voice whispered in my mind. *Look deeper.*

I moved toward a fissure where herbs sprouted, their leaves glowing faintly. The scent was sharp, sweet, and dangerous. I crushed one between my fingers; the juice burned, then cooled.

"Enchanted herbs," I murmured. "The kind that twist wishes."

Holden frowned. "So, someone's harvesting this stuff, either human or Dweller, for money?"

"Or power," Calderis confirmed. "Enough to destroy peace itself."

The air quivered.

"Was the collapse intentional?" I asked quietly.

Calderis rose, his robe darkening. "Perhaps. Or perhaps the Vault resisted the intrusion from someone digging above, causing a cave-in, blocking the path so no one would find the secret chamber."

"Where is the chamber?" I asked.

"Close, invisible to the eye, hidden beneath a veil."

"So, someone was digging above, and someone below turned off the security system. Do you think they're working together?"

"I'm not sure, but I intend to find out." Calderis met my gaze. "I'll reset my security system. Then we'll return to your side. The spiral path is still compromised. With my security system down, Dwellers can cross through the spiral vortex to Wishville above. We need to seal it tonight."

Holden brushed dust from his robe. "Fairy tale's over. Now it's a crime scene."

"No," Calderis said softly. "It was always both."

We turned back, our footsteps echoing in uneasy rhythm.

At the intersection where realms met, Holden touched my arm. "Whoever's behind this," he said, "they're organized. This took planning."

I met his eyes. "And that worries me."

"Someone definitely had help. Only a handful of people would know how to dismantle my security alert system. The good thing is they weren't able to break into the vault itself, but not for lack of trying. It's cracked." Calderis glanced back. "That ends now."

But his words didn't comfort me. Sealing the spiral path to the chamber that housed the Vault wouldn't erase the truth. Something had already started to wake up. I could feel it.

The light rose to meet us, the world of Elarion fading behind. And as the well pulled us upward, I couldn't shake the feeling that this time, we weren't the only ones crossing between worlds.

CHAPTER

Six

THE WHISPER WOODS were never quiet, not truly. Even in the pale hours of dawn, when most of Wishville still slept, the forest hummed with unseen life: the rustle of wings, the trickle of hidden streams, and the groan of branches stretching toward the first light. But that morning, as Holden, Calderis, and I followed the narrow deer path toward the spiral clearing, the woods felt fragile.

Like glass ready to shatter.

Even though it was summer, the woods in the morning could still be chilly. I tugged my jacket tighter. After nights in ceremonial robes, it felt strange to wear human clothes again. Spandex-blend hiking pants, boots, and a dry fit t-shirt were my go-to. I might look normal on the outside, but I was trembling with fear on the inside.

I adjusted my ponytail, and the pendant at my throat warmed against my skin. The feeling was neither gentle, nor comforting. The heat intensified, and my mother's voice threaded faintly through it again, more of an echo than a sound.

Stay away from the Vault. It will cost you everything.

My steps faltered. Had it cost her everything? Did her disappearance have something to do with this vault? Was she even alive still?

Calderis noticed my stumble. He slowed his long stride, the cobalt shadows of his robe traded this morning for dark jeans, boots, and a simple shirt that still managed to look regal on him. His river-colored eyes now a pale blue pinned me in place.

"You feel it," he said quietly. "You weren't supposed to know."

"Yes, I feel it. My mother told me more than she probably should have, but like your father said…we are a team now." My fingers closed over the pendant. "Now that you know that I know, I want answers. No more half-truths. What is the Veiled Vault exactly? Why did my mother warn me?"

Holden stopped beside us, his gaze swinging between us, impatient but sharp. "I'd like those answers too." He cleared his throat. "As the third member of the team, and all."

For once, Calderis didn't deflect. His shoulders squared, and in the filtered dawn light, he looked older than I'd ever seen him. His voice was low and steady, each word deliberate. "The Veiled Vault is a prison. Not for a human. Not even for a Dweller. For a powerful entity. One born of evil and greed, that can possess anyone or anything and manipulate one's mind. The entity is the disembodied, power-hungry consciousness of the First Elder. An ancient Dweller whose attempt to become supreme ruler destroyed his physical form and human sacrifice. Now a parasitic emotional predator, he jumps into vulnerable hosts while hunting for the ultimate vessel: the hybrid between humans and Dwellers that he tried to create centuries ago, believing that body will finally give him a way to return to power."

"A hybrid between humans and Dwellers sounds a lot like Lyra," Holden said with a frown.

"All the more reason to keep it contained." Calderis said, adding, "It's abilities are limited by Dweller rites, strong-willed minds, and the need for emotional cracks to slip through. It cannot be killed, only extracted from its host to be captured then put into a magical sleep. Storing the entity is the Vault's prime purpose."

My mouth went dry. "And now that the Vault has been breached…"

He met my gaze squarely. "It stirs."

Holden's jaw tightened. "You're telling me there's some kind of nightmare force underground stored in a containment unit, and the only thing keeping it there is a magical nap? Why does this feel like The Exorcist meets Ghostbusters on steroids?"

Calderis looked at me confused.

"Never mind him," I said, trying not to roll my eyes. "Explain the nap part."

"Not nap," Calderis said, his tone clipped. "Slumber bound by spells older than both our peoples, but spells weaken. And when mortals stumble upon sacred places, when herbs are harvested and stones are mined…" his voice darkened, "…the binds rattle."

I swallowed hard, the pendant burning hotter. "My mother knew about the entity, didn't she?"

"Yes." His voice softened then, and a shade of respect tinged it. "Serenna was the one who contained the entity and then sealed the vault after the last breach. Stone and spell entwined, sealed with a spiral to draw the evil energy inward rather than let it spill outward. She gave everything to close it again but then vanished soon after. My father ordered me to keep the vault hidden, and to guard the entity until the world forgot." He sighed. "I have failed him."

I shook my head, still processing my mother's involvement. Had she known all along I would be the perfect host? Was she trying to protect me? "If my mother put the entity to sleep, then how is it waking up now?"

Calderis turned his head slightly, his eyes narrowing. "Someone from inside Elarion must have discovered the enchanted herbs and healing stones inside the forbidden area. And someone on your side is working with them. Perhaps Mike stumbled into it. Or perhaps he was more involved by finding something up top. We cannot yet say for certain, but mining the spiral entrance has weakened the Vault seal."

The words stung.

Kindhearted Mike Zaccaria tangled in something so dark? I didn't want to believe it and prayed his being at the Vault had been an unfortunate coincidence, but I'd learned already that wishing didn't make truth kinder.

Who was he involved with?

What other secrets did he have?

We reached the clearing. My cloaking had already worn off. The spiral lay faint beneath dew and moss, but the air around it thrummed, restless.

Holden sighed slowly, his eyes scanning the clearing, and his hand brushing the radio at his belt. "So, what's the plan? Because if that thing wakes up, I don't think handcuffs are gonna cut it."

Calderis stepped forward, his expression unreadable. "The plan, for now, is concealment. Until we can make the sleep permanent again."

He knelt at the center of the spiral, his palms flat against the damp earth. The air shifted, cooler, sharper. I felt the strength of him channeling Illusory Manipulation, shifting the surroundings and making the landscape transform. The energy poured outward, rippling through the soil in waves. The spiral lines glowed faintly blue then darkened, fading until nothing remained but the forest floor. The humming dulled, muffled behind his wards.

"Masked," he said, rising to his feet. His breath was steady, but his eyes were shadowed. "Only we three will know it's location now."

"And whoever was mining the stones and herbs." Holden's hand still hovered near his hip as if expecting trouble.

He didn't have to wait long.

A twig snapped. Then another.

I spun, my heart thudding, just as Lourdes Morales stepped into view. Her ever-present notebook was tucked under her arm, and a camera swung from a strap at her neck. Her lipstick was flawless, and her expression sly.

"Well, well." She tilted her head. "Fancy seeing you three out here before sunrise. Field trip?"

My stomach knotted. "LuLu."

"Don't 'LuLu' me." She smiled thinly. "A beloved town figure turns up dead in these woods, and now I find the WishFest chair, the police chief, and the mysterious detective sneaking around the very same clearing at dawn? I get the chief and detective investigating the area for clues, but what does the WishFest chair have to do with this?"

"I've lived in Wishville much longer than Chief Thorn. He sometimes seeks my help on his cases, and well, I am the one who found the body."

"You don't have to explain yourself, Lyra." Holden's voice hardened. "It's an investigation, Ms. Morales, and *you're* interfering."

LuLu's smile widened, sharklike. "I'm not interfering. I'm bird watching." She held up her camera. "And observing. There's a difference. Besides, the people of Wishville have a right to know what's happening in their own backyard."

"They don't want any part of this," I snapped before I could stop myself.

Her eyes narrowed, glinting with curiosity. "Then there *is* something more going on."

Calderis stepped forward, the dawn light catching the sharp planes of his face. "You should probably leave and let us get back to work."

She blinked, surprised by his bluntness. Then she recovered, tapping her pen against her notebook. "Maybe I will. But maybe I'd be more inclined if someone offered me coffee." Her gaze lingered boldly on Calderis, almost playful.

I expected him to scowl, to dismiss her. Instead, he tilted his head and studied her for a moment. "Very well."

The words hung in the air like a floating feather.

I gaped at him. "Wait, you're going out with her? Like on a date?"

Holden's sharp gaze shot to me briefly before he raised a brow at Calderis.

Calderis shrugged.

LuLu's grin spread wide. "Meet you at *The Twisted Loaf* at 8 AM sharp?"

He nodded once. "I'll be there."

She clicked her pen shut, tucking her notebook away with deliberate slowness. "See you around, boys. Lyra." She vanished back into the trees, leaving silence behind her.

I turned to Calderis, incredulous. "You just agreed to go for *coffee* with Lourdes Morales. She's an investigative journalist, you know."

His gaze met mine, calm and cool. "Better she fixates on me than on what sleeps beneath us."

Holden pinched the bridge of his nose. "This is going to be a nightmare."

I wasn't sure if he meant LuLu or the entity. Probably both.

I exhaled shakily, the dawn light breaking fully through the trees, gilding the clearing in fragile gold.

We had bought ourselves time, but definitely not safety.

By afternoon, the town square was alive again. Summer WishFest rolled on as if nothing dark had happened, laughter and music drifting up the hill into the clearing where tents stood in neat rows. The sun beat down warm and bright, carrying the scents of fried dough, sugared almonds, and kettle corn. To anyone else, it was just another festival day.

To me, the brightness felt like a mask stretched too thin.

Holden was off interviewing Mike's family, digging into his patients, his coworkers, anyone who might've wanted him harmed. Calderis—unbelievably—was still with Lourdes Morales. Their coffee had been hours ago.

What could they possibly still be doing together?

I shook off my unreasonable irritation. That left me as Guardian to make sure WishFest continued running smoothly. The treaty demanded it, even if my heart wasn't in it.

Could Mike really have been involved in something shady?

Children darted past me, sticky with lemonade ice pops, their shrieks of joy cutting through the fiddle music spilling from the main stage. Betsy Plum waved at me from her booth, flour smudged across her cheek as she sold another tray of donuts. Fiona Fitzwhistle tried to push mystery grab bags of books on passing couples. Gus Grimly tipped his hat in greeting, his mustache twitching as he handed out striped bags of popcorn.

On the surface, everything was perfect, but I felt the undercurrent.

I slipped through the crowd until I reached the shady edge of the clearing, where two figures leaned casually against a wooden post strung with bunting. Most people had come to know them as regulars these days, but I knew who they really were. Weylan, the balloon tour operator, and Sparks, the mechanic. Both were tall with different shades of blond hair and fake tattoos. Dwellers that Calderis had allowed to stay as my eyes in the sky and ears on the ground.

"You're late," Sparks said, though his grin softened the words. "That's not like you."

"Busy day," I replied.

Weylan studied me, his eyes sharper than his smile. "We heard. The woods were louder than usual."

I drew them a few steps farther into the shade, lowering my voice. "It's time I told you the truth because I need your help. But you need to swear to me you won't say a word. No one else can know. Not the Wellies, not the locals, not even other Dwellers."

They exchanged a glance. Sparks' grin faded. Weylan's smile vanished completely.

"You have our oath," they both said.

"The Vault is real," I whispered. "The Veiled Vault... It holds an evil entity. One that can't be killed, only kept asleep, but it's waking up. Mike stumbled on the spiral entrance to the forbidden area. Someone had been digging, mining healing stones and enchanted herbs. Someone from Elarion must have found out because the security system on Elarion's side was breached. They're working together."

Sparks swore under his breath, a string of words in Dweller tongue that sparked like flint.

Weylan's expression darkened. "That explains the noise. The earth hasn't been still for weeks."

I nodded. "We don't know if Mike was part of it or if he just wandered too close, but whoever's behind this might be using what they've taken."

Their eyes widened.

"Look around." I gestured back toward the bustle of festival-goers. "See if people are acting strange, and not in the Wellies' usual way."

We walked slowly through the booths. At first, they looked ordinary enough, offering games, wares, food, and laughter. But then patterns began to emerge. At the dunk tank, one of the volunteers climbed out, rubbing his arm. His skin was mottled with a rash, but as I watched, the redness faded too quickly as though soothed by something more than ointment.

At the lemonade stand, a boy with a broken arm flexed his fingers without wincing. His cast was still wrapped around his wrist, but the ease in his movement wasn't natural. His mother fussed over him, scolding him to keep still, but her eyes glittered with relief.

And farther down, a woman clutched a sprig of something silvery-green, inhaling deeply. Her whole posture loosened, with her shoulders dropping as though years of tension had melted away.

Sparks' lips pressed thin. "Those aren't human remedies."

Weylan's voice was grim. "Someone's selling them pieces of our world."

I swallowed hard, my throat dry despite the sticky air. "I think you're right. That's why I need your help. We need to get them all back. Watch and listen. If you see anything—herbs, stones, anyone suddenly stronger or healed too fast—you tell me first. No gossip or rumors. Just me."

Weylan inclined his head.

Sparks lifted his hand in a mock salute, though his grin didn't return. "We'll keep our eyes sharp," he promised.

I let out a puff of air, allowing my shoulders to ease. The festival drums thudded louder, and the crowd broke into cheers for some pie-eating contest on the main stage. Someone here, maybe even standing among the cheering crowd, was profiting from Elarion's riches.

And I had to find them before the entity beneath us woke fully.

A couple hours passed, taking us into late afternoon.

Summer WishFest had always been my favorite of the seasonal festivals: warm weather, strawberry shortcake contests, and strings of paper lanterns swaying in the trees. It was supposed to be a time of joy, gathering, and granting wishes under a summer sky.

I spotted the Wellies draped in flower crowns and handing out daisy "blessings" to people passing by. Their laughter rang out, as harmless as ever, but I couldn't help scanning the petals in their baskets, searching for any trace of silver-tinged leaves.

Just daisies…for now.

Poor Mr. Finch had his hands full, scrambling around the grounds trying to keep up with fixing things the festivalgoers broke, which seemed to be more than usual. Everyone seemed to be hyped up more than normal.

"Guardian." The word reached me like a tug. Sparks had

returned from his loop through the booths. Weylan joined him, taking a break from the balloon tours, scanning the area from above.

"Anything?" I steered us toward the shade behind the pie contest tent.

"Too much," Sparks said grimly. Electricity popped as he pointed toward a group of teenagers chasing each other near the well. One boy leaped higher than he should've been able to, clearing a bench in one bound. His friends whooped, but the look on his face was more startled than triumphant.

"Not natural," Weylan muttered.

"And him." Sparks pointed toward an older man at the lemonade stand. "He was leaning heavily on a cane moments ago but look at him now."

The more the man drank from his cup, the more his grip loosened and his steps smoothed out. Within minutes, he walked almost normally. His wife clapped her hands in delight, but the glow in his eyes told me it wasn't simple sugar water doing the trick.

My stomach tightened. "Healing herbs. Maybe stone dust dissolved."

"Someone's distributing it," Weylan said. "Quietly, but not cautiously."

I rubbed my temple. "We have to track it to the source."

A shout drew my attention back to the main contest stage. A boy had collapsed face-first into his pie, twitching. People rushed forward, but then he sat up, smeared in blueberries, his eyes wide and wild. He sprang to his feet, laughing, his arms outstretched like he could take on the world. His mother shrieked in alarm.

The crowd clapped wildly, thinking it was part of the spectacle, but Sparks leaned close. "That wasn't sugar. That was a stimulant."

I forced a breath, steadying myself. "Keep eyes on him. See who he goes to afterward."

Sparks nodded, already sliding into the crowd.

Weylan lingered, his gaze heavy on mine. "This isn't just curiosity. Whoever's doing this is testing the wares, seeing who reacts, and how much to give."

The words chilled me. He was right. It wasn't random. It was distribution disguised as festival indulgence. I thanked him quietly and moved on, weaving through the crowd with my senses wide open. The faint bounce of my pendant at my throat was a constant reminder of how disappointed my mother would be if she could see what was happening to our little town.

At the dunk tank, I overheard two women gossiping. "Swore her gout was gone in a day," one said, lowering her voice. "And no doctor did that. Said it was a special tea she got from a 'friend.'"

My pulse quickened. "Special tea," in Wishville, could only mean one thing—herbs not from this world.

By the craft booths, a child sat cross-legged, stacking stones into a tower higher than his head. He clapped his hands and the topmost rock wobbled, glowing faintly before settling back into place. His parents looked delighted, snapping photos, unaware that their son's game reeked of borrowed magic.

I crouched nearby, smiling gently. "That's a very good tower. Where did you get those?"

"My parents." He beamed. "The rocks like me!"

I touched the ground. He wasn't wrong. The vibrations in those stones were not ordinary. They carried traces of Elarion's healing stones, sensitive to touch, eager to respond. His parents had given him fragments to play with, treating dangerous relics like toys. I would have to find a way to confiscate everything without sounding the alarm and jeopardizing WishFest.

I forced myself to move on, though dread curled deep in my stomach.

Soon, the festival's energy swelled with fiddlers tuning up for the evening dance, children darting around with balloon animals, and vendors hawking maple flavored everything. But I saw it everywhere now: faint glows, too-fast recoveries, and strength that shouldn't belong.

I met Sparks again near the Ferris wheel, its colorful cars creaking as riders laughed overhead. He kept his voice low. "The boy from the pie contest? He met up with someone near the cider booth. I couldn't tell if it was a man or woman. They wore a big coat with the hood pulled low even in the heat. They slipped him something small. Stone dust, maybe."

My jaw tightened. "We need a name."

"Working on it," he said. "They're gone now."

Weylan reappeared, shaking his head. "It's worse than you think. I checked the healer's tent. Half the remedies in there carry traces of herbs not found in Wishville. He says he got them from a pop-up holistic stand. It's not there anymore, of course. Whoever's behind this isn't just distributing. They're laundering them through the festival booths."

A chill spread through me. It was organized and systematic.

"Both of you," I said firmly, "this stays between us. We find the proof first, then we act. If people start suspecting something is wrong, panic will spread faster than the herbs."

They nodded, with Weylan solemn and Sparks sharp-eyed.

The fiddlers struck up a lively tune, and couples spun around the dance floor. The crowd clapped along, the air thick with merriment, but all I could see were the cracks in the mask. The Vault's shadow was already seeping through.

I feared evil wouldn't be far behind.

CHAPTER
Seven

THE SECOND NIGHT of WishFest lingered in the air like smoke after fireworks. The scent of kettle corn and roasted nuts drifting up from Main Street. Down the hill, laughter echoed in pockets, tipsy festivalgoers lingering in clusters of lantern light. Those lanterns swayed gently in the evening breeze, their paper skins creaking on their strings.

Belle's pigeons circled above the bakery in chaotic formation, refusing to roost no matter how she whistled. Their wings cut the quiet with frantic flutters, a reminder that even the birds were restless.

I made my way home, slipped into comfy clothes, ate leftovers, and fed Vex. Peace and quiet was what I needed most. I had just finished stacking dishes and wiping down my little kitchen table when a knock rattled my door.

Firm. Steady. Holden.

Vex flicked an ear from his perch on the sill. *The grumpy one again,* he remarked, before tucking his nose beneath his paw.

I opened the door and found Holden standing in the porch light, looking better than a man had a right to even in his disheveled state. His gray suit coat was creased, the collar slightly askew, and his notebook bulged thick with scribbles. The faintest dusting of glitter—flower crown shrapnel, no doubt—clung stubbornly to his lapel. He looked worn down by festival chaos, his shoulders slumped, but his eyes remained sharp and cutting.

"Evening," he said in a voice rough around the edges.

"Come in before Belle's birds head this far and mistake you for target practice." I laughed, trying to lighten the moment before I did something stupid like hug him. Even though we had grown closer and flirted a little, we still hadn't crossed the line from friends to something more. I never quite knew what to say or do when we weren't working.

A soft snort escaped him over my pigeon comment. He stepped inside, bringing the cool night air with him. My house wrapped around him in warmth with the low glow of a candle, the scent of lavender bundles drying on a windowsill, and the faint trace of sage I'd burned earlier.

He glanced around. "How are the renovations holding up?"

"Good, thanks to you." I smiled.

He nodded as he lowered himself onto the couch with the kind of sigh that spoke of chasing children from dunk tanks and breaking up too many pie-eating disputes. I moved automatically to the kettle, but he waved it off.

"Coffee." He rubbed his forehead. "If you've got it."

That caught me off guard. Holden Thorn rarely asked for anything. Happy to help in some small way, I obliged him by pulling out the small tin of dark roast I kept for emergencies. The aroma bloomed as it brewed, rich and grounding. I poured it into my sturdiest mug and handed it to him, our fingers brushing.

I quickly let go.

He cupped it like a lifeline, the steam fogging his face as he took a long sip. Only then did he pull out his notebook. "I've been talking to people. Figured you'd want to know where the family was when Mike disappeared."

I curled into the armchair opposite him with a notebook on my lap and my pen poised. "Go ahead."

"Kim," he began. "She was with the boys at camp, handling

activities and making sure the schedule for the day stayed on track. Multiple people saw her go in and out of the lodge that morning before she returned to her campsite in search of Mike."

I nodded.

"Tony was supposed to be setting up the lifeguard station that day," Holden continued. His tone was flat and even, like he was just reporting facts. "He left his post for a while and told his friends he was going for a run. He went back to his campsite before his shift when his mother told him his father was missing."

I scribbled quickly, the scratch of my pen loud in the quiet.

"Joey was supposed to be fishing," Holden flipped a page, "but he wandered off for a few hours then came back with a story about losing track of time. His mother chalked it up to typical teenage stuff."

"Typical teenage stuff doesn't usually involve murder," I muttered.

He didn't respond, just made a note. His voice stayed steady. "So that's the family. Kim, Tony, and Joey. All accounted for, technically, but all with gaps if you look closely. Nothing airtight."

The candle flickered, casting shadows around the room.

Holden flipped another page. "Outside of the family we've got Ingrid Peelman, a rival chiropractor. She claims she was visiting her sister over in Pine Hollow the morning of the murder, but her sister wasn't home so there's nobody to vouch for her. And Evan Teller, a former patient who still carries a grudge. He said he was fishing alone at a nearby lake."

"Do you believe them?" I asked.

"Not sure yet." Holden's eyes narrowed. "Neither of them looked rattled when I asked their whereabouts the morning of the murder." He leaned back, rubbing his beard with one hand, the coffee mug still steaming in the other. "Park Ranger Tiana Ellison mentioned something else. Strange activity up around Lake Mistfall before the festival even started. She sometimes calls in that tracker who lives off the grid. He helps her with things like missing pets, hikers, and poachers in exchange for her leaving him alone. He knows the woods better than anyone."

I sat straighter. "The hermit?"

"Yeah. Odd fellow. Keeps to himself, but if he's around, he's a pair of eyes I'd like to question."

I let that settle, then said quietly, "I checked in with Sparks and Weylan."

Holden's attention snapped to me.

"They think more rebel Dwellers may be hiding among us," I explained. "Maybe in disguise. They could have slipped through the Vault's spiral exit when the security system was down. If that's true..." I folded my arms tight. "Wishville isn't as safe as we thought."

Holden's eyes narrowed further. His pen tapped against the open page, steady and controlled, then he nodded. "All right. If rebels are here, we'll keep watch." He tilted his head. "Do you think the hermit could be one?"

"Maybe. I'll know more when I meet him."

His frown deepened. "Don't go rogue again, Wells."

"I wouldn't dream of it." My tone was innocent, but Vex's flicking tail said he wasn't buying it any more than Holden.

Holden sighed with resignation and worry. "Anything else?"

I hesitated. "Lauren. She told me she was going to hike with her dogs on the same path Mike was on the morning he vanished, but something was off. I guess Sully ran off the path, leading her in the opposite direction. She said he never does that. He's the lazy one and never leaves her side. Something must have distracted him. She said she spent hours looking for him in unfamiliar areas. It rattled her."

Holden's brow furrowed.

"She looked shaken," I added softly.

"What about her husband?"

"Matt?" I shrugged. "He was at the high school. Teaching, grading, doing his usual. That's why Lauren showed up late at the clinic, with the dogs still in tow."

Holden jotted it down, then shut his notebook with a snap. The sound echoed, sharp as flint. "That's the shape of it, then. A family with gaps in their stories. A rival chiropractor, a disgruntled patient, a mysterious businessman, and maybe a hermit who knows more than he should. And on top of it all, possible rebel Dwellers in disguise."

Outside, the rustle of leaves in the trees sounded suddenly loud. The pigeons had made their way this far after all, their cooing carrying faintly through the open window, stubborn and unsettled.

I stared past Holden, out the window where the sky stretched wide and black, thick with stars. "We need to figure this case out, even if it means chasing whispers."

Holden's gaze met mine, steady and level, the coffee still steaming in his hands. "Then we'd better start listening."

Morning sunlight filtered through the canopy, gilding the forest floor in shards of gold and shadow. The air smelled of pine needles crushed under foot, and damp moss laced with faint smoke still drifting from festival fires. Wishville was only just stirring, but Holden and I followed Ranger Tiana Ellison deeper into the woods, leaving the sound of vendors prepping for the day behind us.

Tiana's long box-braids, with a streak of forest green threaded through them, swung against the back of her short-sleeved button-up gray collared shirt that was tucked into belted green trousers over sturdy shoes. She carried her tan hat in her hands.

"You know he doesn't just live in a cabin you can knock on." She glanced back at us. "The hermit shows himself when he wants to. When I need him, I wander. He finds me."

"Like calling a stray cat," Holden muttered.

"More like a fox," Tiana corrected. "If he doesn't want to be seen, you won't see him. Period."

We reached a clearing ringed with spruce, where Lake Mistfall gleamed through the trees. She gave a three-note whistle, sharp and clipped, then crossed her arms. "Now we wait."

Holden shifted, restless, but I already felt it—a charge under my skin like the air before a storm. My Dweller half stirred. Someone was nearby.

From the tree line, a figure emerged. Broad-shouldered, wrapped in green cotton, with a beard wild as the undergrowth and eyes dark as a crow's. I squinted, studying him, and knew for certain he wore a glamor meant to disguise him. He moved like he belonged to the forest itself, barely disturbing the needles underfoot.

"You called," he said, his voice gravel deep.

Tiana tipped her chin. "They wanted a word." She gestured in our direction. "Chief Thorn and Lyra Wells."

He studied us with an unreadable expression.

"Okay, then," Tiana said. "I'll leave you to it."

"Appreciate it." Holden nodded once.

She nodded back, then disappeared down the trail, her footsteps fading away.

I walked forward. "You don't have to keep up the hermit act with me."

His gaze snapped to mine. "Act?"

"You're a Dweller," I said plainly. "I can feel it. And Holden already knows about Elarion."

Holden's jaw ticked, but he didn't stop me.

For a heartbeat, the wild man was still. Then his lips curved into something between amusement and warning. "Brave, Guardian, to say that aloud. I didn't expect it." He looked at Holden, then back to me, his eyes glinting. "I've heard whispers of The Covenant Three. Word travels, even to those of us cut off from Elarion."

Holden frowned, his lips parting as if he were about to speak.

I beat him to it. "Then you know why we're here."

"I know enough." The man straightened, his shoulders rigid.

"Name's Alden. I was cast out to the outer ring long ago. I'm not a rebel. I'm an exile. I slipped through the well portal centuries ago and have walked these woods for years, unnoticed. My place is here, living apart from everyone. That's the way I like it."

"You like watching," Holden said flatly. "You watched Mike Zaccaria, didn't you?"

Alden's eyes hardened. "Your healer was reckless. He dug at the spiral entrance and collected old stones. Dangerous stones. He caused a cave-in and nearly buried himself, but he kept coming back. Meeting people. Trading things."

"Who was he meeting?" Holden pressed. "I need names."

Alden's mouth twisted into something sharp. "You think he told me? I don't waste time with men who trespass where they don't belong."

Holden's temper flared in the twitch of his jaw.

I jumped in before he could say something he might regret. "You *saw* something, though. Didn't you?"

For the first time, Alden's expression shifted—testing me. Then, with a small motion, he bent and pressed his palm to the earth.

The air tightened, humming low in my bones. A thin green glow spread like veins through the grass, winding outward in a spiral before fading. The ground rumbled almost sounding like a growl. The scent of damp stone rose sharp and metallic. Holden stiffened beside me with one hand on his holster, though his eyes were wide.

"That's dark magic," I whispered, my throat dry. "Trickery."

"Not a trick." Alden straightened. "A warning. I've been around a long time. I remember the stories of the creature. It stirs when disturbed. I'm assuming the Vault must be somewhere beneath the spiral. Zaccaria must have cracked the Vault's shell after the cave-in from his digging. You've felt it's energy, Guardian. Don't deny it."

I swallowed hard. "I have."

Holden's gaze cut between us with suspicion and something like unease flickering there. "You could've stopped Mike."

"I did what I could," Alden said evenly. "I kept close. I scared off what men I could, but he was stubborn. Curious. And curiosity is a dangerous thing near the Vault."

The forest hushed around us, even the birds had quieted.

"You don't know if other Dwellers came through," I said carefully, "but you think it's possible."

Alden's eyes darkened. "Possible, yes. And if so, they won't care about your festival or your families. They'll care about the Vault and what's inside. And if they manage to open it…" He let the words trail off, his silence heavier than any answer.

Holden scribbled in his notebook, though I noticed his hand shook just slightly. I stood rooted, my Dweller blood humming like a struck chord. For the first time, I wondered if Alden was more than an outcast.

Maybe a harbinger.

The woods had gone too still. Even Vex, crouched on my shoulder, had gone rigid, his tail flicking in short, tense jerks.

Holden cleared his throat. "If you know more, now's the time to say it. Names. Who Mike met. What they traded. Don't dance around it."

Alden's gaze slid to him like he was weighing Holden's worth. "Chief Thorn, you want everything labeled and filed, but the forest doesn't work that way. Some truths can't be spoken. They can only be felt."

Holden's pen dug into his notebook. "That's not an answer."

A faint smile touched Alden's lips. "No, but it's all you'll get tonight."

Before Holden could snap back, Alden shifted, his t-shirt stretching taut. He crouched, pressed his palm to the earth again, and the grass at his feet glowed faintly green. Then, like the flash of a camera, he was gone. The glow sank into the ground, leaving only damp leaves and pine needles undisturbed.

Holden swore under his breath and stepped forward, scanning the tree line. "He couldn't have just—"

"He did," I said softly. My chest still buzzed with the echo of Dweller magic, my half-blood humming in recognition. "He vanished the way some Dwellers do in Elarion, between light and shadow."

Holden turned toward me with raised eyebrows. "So, he's a Dweller and not just a hermit? I thought they weren't allowed in Wishville."

"Yes, and they're not. That's the problem." My throat tightened. "At least he's an outcast and not a rebel like Thayn was… but if he's a friend or foe remains to be seen."

Holden's jaw worked, but for once, he didn't speak. He just looked at the spot where Alden had been, his notebook limp at his side and gray eyes unsettled in a way I rarely saw. The forest hummed around us again like wind through spruce. A crow called overhead, and distant water lapped against Lake Mistfall's shore, but it all felt different now.

Like Alden had pulled back a curtain, and something was watching.

"We need to find out who Mike was meeting. Alden said *men*. What men?"

Holden finally pocketed his notebook. "It's about time we found out."

CHAPTER
Eight

THE WISHBONE CAFÉ smelled like comfort.

Rosemary and garlic simmered in the air, weaving through the darker scents of roasted coffee and baked bread. Mismatched chairs scraped against reclaimed wood floors, every table carrying its own history of rings and scratches. Low jazz hummed from speakers tucked into the corners, a saxophone and piano threading lazily through the conversations of locals who had claimed their favorite booths years ago.

It was cozy and dim.

Bart the butcher was delivering fresh cuts of meat to Willa for the café's dinner menu. He gave a head nod to Trip, who had cornered Holden's deputies in their booth, giving unsolicited help during their lunch break. When he took a moment to wave with his wand flashlight at us, they quickly slipped out and headed for the door before he could stop them. Setting his sights on Mayor Doug Delaney and his assistant, Laisira, he made a beeline for their table next.

I slid into a booth near the back with Vex curling himself into the seat beside me. His tail flicked once before settling, and his eyes glowed faintly in the shadows. Everyone knew he was my emotional support animal and turned a blind eye when he accompanied me.

"Behave," I whispered under my breath, knowing he would do whatever he pleased. I didn't own him any more than he owned me. We were equals and allies, he was just the snarkier one.

Holden had gone deeper into the mess of Mike's disappearance, digging through records and witness statements with his usual grim focus. That left me free—or at least freer than usual—to meet Lourdes Morales for lunch. I'd been meaning to. The woman had a way of orbiting close to every lead like a planet determined not to fall out of rotation. And while the Wellies adored her, I knew better than to trust too quickly.

I always looked into newcomers. That was part of my job as Guardian, though of course, I couldn't exactly write *background checks on humans who might stumble into immortal business* on any official list of duties. So, I'd done what I always did…I dug.

And what I'd found had left me unsettled.

LuLu had made her name in Miami as an investigative journalist, sharp and fearless. But some scandal had happened, and she became the scapegoat. Her reputation had been shattered, and the newsroom turned on her faster than wolves scenting blood.

She'd said that she was doing a favor for Ernie Maddox, but the truth was worse. Ernie hadn't reached out to anyone for help. Her boss had begged him to take her on and give her a place to lie low until the scandal cooled. She wasn't here just to fill in for Marin. She was here because she had nowhere else to go.

And she was determined to claw her way back.

That much I could see in her eyes every time she circled me with questions, and every time she scribbled in that ever-present notebook. She wanted the story of the year. And if she ever found out Elarion was real—ever glimpsed Dwellers—she'd run with it and never look back.

I told myself to be careful. That this lunch was my chance to feel her out and decide how much of a risk she really was.

When she walked in, heads turned. Not because she was flashy. She wasn't. But because she carried herself like she belonged anywhere she stood. Espresso-dark hair framed her face in loose waves as usual, with her brown eyes snapping sharp and bright even when she smiled. She spotted me and lifted her hand in a small wave as she wove through the tables.

"Hope you don't mind," she said as she slid across from me, "but I called ahead and ordered us a plate of garlic knots. Willa swore they'd change my life."

"They just might." I smiled despite myself.

Willa Hartman had been running this place for decades, and if anyone knew the power of garlic knots, it was her. For a moment, we sat in comfortable silence with the clink of silverware and low murmur of voices around us.

Then LuLu leaned forward, resting her elbows on the table. "Look, Lyra…we got off on the wrong foot."

I blinked. That wasn't the line I'd expected.

"I really like you," she continued, her voice softer now, stripped of the brisk reporter's edge. "And, honestly, I could use a friend."

I studied her face, searching for the trap. But she only looked tired, honest, and maybe even a little raw. "I like you, too. And for the record, I'm a good listener if you're in need."

She hesitated a moment and then exhaled slowly. "Back in Miami I screwed up. I went public with a story that wasn't true. My source lied, and I didn't double-check like I should have. Everything fell apart after that. People I thought had my back? They didn't." She sighed. "My name was trash."

So she hadn't lied. She'd been betrayed. "Oh, Lu, I'm sorry. That had to have been rough."

"It was." She nodded. "My boss shipped me out here under the guise of a favor to Ernie, but really, he just wanted me gone before the fallout landed on him. So here I am. In a town no one's heard of, trying to scrape together the pieces of my career. That's why I've been pushing so hard, asking too many questions. I need to prove myself again. Prove I'm still worthy of doing the work I love."

I had asked her to lunch, planning on confronting her. I hadn't expected her to open up to me first. I'd been ready to challenge her and demand to know her intentions. But instead, she'd beaten me to it, laying herself bare.

"I get it," I said quietly.

Her brows arched. "You do?"

I nodded, my fingers worrying the rim of my water glass. "Every mistake with WishFest? Every banner hung crooked or booth misplaced? It all comes down on me. I'm chair of the festival. Everyone looks at me like I'm the problem. Like I'm not enough." Which was the truth, even if it wasn't the *whole* truth.

The Council of Elders never let me forget that I wasn't a full Dweller. That no matter what I did, some part of me would never measure up. I couldn't tell LuLu that, but I could let her see the shadow of it.

She tilted her head, her expression softening. "So, you know what it's like. Always having to prove yourself."

I gave a short laugh. "Yeah. More than I'd like."

Something eased between us then. The garlic knots arrived, steaming and fragrant. We placed our orders and then both tore into the appetizer like we hadn't eaten in days. By the time our salads came, we were laughing over the Wellies' latest antics, and it felt less like a test and more like the beginning of a friendship.

"Let's start over." She held out her hand across the table. "No more walls or secrets. Just friends."

I hesitated, knowing there was one secret I had to keep, then clasped her hand. "Friends." It felt good. Vulnerable, maybe, but good.

We lingered until the lunch crowd began to thin, the jazz softening into a slower melody. I was about to suggest coffee refills when movement near the door caught my eye.

Kim Zaccaria stood just inside, her tote clutched tight against her side. She looked composed at first glance, but her fingers twisted the strap of her bag, and her eyes darted around nervously.

She wasn't alone.

Three men stood with her, commanding the space without even trying. The first was wiry, late fifties, with sharp hawklike features that seemed to cut through the dim café light. His graying hair was slicked back with meticulous care, every strand disciplined, but the precision only emphasized the restless energy in his darting eyes. His suit was tailored but just a touch too flashy—deep jewel tones, gold cufflinks, and a silk scarf knotted at his throat. He looked more showman than businessman, his smooth, persuasive voice carrying across the café like oil spreading across water.

Flanking him were two giants who might have been mistaken for professional bodybuilders if not for the menace in their posture. One was bald with a jagged scar carving a line from his temple to his jaw, giving him a permanent sneer. The other had a mane of dark hair pulled into a slick ponytail, his heavy brow shadowing eyes that were too small. Their suits strained against corded arms, and they moved with the swagger of men who knew their size unsettled people.

I leaned forward slightly, straining to catch his words, but the low jazz and the hum of the café swallowed them.

Kim nodded along, her smile brittle. When the wiry man touched her elbow, she flinched almost imperceptibly, then pulled away with a hasty excuse. She slipped out the door, her face flushed and her steps too quick.

The men lingered.

That's when Brittany Voss bounced in, all blonde curls and endless energy. She didn't hesitate a second, beaming as she slid her business card into the scarred man's hand. I watched her gesture toward the ponytailed brute and the wiry hawk-faced leader, her voice too bright to be casual. She was no fool…

She was pitching them her gym.

The men listened with interest, the hawk-faced one smiling in that smooth, oily way that made my skin crawl.

LuLu leaned close, her voice barely above a whisper. "Who are they?"

"I don't know," I admitted, my gut tightening, "but I intend to find out." Because whatever conversation Kim Zaccaria had just fled from…

It hadn't been about garlic knots.

By evening, the festival had shifted gears into something dreamlike.

Lanterns strung between poles and trees cast warm pools of light across the green, their glow mingling with the flicker of fire pits where townsfolk roasted skewers of hotdogs or marshmallows. The hum of laughter and fiddles drifted through the summer air, mingling with the tang of maple butter corn and candied almonds. Children darted through the crowd with glowing necklaces bouncing against their shirts, while the Wellies paraded about in flower crowns as though they'd been officially appointed priestesses of the solstice.

It should have felt safe. It should have felt normal. But Mike's absence hung over everything like a ghost, and the shadows at the edges of the festival grounds felt spookier tonight.

I stood near the lemonade stand, pretending to be absorbed in Tilly's lecture on how lavender sprigs tucked behind your ear would prevent bad fortune. I felt Holden's presence before I saw him. He moved through the crowd with his usual mix of quiet authority and mild exasperation, his shoulders squared and storm-gray eyes scanning the festival for threats.

"Wells," he said when he reached me, his deep tone vibrating through me.

"Chief," I said, my heart softening more than I cared to admit. "I wondered when you would show up."

"Had things to check." His gaze slid past me, taking in the booths, families, and festival glow. "Found out something you're not going to like."

I crossed my arms. "When do I ever like what you dig up?"

He leaned closer, lowering his voice. "Kim Zaccaria took out a life insurance policy on Mike. Right before the camping trip."

My stomach clenched. "That doesn't mean—"

"It doesn't mean she killed him," he cut in, "but it sure does mean she was preparing for the possibility he might not come back."

I swallowed hard.

Before I could reply, he added, "And that's not all. I traced Mike's movements over the past month. He met multiple times with an artifact collector named Rufus Graymoor. Mike has been seen with some questionable characters."

Questionable characters?

"I think I saw him today," I said quickly. "LuLu and I were at *The Wishbone Café* for lunch, and Kim was there with three men. One wiry, flashy older guy and two human tanks who looked like they'd been hired to scare people just by standing still. Kim looked rattled when she left. Then Brittany swooped in, trying to sell them gym memberships."

Holden's jaw tightened. "Sounds like our men."

As if conjured by our words, I spotted them near the edge of the crowd, standing out like wolves in a flock of sheep. The wiry man wore a suit in deep emerald tonight, his scarf knotted with careless precision. He laughed smoothly at something one of his hulking shadows said, his hands spread in that salesman's way that made every gesture look rehearsed. The scarred brute scanned the crowd with sharp eyes, while the one with the pony-tail loomed, his arms folded as if daring anyone to approach.

Holden followed my gaze. "Let's pay Mr. Graymoor a visit."

We cut through the festival, weaving past stalls selling maple cotton candy and bundles of rosemary. The closer we got, the heavier the air felt, like the music dimmed around us. Rufus noticed first, his sharp eyes sweeping toward us, amusement curling his lips.

"Chief Thorn," he said smoothly, his voice as polished as his cufflinks. "And Ms. Wells. To what do I owe the pleasure?"

It didn't surprise me that he knew who we were.

Holden didn't waste time. "You're Rufus Graymoor." It wasn't a question.

The man dipped his chin, the silk scarf catching the lantern light. "I am."

"What was your business with Mike Zaccaria." Holden's tone was all iron, no courtesy.

Rufus' smile didn't falter. "Ah, Mike. Fine man. He contacted me himself, you know. Said he had some rare artifacts he wanted to sell. Interesting pieces, quite valuable. We spoke at length, but in the end, he backed out. Said he'd found another interested party, though he never named who."

"Convenient," Holden said flatly. "Where were you the morning of his death?"

"An estate sale in Burlington," Rufus answered smoothly, without hesitation. "I adore them. They're full of treasures if you know where to look. But alas, I didn't buy anything that day." His smile widened, daring Holden to challenge him.

Holden's eyes narrowed. "No log, no receipt, nothing to tether you to the place. So, we just have your word." He paused, shooting Rufus a disbelieving stare. "Like I said, convenient."

"An honest man's word." Rufus spread his hands, charm dripping from every word. "I am, after all, a businessman. Not a murderer."

I shifted, unable to hold back. "Then what were you doing with Mike's widow, Kim, earlier? She looked upset."

For the first time, Rufus' smile thinned. "Simply inquiring whether she knew anything about her husband's artifacts. Whether she might be willing to part with them, should she come across some. She claimed she knew nothing, of course. I believed her."

The way he said it—oily, dismissive—made my skin prickle.

Holden's voice dropped lower, steel sharpening his words. "Stay close, Mr. Graymoor. Don't give me a reason to drag you in."

Rufus gave a small, mocking bow. "Of course, Chief. I wouldn't dream of interfering in your investigation."

The scarred man sneered, the ponytailed brute chuckled under his breath, and the three of them melted back into the shadows of the festival, leaving behind the faint scent of expensive cologne.

Vex's voice whispered in my head, low and warning. *The Collector is never empty-handed. He carries more than he shows.*

I wrapped my arms tighter around myself. Rufus Graymoor might not have killed Mike with his own hands, but he was tangled in this web. And the closer he drew to Kim—and her secrets—the more I feared what else he was capable of.

"We need to talk to Kim again," I said.

"You took the words right out of my mouth." Holden's eyes still lingered on the shadows where the snakes had disappeared. "But first, we need to update Calderis on these artifacts. Something tells me the breach surrounding the Vault is bigger than we thought."

CHAPTER
Nine

CROSSING into Elarion always felt like stepping into another lifetime. Late that night, the well's light swallowed us whole, cool and weightless. When I blinked again, we stood in the underground world that pulsed with its own rhythm. Moss and marble, crystalline light, the hush of waterfalls echoing through caverns. Even after centuries, it still left me breathless.

But I didn't lead Holden straight to Calderis this time.

"Where are we going?" His boots squeaked lightly on the marble path that glowed faintly beneath our feet.

"My mother's house first." I led the way.

The path took us into the *Stonemasons' Quarter*, one of the oldest neighborhoods in Elarion. Homes had been carved directly into the rock walls generations ago, their archways shaped with impossible precision. Intricate carvings ran across facades like living vines: scenes of battles, festivals, and families etched into the stone itself. Colorful mosaics of enchanted glass adorned entryways, glimmering faintly under the bioluminescent glow. Each house bore charms and symbols to reflect the family's skill and lineage. Spirals for masons, constellations for stargazers, and blades for warriors.

My mother's family dwelling was quiet, as it always was. The door etched with a stylized willow tree rooted in stone, the branches arching into the shape of a spiral. She came from a long line of masons and Guardians. I brushed my fingers against it, half hoping the wood would give way to some hidden truth.

Inside, the air was still. Dust hung in the light spilling through crystalline sconces, the rooms untouched since my mother had vanished and I took her place as the Guardian. Shelves were still lined with scrolls, and herbs long since withered were in jars. I moved slowly, scanning carvings, corners, anything that might hold another clue to what happened to her after she sealed the Vault.

Holden lingered by the doorway, respectful but restless. "You've been here before. What are you hoping to find now?"

"Anything I missed." A lump filled my throat. "She warned me to stay away from the Vault. Now I know why. But what I don't know is what it took from her. There has to be something she left behind."

I searched the study, kneeling by the desk where she'd written her council reports. No hidden compartments, and no folded scraps waiting for discovery. Just the faint smell of ink long faded. In the bedroom, her pendant box sat empty on the shelf, its velvet lining worn smooth. I'd already taken the necklace years ago, the one that still vibrated against my skin when the Vault stirred.

But tonight, something else caught my eye.

A carving on the wall I'd never noticed before, nearly swallowed by the shadows. A spiral, etched faint and shallow, almost like she hadn't wanted anyone to see it. My pulse quickened as I ran my fingers over the grooves. It had a distinctive split down the middle. Had she known there would be a breech?

"Another Vault clue?" Holden asked, stepping closer.

"Maybe." I pressed my palm against it, but no magic stirred. Just cold stone. Disappointment lodged in my chest. Maybe it was just habit, her hand carving spirals the way other people doodled. Maybe her knife had slipped and made the line down the middle. Or maybe it meant more, and I still didn't understand. I forced myself to rise. "There's nothing useful here. Let's go."

Holden didn't argue, but his gaze lingered on the carving before we left.

It didn't take us long to reach Calderis. His quarters were carved higher into the cavern walls, overlooking the Dreamroot Forest's silver canopy. The Enforcer's home was austere, all sharp lines and precise order, but there was a weight to it, like every item had been placed with care.

His mother, Elanith, and sister, Lumira, spoke in hushed tones just outside his door, looking worried. When they spotted us, they gave Calderis a hug, bowed, and then quickly left.

After they disappeared from sight, Calderis turned and motioned us forward, his robe tonight a deep cobalt trimmed in bright azure. "Lyra. Thorn." His bow was formal, but his pale eyes softened fractionally when they met mine. "You come with news."

"We do," Holden said grimly. "Mike Zaccaria was more than a missing person who died. It's as we feared. He was in possession of rare artifacts. Lyra thinks they were the enchanted herbs and healing stones from the forbidden area surrounding the Vault."

Calderis' expression hardened. "The security system has been restored and the spiral entrance resealed."

"Yes, temporarily," I said quickly, though my mother's warning still burned in my memory. "And people at WishFest are acting strange—miraculously healed yet angrier and restless. I think the artifacts are poisoning them, twisting them."

Calderis paced slowly across the chamber. "How did this man come to possess such things on his own?"

"That's what we're trying to piece together," Holden said. "A hermit saw Mike meeting with people. Then Rufus Graymoor, a so-called artifact collector, told us Mike tried to sell to him but then backed out. He said he had another interested party, whatever that means."

"Hermit?" Calderis frowned.

"No one of importance," I said. My gut told me Alden wasn't a threat. I would deal with him later. For now, we needed to stay focused. "Have you heard anything? Any whispers down here?"

Calderis' gaze moved to the window, the marble path below lit with bioluminescent threads leading toward the city center. "Not in the Council chamber, but the market has ears. My mother and sister were just filling me in. Come. I'll take you."

Following his lead, we soon reached our destination.

Market Square was already bustling when we arrived. Lantern globes floated overhead, glowing in hues of emerald and sapphire, lighting up the stalls that were carved into the cavern walls. The scents of crushed herbs, spiced stews, and burning crystal incense filled the air. Stalls overflowed with enchanted goods—flasks of glowing liquid, charms strung with silver thread, and stones that hummed faintly when held.

This was Elarion's heart. A place where information traded as freely as goods.

"Stay close," Calderis murmured as we threaded through the crowd.

I did, though Vex had already slipped from shadow to shadow, his fur gleaming faintly like oil-slick light, in search of his Whispen girlfriend, Fenrin, no doubt. Holden kept his eyes sharp, though I could tell the market's surreal glow unsettled him.

Calderis led us to a spice merchant's stall. A Dweller woman with hair like silver wheat and eyes of stormlight measured herbs into a scale. She brightened when she saw him. "Chief Calderis. Twice in one week. That can't bode well."

"Tell me what you've heard, Meridessa," he said evenly. "I just spoke with my mother and sister, so don't bother lying."

She hesitated, glancing at Holden and me, then shrugged. "Rumors that the Veiled Vault from the legend is real. Rumors of pieces from our world working their way up through the soil. Rumors of someone in the Whisper Woods digging. Rumors the rebels were looking for the Vault, thought they found it after vibrations from a cave-in in the forbidden area, and then they never returned."

Mike. The word pulsed through me like a bruise.

"Who helped him?" I asked.

Her lips pursed. "No one knows for certain, but the collector's name comes up often. He has the muscle for a job like that. The manpower. The greed. If he was cut out of the deal, then someone else stepped in. If that person was cut out..." She spread her hands. "Rebels don't take kindly to betrayal."

Holden swore under his breath.

We thanked her and moved on, Calderis steering us deeper into the market where gossip hummed like background music. We overheard a group of apprentices hunched around a brazier, talking about rebels seen sneaking into caverns. A jeweler muttered that he traded precious gems for healing stones only to have those stolen from his stall weeks ago, vanishing without a trace. A brewer claimed to have been commissioned to brew a special batch of tea from enchanted herbs.

Every thread wound back to the same weave: Mike had cracked the seal hiding the Vault through his digging up top and finding artifacts he didn't recognize, rebels had obviously been aiding him by gathering more artifacts he couldn't access from Elarion, and a mastermind was overseeing everything. By the time we emerged from the market's glow, my chest ached with the weight of it all.

Calderis' jaw was set. "If the rebels truly know the Vault exists and they've breeched the forbidden area, they must have an established passage between the two realms. We can't risk the entity escaping, and we cannot allow more artifacts to escape. Humans have no idea what kind of power they're dealing with."

"We won't," I said, fiercer than I meant to. "We'll stop whoever is distributing them and get the rest back. Every last piece." But inside, my mother's spiral carving floated through my thoughts. She had known something more about the Vault. And now, her warnings felt less like protection and more like fore-shadowing.

The next morning, the sunlight spilled bright and golden across Wishville, warming the festival grounds while the banners fluttered in a playful breeze. Day four of WishFest promised another long list of activities, but my feet carried me away from the laughter and music, across town to the Zaccarias' house.

I balanced the covered dish in both hands as I walked up the path. Willa Hartman had insisted I take it, clucking about how no woman should have to think about feeding her family in the middle of grief. Garlic chicken, rosemary potatoes, green beans tossed with almonds—comfort food in its purest form.

I'd learned not to argue with Willa, so here I was, ferrying condolences in a casserole dish.

It had been three days since Mike's death. The medical examiner had released his body yesterday, and Kim was already planning the funeral. I'd avoided her until now, partly out of respect and partly because I needed to approach her carefully. Kim Zaccaria was normally polished to perfection on the outside, all smiles and gracious manners, but underneath her edges had begun to fray and it had started to show.

I knocked, and the door opened almost immediately. Kim stood there, her brown hair pulled into a neat twist, her linen blouse immaculate despite the shadows beneath her blue eyes.

"Lyra." She forced a smile that trembled. "This is kind of you."

I held out the dish. "From Willa, but with my condolences. I wanted to see if you needed anything."

"Thank you." She took it automatically, then stepped aside. "Come in."

The house was quiet, hushed in that uncomfortable way grief made spaces feel. The scent of pine cleaner polish lingered faintly, though the tidy living room looked untouched, as if Kim hadn't had the strength to disturb it. She set the dish down on the counter and fussed with the lid a moment longer than necessary, avoiding my gaze.

When she turned back, my eyes caught on the necklace around her throat. A simple chain with a small oval locket. Innocent enough except when the morning sunlight caught it, my Dual Sight flared, allowing me to see what others couldn't in both realms. A glow pulsed faintly from within, unmistakable.

A tiny vial was tucked inside the locket, alive with energy.

My heart stuttered. I forced my voice to stay even. "That's a beautiful locket."

Kim's hand flew to it instinctively, as if she hadn't realized she was wearing it until I pointed it out. "A keepsake." She quickly smoothed her blouse over it. "Family piece."

I let it go for now.

Instead, I asked softly, "Kim…was everything okay between you and Mike before he died?"

The question hung in the air, weighted.

Kim hesitated just a beat too long, her mouth tightening before she smoothed it into another brittle smile. "Of course. Everything was great."

I didn't move, holding her gaze gentle but steady, trying to see if she would reveal anything more to me. "Then why did you take out a life insurance policy on him right before your trip?"

Her composure cracked like porcelain under strain. Tears welled in her eyes, and she pressed her lips together before they trembled apart. "Because…" She sank into a chair, her shoulders shaking. "Because I was scared. He wasn't himself. He went on so many solo hiking trips and would be gone for hours, sometimes days. He'd started keeping secrets. The man could barely keep a birthday surprise, yet he was keeping secrets from me."

"Secrets like meeting with an artifact collector?" I watched her closely. "The men I saw you with at the café?"

She blinked her eyes wide, then she hoisted her chin high. "Like I told those men, I don't know anything." She cleared her throat. "I thought…I thought Mike was cheating on me."

"Oh, I'm so sorry, Kim." I felt horrible for her.

Her voice broke. "I didn't know what to do. I even hired a private investigator. I was angry, but mostly I was terrified. I couldn't shake the feeling something bad was coming. That's the only reason I took out the insurance policy. Not because I wanted him gone."

I slipped into the chair opposite her, lowering my voice. "Kim, no one's saying you did. You're protecting your family. I understand."

She nodded, brushing away tears, desperate to reclaim her composure. Her fingers fiddled with the locket again, almost unconsciously, until she noticed me watching. She tucked it quickly beneath her blouse once more and rose. "I should…thank you for coming, Lyra. Really. But I have so much to do for the funeral. The boys will need me."

The dismissal was polite but final.

I rose and smoothed my pants, giving her space. "If you need anything, call me."

Her smile was a shadow of itself. "I will."

I stepped outside, blinking against the sunlight, the warmth clashing with the chill in my chest as she closed the front door. From the driveway, the garage door stood ajar. Voices drifted out, muffled and tense. I followed them, curiosity guiding me like a magnet.

Inside, Tony and Joey were hunched over a workbench. The air smelled faintly of oil and cut wood, boyhood projects abandoned among clutter. Tony startled when he saw me, snapping a leather-bound journal shut so fast the sound echoed. But not before I caught a glimpse of what lay inside—spiral sketches, familiar and haunting, and coded symbols inked across the pages.

My pulse leaped. "What was that?" I tried to keep my tone calm yet careful.

"Nothing." Tony quickly shoved the journal in a backpack.

I tilted my head. "Where did you go the morning your father died, Tony? You were gone for hours."

His jaw tightened. "I went for a run."

Joey's voice piped up, unguarded. "You followed, Dad. Don't lie."

"Shut up!" Tony snapped, turning on him. His face flushed red. "I knew *he* was lying!" Tony's voice cracked, louder now. "Dad wasn't where he said he was. I had to know the truth."

Joey squared his shoulders, defiantly. "You *stole* his journal."

"You should talk. You *stole* that fancy stone—" Before Tony could finish, Joey jammed his hand into his pocket, hiding whatever he'd been playing with.

My eyes narrowed. "Stone?"

"It's nothing!" Joey blurted.

Tony's fists clenched. "You're one to talk, Joey. You think Mom doesn't notice when you disappear? You hide things, too."

They both shouted over each other, the raw grief of losing their father bleeding out in anger.

"Enough!" Kim's voice cut sharp from the back door. "Inside. Now."

The boys froze, then Tony grabbed his backpack and stalked past me. Joey hurried after him, both with their shoulders slumped. I followed them out of the garage. Tony glared at Joey and Joey scowled at Tony, both of them carrying secrets heavier than they knew how to bear. Kim gathered them up with efficiency, ushering them into the house without another word to me, shutting me out.

The blinds snapped shut.

I stood there a long moment, staring at the closed door, with my heart hammering. It made me sad that they'd tried to hide things from me specifically when all I wanted to do was help them. A locket that glowed with hidden power. A journal filled with Vault spirals and strange numbers. A boy with a stone that pulsed like a heartbeat, even after he thought he'd hidden it.

Secrets stacked on secrets.

And I was running out of time to untangle them before they tore this family—and Wishville—apart.

CHAPTER

Ten

THE SUMMER SUN gleamed off Lake Champlain as Holden and I rolled into Burlington in the afternoon. The water sparkled beneath the wide sky, sailboats bobbing lazily in the harbor. Church Street was alive with people. College kids in shorts and sandals, families pushing strollers, and street musicians strumming guitars beneath hanging flower baskets. Compared to quiet Wishville, the city felt vibrant, restless even.

I should have been charmed by the energy, but all I could think about was why we were here.

After talking with Kim, I'd had to put out fires at the festival as Victoria's chemistry station blew up in her face, staining her blonde hair a neon green. She insisted one of her students must have added an extra ingredient to the demonstration, but the kids weren't talking. Mr. Finch was fixing the booth, and LuLu was assisting the mayor and Laisira in getting the festival back on track so I could run this errand with Holden.

I'd filled him in on my conversations with Kim and the boys. It didn't take him long to track down her private investigator. We found Frankie Malloy's office tucked into a narrow brick building just off the main drag, wedged between a tattoo parlor and a secondhand bookstore. A weathered sign over the door read

Malloy Investigations: Discretion with Results, though the fading paint suggested neither the discretion nor the results had budgeted for marketing.

Inside, the place smelled faintly of coffee, paper, and a hint of vanilla candle. The waiting area was a jumble of mismatched chairs, and the desk beyond was covered in files, a cracked lava lamp, and a ceramic skull that doubled as a pen holder. Stickers plastered the filing cabinet in the corner.

Trust No One, Coffee is my Spirit Animal, and my favorite, *World's Okayest PI.*

Frankie Malloy was exactly what her office promised. Spiky pink hair, leather boots, a fitted jacket, and a can of Monster sweating rings onto a stack of manila folders. She looked up, flashing a grin like she'd been expecting us all along.

"Well, if it isn't the Wishville delegation." She kicked her boots off the desk.

Holden said nothing, just looked at her with a raised brow. His silence usually carried more weight than words.

"I've seen you on the news," she added by way of explanation. "After Mike Zaccaria's murder, I knew it wouldn't take you long to come calling on me. Come for the tourist traps, stay for the dirty laundry?"

"Cut to the chase, Frankie." I slid into the chair opposite her as I summoned my inner sleuth. "You know why we're here."

Holden raised an eyebrow at me.

I ignored him.

Her grin widened. "I always cut to the chase, sweetheart. Comes with the territory." She leaned forward, lacing her fingers, and her tone sharpened. "Your friend Kim? She came to me months ago, convinced her husband was stepping out. Classic signs like late nights, vague excuses, and a gut feeling that wouldn't quit. So, she hired me to dig."

"An affair." Holden nodded. "Kim suggested as much to us as well."

"I can't imagine Mike doing something like that." I shook my head.

She drummed black-painted nails against the desk. "I tailed him. Kept notes. I'm with you. Kim was barking up the wrong tree. There were no secret dinners, no motels, and no lipstick-on-collars. He did meet a woman, but not the kind Kim imagined. She wore her hood pulled low, coat tight, and kept her head down the whole time. The only clue I caught was a strand of long blonde hair slipping free as she walked away."

I felt my pulse skip. Could it be the same hooded person distributing goods at the festival? "Lauren Glaub?" The name slipped out before I could stop it.

Frankie tilted her head, studying me like she was gauging how much I already knew. "Mike's assistant? Could be. But if you're thinking romance, forget it. There was no touching, no flirting. He looked like he'd rather be anywhere else. He kept things strictly business."

Holden leaned forward, his jaw tight. "What kind of business?"

Frankie's mouth quirked. "The shady kind. He gave her cash. She gave him a package—small, wrapped in brown paper, and tied with string. Old-school cloak-and-dagger. I never saw what was inside, but he guarded it like it was priceless."

A cold ripple ran down my spine, that half-human, half-Dweller instinct that hummed whenever something from Elarion brushed against the edges of Wishville. Packages wrapped in brown paper shouldn't have set me off, but I couldn't shake the prickle beneath my skin. I told myself it could've been anything like documents, medicine, or even contraband.

But my gut whispered otherwise.

"How many times?" Holden asked.

"Several." Frankie shrugged. "Always the same woman and same routine. Quick, careful, and absolutely not romantic." She leaned back, smirking again. "So, if Kim thought she had a cheating husband, she was wrong. But if you ask me? What she did have was a husband in over his head with something he didn't want her or anyone knowing about. And that, sweetheart, is far more problematic."

The words lingered in the air. I could feel Holden's tension radiating beside me, see the storm in his eyes though he kept his face neutral. For me, the unease went deeper. If Mike wasn't straying, then what had he gotten tangled up in? Every nerve in my body whispered that whatever was in that package wasn't entirely from this planet…

And Mike was in deeper than we ever imagined.

We thanked Frankie and left Burlington as the sky blushed gold over the lake. Holden drove in silence at first, the hum of the tires filling the car as the city gave way to rolling fields and pine-dotted hills. I stared out the window, my thoughts running faster than the passing scenery.

Finally, he spoke. "So. Lauren Glaub." His voice was low, but there was no mistaking the weight behind it.

"Maybe." I kept my eyes on the horizon, thinking. "Frankie wasn't certain. And even if it was Lauren, she's right. There was nothing romantic going on. This wasn't about love."

"Cash. Packages. Hooded meetings." He tightened his grip on the wheel. "That doesn't sound like a man having an affair. That sounds like a man caught in something dangerous."

I pressed my palms against my thighs, grounding myself. "Dangerous for him…or for all of us?"

Holden shot me a sidelong glance, the question hanging unspoken between us. I didn't answer, but deep down, my Dweller side already knew. Whatever Mike Zaccaria had gotten himself into, it was connected to the forbidden area surrounding the Vault, just as we all suspected. And the thought of Elarion's secrets bleeding out into the open made my stomach twist.

Neither of us spoke again as the sun faded to rain and the Vermont countryside slid past, green and deceptively peaceful, like a stage hiding a trapdoor.

The storm that had hammered Wishville all afternoon had finally loosened its grip.

By the time Lourdes came over, the downpour had thinned into a drizzle that pressed the night against the windows like damp velvet. The air smelled faintly of wet earth and pine, and the faint pinging of rain on the glass was steady as a ticking clock. I poured two glasses of red wine, the good kind I usually saved for company, and slid one across the table to her.

LuLu accepted it, but instead of taking a sip, she set her phone face-down on the table like it was dangerous to even touch. She leaned back, her arms folded and eyes darting toward the window as though checking for eavesdroppers.

"You're twitchy." I settled into my chair, curling my legs beneath me. "Did something else happen at the festival?"

Her mouth curved in that sly, conspiratorial way she had when she was about to tell me something she shouldn't. "Not the festival." She tapped her nail against the wineglass. "This is bigger. This comes from Marco."

I frowned. "Marco?"

"Kim Zaccaria's grad intern," LuLu explained. "The one she hired at that consulting firm she works at. Bright kid, good with data, but green as grass. He books time at the university's core facility—all the toys they keep locked away unless you're on a schedule." She smirked. "Turns out Kim leaned on him. She convinced him to give her his slot by promising to give him edits on his thesis, a glowing letter of recommendation, and maybe even co-authorship if she spun it right. He idolizes her, poor thing."

The wine in my glass suddenly tasted sour. "So, he gave her his time."

"He did. She borrowed his toolbox and used his password to get in," LuLu said. "She obviously didn't want to run any off-the-book toxicology tests where she works. But here's the thing…he didn't trust her. So, he planted a little motion camera in his toolbox before he gave it to her and at his assigned work station. He figured if she crossed a line, he'd have proof he didn't know about it and wasn't in on it." She paused, savoring the moment. "And when he saw what she did, he panicked."

My stomach tightened. "Panicked enough to come to you?"

Her grin widened, full of satisfaction. "You know me. I asked the right questions, fluttered the right lashes. He's terrified. He thinks his career will implode if anyone finds out he gave her that time slot. He met me in the parking lot behind the café like he was dealing contraband." She lowered her voice in imitation of his. "'I can't sit on this, but I can't be tied to it either. You're the only one I trust to handle it.'"

I blinked. "He said that?"

She nodded, swirling her wine and finally taking a sip. "He shoved me the card like it was burning his fingers, then he begged me not to burn Kim. He said, 'I like her. I don't want to ruin her, but if this gets out, it ruins me too.' He looked like a man about to confess to murder when all he'd really done was give away a time slot."

"Poor kid," I murmured.

"Clever kid." LuLu flipped her phone over and tapped the screen. "Because he gave me this."

The screen filled with grainy, timestamped footage: June nineteenth, just past midnight.

Kim appeared, slipping into the university lab with the furtive air of someone breaking curfew. Her hair was tied in a messy knot, her appearance hidden beneath a lab coat. She held a small amber vial like it might burn through her gloves.

She glanced around the empty room and made her way to his work station, her every movement sharp with nerves, then slid the vial into the autosampler tray. The machine blinked awake, humming, its green glow washing her face into a mask of angles.

The microphone picked up her voice—soft, deliberate, then fraying as she spoke into the silence.

"Sample: bourbon bottle, June nineteenth... Metals screen clean. GC-MS—just ethanol, typical bourbon congeners..."

She rubbed her mouth with the back of her hand, her eyes flicking nervously over the chromatogram.

"HPLC fingerprint inconsistent—extra peaks...LC-HRMS shows unknowns at four-eleven point one eight three two...no database match."

Her voice cracked on the last word.

On the screen she sagged back in the chair, whispering like a woman afraid of her own thoughts. "What on earth did you get yourself into, Mike?"

My pulse thudded in my ears.

Kim folded the printout and slipped it into her purse. For a moment she hovered, staring at the vial with a look of devastation, then muttered, "I should turn this in. God help me, I should...but..." Her voice broke into silence.

She wiped the counters, powered everything down, and hurried from the frame.

The timestamp blinked and the feed ended.

LuLu locked her phone again and leaned back, her bracelets chiming against one another. "Marco said she looked fragile. He said it broke his heart to watch her, but it scared him, too. He told me, 'She's carrying something she can't handle, and I don't want to get dragged under with her.' So, he handed it to me. The footage. The memo. Everything."

"The memo?" My voice was thin.

LuLu reached into her oversized satchel and slid a folded sheet across the table. "She drafted it before she scrubbed it from the server. Marco pulled a copy. He didn't want it tied to him. He said, 'Please, don't bury me with her mistake.'"

I hesitated, then unfolded the page.

Lab Memo — Confidential Draft

Author: Dr. Kimberly Zaccaria, Toxicology Division
Date/Time: 6/19, 00:42 hours
Subject: Unknown liquid sample (amber, bourbon matrix)
Analyses Performed:

- ICP-MS (priority metals): No detects for arsenic, cadmium, or mercury. Lead < 5 ppb.
- GC-MS (volatiles/semi-volatiles): Ethanol matrix consistent with bourbon. No methanol, ketones, or chlorinated solvents.
- HPLC-DAD (botanical profile): Chromatographic fingerprint inconsistent with reference bourbon standards; additional late-eluting peaks observed.
- LC-HRMS (untargeted screen): Multiple unknown features present. Highest intensity at m/z 411.1832 (RT 7.42 min).
  - No database match in NIST, mzCloud, or in-house plant compound library.
  - Fragmentation spectra inconclusive.
  - Isotopic distribution atypical for natural products.

Preliminary Interpretation:

- Non-routine constituents detected.
- Unknown compound(s) may be plant-derived but not recognized by standard libraries.
- Toxicological properties indeterminate.
- Recommend further structural elucidation (NMR) if escalation approved.

Personal Note (verbal transcription captured):
"What on earth did you get yourself into, Mike?"

Status: Draft only. Not submitted through official reporting channels.

I read the last line twice, my throat tightening. The memo seemed to hum with unease, like a secret struggling to leap from the page.

"She ran this before WishFest," I whispered. "And she didn't send it through. She carried this with her like a weight around her neck. She went on vacation with her family knowing this was in her purse." I closed my eyes, bile rising. "Did she…did she kill Mike to keep it buried?"

LuLu leaned forward, her bracelets glinting under the lamp. "She was protecting him, or herself. Either way, it's dynamite. If it gets out, it's not just Mike. It's the town. Marco knew that. He told me flat out, 'If people find out she tested something dangerous in secret, they'll trace it to me for letting her in.' He looked like he hadn't slept in days. Said he just wanted to hand it off to someone and be done with it."

I pressed my palm flat to the memo, as though I could stop the danger from spilling off the page.

She swirled her wine and sipped again, her gaze sharp. "So? Proof of an unknown tonic, probably black-market science. But you—" she tilted her head "—you look like you've swallowed glass. What do you see that Kim doesn't?"

The memory of the herb shimmered in my blood—the way its leaves glowed faintly near the Veiled Vault, the hum that wasn't earthly but something deeper. An ordinary scientist would see data that didn't fit a database.

I knew better.

"If Kim takes this public, she'll spark panic," I said carefully. "And whoever Mike was working with will vanish before we can find them."

LuLu arched a brow. "So, you want me to bury this. Sit on a scoop that could put me back on the map. After everything I've told you about my career hanging by a thread."

I met her eyes, my voice raw. "I want you to hold it until we know the truth. If this leaks, we lose our chance to stop whoever was pulling Mike's strings. And Kim—and her children—will be collateral."

For a long moment, the only sound was the rain hitting the glass. Finally, LuLu released the breath she'd been holding. "You're asking a lot, Lyra, but you're right. Sometimes the story's bigger than the headline."

I folded the memo into my case notes, its weight enormous for such thin paper. "Then we find out who Mike was working with," I said, "before Kim or anyone else pays the price."

Outside, the drizzle hushed into silence.

Inside, the two of us sealed a pact to follow the quieter, riskier path and dig out the truth before the town paid the cost of curiosity.

CHAPTER
Eleven

THE MORNING BROKE SO bright and sharp it almost hurt to look at. When I cracked open my window, the air rushed in cold and laced with pine and damp cedar. But the hollowness inside my chest sharpened. Holden had left Wishville before dawn, sending me a simple text message.

Burlington. Rufus. Alibi.

That left me on my own, free to chase my own lead. Kim Zaccaria.

I paced my living room, my bare feet brushing over the braided rug, each step punctuated by the low hum of the orb phone on the table. The sphere pulsed faintly, like a heart that belonged to no one, its glow waxing and waning in time. Dweller inventions always straddled the line between wonder and unease.

Part machine, part spell work, and shaped like a crystal ball but alive in its own way.

I pressed my palm to it. The surface rippled like water. Light webbed outward in a slow bloom until Calderis' image sharpened into view. His angular features were carved with precision, his eyes were the cool shade of storm glass, and his cobalt robes glowed faintly as though touched by another sun. The sound of his voice carried distortion, like speaking beneath the water.

"Wells."

Hearing my surname in his clipped cadence always tightened something in me.

"I need you." I cleared my voice over the subtle change in his expression. "Here, in Wishville as Detective Cal Deris," I clarified.

His pale brows drew together. "What has happened?"

"Holden is gone, and I can't wait for him. Kim Zaccaria has something she's hiding—something important. I need backup. Someone who can read her without giving too much away."

A pause stretched.

Then the orb hummed softly, casting fractured light across the walls. Calderis' gaze never wavered, though a muscle flickered in his jaw. He hated slipping into his human guise, considering it beneath him like wearing a chain around his true nature.

But after breathing out a sigh that seemed to scrape the edges of his pride, he inclined his head. "Send me the coordinates. I will come."

The orb dimmed, leaving only my reflection, pale and sharp-eyed in the fading glow. Relief seeped into my shoulders, loosening the tight band of tension. For a moment, I just stood there listening to the tick of the clock and the faint groan of the old house settling.

Finally, I grabbed my purse and headed out the door.

Before long, I reached the firm where Kim worked. Calderis was already there when I walked inside.

The lab felt too clean, too sharp, the sting of disinfectant barely softened by air freshener that clung to the back of the throat. Fluorescent lights buzzed overhead, reflecting off glass partitions and polished tile floors.

Behind the front desk, a man froze the moment we entered. His eyes were too wide, blinking rapidly as though his brain had skipped a beat. Thin fingers tapped against the laminate counter, a nervous staccato that carried through the quiet room. He looked like a man waiting for the first excuse to run.

LuLu had mentioned Marco was an intern here. I was willing

to bet this was him. His Adam's apple bobbed as he swallowed hard, then snapped his gaze to the monitor in front of him, pretending he hadn't noticed me.

Beside me, Calderis had already become his glamour. The transformation was uncanny: a tall man in a dark blazer, his posture ramrod straight and hair tied neatly back, and glasses perched on the bridge of his nose.

I grinned over the addition. Dwellers had perfect vision.

He looked every inch the seasoned detective, and yet his Dweller essence clung to him like static. Even muted, it made people shift in their seats, straighten their backs, and avert their eyes. Instinct whispered that he was not to be crossed.

"Let's make this quick," I murmured under my breath.

The man jolted when Kim's voice floated down the hall. "Lyra? What are you doing here?"

She appeared with brisk steps, her white lab coat swishing around her thighs. Her brown hair was pulled into a severe pony-tail, but it couldn't hide the pallor of her skin or the heavy shadows under her eyes. Stress clung to her like a second garment.

"Can we talk?" I asked.

Her gaze passed between Calderis and me, hesitation warring with exhaustion. At last, she nodded. "Sure. I'll take my break and meet you out back."

We made our way around the building to wait for her. The back lot was quieter, though the hum of traffic carried faintly from the main road. A spindly maple shaded a worn picnic table. The air smelled of damp bark, fresh-cut grass, and faintly of gasoline from the delivery trucks idling nearby.

Kim joined us, sitting on the bench as though her bones were made of lead. She smoothed her coat over her legs, but her hands betrayed her—fidgeting, tugging at her sleeves, and twisting in her lap.

"What's this about?" Her voice was thin.

I slid the lab report onto the table. The paper looked stark and incriminating against the wood.

Her face drained of color. She clutched at the locket around her neck, her fingers tightening so hard her knuckles whitened. "Where did you get that?"

"That's not important," I said softly. "What matters is why you didn't turn it in."

Her gaze darted between us. Her breath came shallow and fast. "I...I didn't know what to do. I found a solution hidden in an empty whisky bottle in our garage."

"You tested it." Calderis' voice was smooth and low, carrying the weight of truth. "You knew it wasn't natural."

Kim's lips trembled. "Yes. I took it to a lab away from here. I thought maybe it was experimental—something cutting-edge. But the results didn't match anything. Nothing. It was like...like it wasn't from this world."

My chest tightened. She was closer to the truth than she realized.

"So, you kept it," I pressed.

Tears welled in her eyes, blurring the sharp lines of her face. "What else was I supposed to do? If I turned it in, it would ruin us. Mike's patients, his reputation—gone. And my boys..." Her voice cracked on the word. "I just wanted to protect them."

I leaned closer, softening my tone. "Kim, I believe you. But hiding this doesn't just endanger your family. It endangers every-one. I'm sure you've seen the changes at WishFest. People are short-tempered, restless. This stuff is dangerous."

She shook her head, her tears slipping free. "I had no idea it was dangerous. I had my suspicions that it wasn't normal, but the tests didn't show any toxins I recognized. Whatever is in there, isn't a known substance." Her fingers clutched the locket tighter, as if the chain itself could hold her together. "Please don't turn me in. If I give you the vial—if I stay quiet—will you keep my secret? Let me protect my family while you figure out who Mike was working with."

I glanced at Calderis. His expression was unreadable marble, but he didn't interrupt. He was letting me choose.

I reached across the table, covering her trembling hand with mine. Her skin was cold and damp with nervous sweat. "I can't promise to be quiet forever, but I won't say anything yet. Give us the vial. Keep quiet. We'll find out the truth. But if you hide anything else, Kim—anything that puts people in danger—I won't be able to protect you."

Her shoulders sagged, relief and despair colliding in her eyes. With shaking fingers, she unclasped the locket. The chain slipped through her hand like a lifeline breaking. She pressed it into my palm. The metal thrummed faintly, almost imperceptibly alive.

"Thank you," she whispered.

I tucked it into my pocket. Even through the fabric, I felt the faint glow pulsing against my leg.

Kim stood abruptly, brushing her tears in sharp, almost angry motions. "I have to go to work. Make funeral arrangements. Everything—" Her voice broke, and she turned away, retreating toward the side door without another word.

The silence left behind was deafening. A breeze stirred the maple branches, scattering droplets that pattered onto the table. Somewhere, unseen wildflowers gave off a faint, sweet perfume.

Calderis finally spoke. "She is not guilty, but she is entangled."

"She's scared." I stared at the pocket that held the locket. "And scared people make mistakes."

His pale eyes lingered on me. "So do those who care too much."

I stood, slipping the locket deeper into my pocket. "Then let's make sure neither of us does."

The Twisted Loaf had a way of making me almost forget the heaviness in my pocket.

Almost.

The little bakery café had become a beating heart of WishFest, its windows thrown open to let in the bright air and the babble of festival music from up the hill. The smell hit me first—thick, warm, and intoxicating. Fresh yeast and baking sugar, the tang of roasted coffee beans, and the buttery sweetness of cinnamon-swirled loaves cooling on racks behind the counter.

The scent clung to everything, my hair, clothes, and even my tongue, until it felt like sugar lived in my every cell.

Inside, the place was crowded.

Locals queued shoulder to shoulder, pressed close as they eyed the glass cases. Each shelf gleamed with festival specials like twisted breads dusted in powdered sugar, knots glazed with golden honey, and the bakery's signature chocolate-orange loaf marbled dark and bright like the inside of a gemstone. Children smeared with sugar granules clutched paper bags, tugging on their parents' hands. Teenagers leaned against the counter, pretending not to flirt while they ordered double-shot lattes. Every table was full of people whose voices collided with the hiss of steaming milk and the chime of the register.

And then Calderis walked in.

Even wrapped in his glamour, he carried himself like a blade unsheathed. Tall, broad-shouldered, with edges sharpened by habit and not choice. People parted without realizing it, stepping out of his path, their voices dropping as though the air had shifted. He didn't try to soften his edge. I wasn't even sure he would know how. The human mask hid his features but not his essence.

I tugged him toward the counter, keeping my voice brisk. "Two coffees, and the chocolate-orange loaf."

The barista, a college student with a nose ring, flushed as she met his gaze and fumbled with the cups. I hid my smile, collected our order, and steered Calderis toward the corner booth where lace curtains filtered sunlight into fractured gold.

The coffee was strong and dark, steam curling upward. Calderis studied his mug as if it were a relic unearthed from ruins. His first sip ended with his lips tightening in faint disdain.

"Still bitter," he muttered.

"That's the point." I tore into the loaf, the crust crackling under my fingers, releasing a ribbon of steam scented with orange peel and melted chocolate. The first bite was warm and rich, the sugar melting on my tongue. "It balances the sweetness."

He didn't answer. He was too focused on me—or rather, on the pocket where the locket weighed against my leg. His pale eyes kept glancing at it.

"The elixir," he said, his voice low.

I leaned closer, dropping mine. "As you know, when Kim tested it, her machine didn't recognize a single compound, which makes sense. Anything from Elarion wouldn't register on human equipment."

He inclined his head slightly, like a scholar conceding a point. "But someone altered it. Refined the herbs and stones to make them into a tonic. That takes skill."

"Exactly." I traced the rim of my cup with my finger, thinking. "Mike couldn't have done that alone. Someone had to grind the stones, balance the elements, stabilize the mix. That kind of precision requires training. Chemistry. Alchemy. Both."

"You said in your update that Frankie Malloy saw him with a woman," Calderis said. "A blonde. Mike gave her money, and she gave him a package. More than once."

My mind ticked through suspects like beads on a rosary. Victoria Lynch, with her chemistry background. Brittany, always dabbling in wellness concoctions. Or maybe someone no one suspected, someone whose public life was spotless. Hiding in plain sight.

"Whoever it is," Calderis continued, his voice flattening like a blade pressed to stone, "they must be stopped and all the tonic found. Every vial. Every herb. Every stone. All must be returned."

The enormity pressed against my chest. "We don't even know how much of it is out there."

And then the bell over the door chimed.

I didn't need to look to know who had arrived. The air itself seemed to shift, charged with perfume, chatter, and the rattle of too many bangles.

The Wellies.

They swept in like a parade float—Tilly in a sunflower-yellow dress and hat to match, Belle with braids laced in ribbons of green and pink, and Dot wrapped in a shawl so loaded down with charms it jingled every time she moved. Festival finery clung to them like second skins with ribbons trailing and skirts swishing. They filled the café instantly, their voices rising over the din, and their laughter spilling out like champagne bubbles.

They flocked to the counter, ordering pastries and gossip in the same breath. The poor barista tried to keep up, her pen scratching frantically while Tilly demanded extra glaze, Belle asked about the origin of the cocoa, and Dot quizzed her on the astrological compatibility of cinnamon with Taurus energy.

Betsy just rolled her eyes and jumped in to help her employee.

It was only a matter of time before Belle spotted me. She waved so hard her bracelets clinked like bells. "Lyra, darling! There you are!"

I groaned under my breath.

Calderis arched a brow, amusement tugging faintly at the corner of his mouth.

The Wellies didn't wait.

They descended on our booth like a brightly plumed flock, dragging chairs, bags, and paper cups. Dot's shawl brushed Calderis' knee as she plopped down, jingling like a carnival. Tilly squeezed in on my side, nearly toppling my coffee. Belle slid across from me with the energy of someone about to deliver state secrets.

"We were just saying," Tilly began breathlessly, "the energy at this season's festival is extraordinary. Everyone's buzzing. Don't you feel it? Like the whole town is humming?"

My stomach dipped.

Belle rummaged in her bag and produced a vial. She held it aloft with triumph, the liquid inside shimmering faintly, betraying its unnatural origin. "And these are everywhere! Festival Fixers they're calling them. Best energy shots I've ever had."

My pulse jumped. "Where did you get that?"

"Oh, from a booth in the clearing," Belle chirped, oblivious. "Blue canopy. Very official-looking, but surely you know as chair of the festival. The young man said it was a health initiative. My knees haven't twinged once since I tried it."

Dot fished another from her shawl, holding it up with glee. "I got mine free in the dunk tank line. Isn't that marvelous? A little festival spirit in a bottle!"

Calderis' jaw tightened. His eyes were shards of ice.

"No, I didn't know about this, and that has me worried. Do you have more?" I asked, my voice sharper than I meant.

"Of course." Tilly patted her oversized bag. "We stocked up. You never know when you'll need a boost."

I extended my hand. "Give them to me."

They blinked in unison. "Why?" Dot asked, sounding suspicious.

"Because they're dangerous," I replied firmly. "You don't know what's in them. You're putting yourselves at risk."

Belle pursed her lips, unimpressed. "You always were dramatic, Lyra."

But something in my tone must have cut through. Slowly, reluctantly, they surrendered their vials—six in total, each glowing faintly in the café light. They clinked against the table like captured fireflies.

I swept them into my bag with hands that shook. The smell of cinnamon and orange peel around us suddenly felt suffocating.

"All over the festival," Calderis murmured, his voice sounding like stone cracking.

Tilly leaned forward, lowering her voice conspiratorially, though she was still loud enough to turn heads. "If you want more, just head to the clearing. Everyone has them. It's the newest craze."

I forced a smile. "Thank you. Please don't drink any more. Promise me."

The Wellies exchanged glances, then sighed in dramatic unison. "Fine," Belle relented. "But if my knees creak again, that's on you."

With that, they bustled outside, their shawls jingling, skirts swishing, and lavender perfume trailing. They left behind a mess of crumbs, empty cups, and the faint echo of their laughter.

I stared at the bag in my lap, heavy now with glowing glass. My pulse thudded hard in my ears. "They've already spread," I whispered. "All through WishFest."

Calderis laid a steadying hand over mine. His skin was warm and comforting, grounding me. "Then we gather them, every last one, before more damage can be done."

His voice was a vow, iron-strong. And yet, fear coiled deep in my chest. Because if the Wellies had them, then so did half the town. And finding them all before the festival ended might already be impossible.

CHAPTER

Twelve

THE TOWN HALL WAS PACKED. Folding chairs had been set up in hasty rows across the parquet floor, and every seat was taken—shopkeepers in aprons, teenagers in WishFest volunteer tees, and the Wellies in their coordinated floral cardigans as if they'd dressed for combat by way of the church bazaar.

Holden stood along the side wall near the bulletin board, his arms crossed and jaw a stone outcrop beneath the fluorescent lights. LuLu had snagged a seat in the second row, her reporter's notebook already open with her pen poised like a stinger. Trip occupied an aisle spot, his legs too long for the chair, his home-made Wish Sheriff badge catching the light whenever he shifted.

At the front, Mayor Doug Delaney tapped the microphone, grimaced at the feedback, and lifted his hands in a pleading gesture for quiet. There were two perpetual headaches of Wishville: festival logistics and the way the town could turn on a dime when gossip caught fire.

"All right, folks." His voice was full of frustration and weariness. "We'll keep this brief, but we needed to share an update."

Laisira handed him several pages of notes.

"'Brief,' he says," Tilly murmured from behind me, the word fluffed like a goose down pillow.

Belle shushed her.

That invited Dot to whisper, "Brief like those shorts I told you not to buy for your grandson."

They snickered.

I resisted the urge to turn around and join them.

"First order of business is Dr. Ethan Bellamy's report." Doug glanced at Holden, who didn't move to the microphone.

No surprise.

Holden hated being the one to carry bad news into rooms.

Doug cleared his throat and continued. "As you all know, Michael Zaccaria was found deceased in the Whisper Woods."

An uneasy ripple went through the audience.

"Dr. Bellamy's preliminary findings indicate blunt force trauma to the back of the head as the cause of death." Doug softened the phrase with a wince. "Estimated time of death places it between six and eight in the morning the day he went missing. There were defensive wounds consistent with a struggle. Toxicology is pending, but there were trace residues on the skin and clothing that Dr. Bellamy is analyzing—unidentified compounds at this time."

LuLu's pen scratched faster. "Unidentified…as in synthetic?" she called, without waiting for permission.

Before Doug could answer, Holden stepped forward into the front aisle, letting his height and stillness draw attention. "We're not ready to characterize the compounds," he said, the words weighted like bullets before they left his mouth. "We'll know more when the tox screen comes back."

I had a feeling the tox screens would match the vial Kim had secretly tested.

A hand shot up from Betsy, flour still dusting her sleeve. "Was it a mugging? Did he have anything missing?"

Holden's gaze locked onto mine for a moment, an unspoken check on how much to say. I shook my head fractionally. We didn't have the right to dump half-formed theories into this room like kindling.

"No evidence supports robbery as a motive," Holden said. "We're following multiple leads, including activity near the trailhead." His tone cooled a degree. "We ask that folks keep clear of that area until Ranger Ellison reopens it. The woods might be dangerous, and we don't want to take any more chances."

Trip leaned forward in his seat. "And while this is a tragedy for Mike's family and the community," he said in his best business-voice, "we want to assure everyone that Summer WishFest will continue. Right, Chief?"

"Yes. I've got it from here, Trip." Holden paused as if counting to ten. "We've postponed the trail run and the campfire singalong events, yes, but Main Street programming is proceeding as well as the festival grounds. The vendors are already set up, and the schedule—"

"About the vendors," I said, rising before I lost my nerve.

My heart thumped once, hard. Every head swiveled; the room's current shifted toward me. I felt Vex's absence like a soft weight missing from my lap, and in my head.

I steadied myself on the back of my chair instead. "I need to make a public warning."

Doug's eyebrows went up. He nodded in a get-it-over-with way.

I stepped into the aisle, halfway between the Wellies and Holden, exactly where I always seemed to land—between humans and the well. "There's a tonic being sold at the festival under the name Festival Fixers." I projected my voice so the people clustered by the doors could hear. "It's being marketed as a cure-all for fatigue, pain, and the dreaded 'WishFest hangover.' I know several of you have tried it." I let my gaze skim faces, looking for guilty culprits. "Do not use it. We have reason to believe it isn't safe."

A collective inhale drew the walls closer.

From halfway back, Brittany stood. She was tan, ponytailed, and beautiful in that sculpted way that made me think of marble statues and protein powder. As the owner of a gym on the east side of town, she'd been all charm and giveaways yesterday—free smoothie coupons and two-week trial passes slipped into people's hands.

She hooked her thumbs in the waistband of her leggings and smiled the kind of smile that invited cameras. "Lyra." Her tone was bright enough to be cordial but edged enough to cut. "I'm selling it at my gym, and my people love it. They're not dropping like flies, so, it can't be all bad, right?"

A few snorts of laughter broke the tension. The town liked bravado almost as much as it liked pie.

I measured my reply. "*Not dropping like flies* is a low bar for safety."

Tilly clucked approvingly. "Amen."

I tried again. "Look, I get it. We're tired. It's been weeks of planning for this festival, and the past several days have been… hard." I swallowed. The image of Mike's wife by his body in the woods pressed against my throat. "Quick fixes look like kindness when you're running on fumes. But I've seen what happens when people don't know what they're putting in their bodies. Dr. Bellamy found unidentified compounds on Mike's clothes. *Unidentified.* That should give us all pause."

I wasn't giving away that the unidentified compounds were part of enchanted herbs and healing stones from Elarion. I was simply suggesting that people might not want to drink something foreign. It could be laced with drugs or poison for all they knew.

Brittany's smile didn't budge, but the muscles in her jaw twinged like a shadow of thought. "Correlation isn't causation. You can't link my product to what happened to Mike. And I resent the implication." She turned slightly so the crowd could admire her profile and its righteous indignation. "Festival Fixers is a blend of legal, natural ingredients. Turmeric, ginger, ginseng, electrolytes—"

"And?" Holden said so quietly the room shivered.

He had moved to stand near me, looking like a united front. I greatly appreciated him having my back.

"If they're all natural, then you shouldn't have a problem listing all of the ingredients," he continued.

"Trade secret." Brittany's voice was as crisp as a new bill. "Like Betsy's cinnamon twist."

Betsy bristled. "My recipe isn't a mood-altering compound, sweetheart. It's filled with flour and sugar and regret."

Laughter bubbled, defusing the moment.

LuLu rose, too, as if her reporter instincts sensed blood. "Brittany, would you be willing to provide a sample for independent testing? If it's as benign as you claim, that would clear things up. Transparency builds trust."

Brittany didn't even glance at her. "Look, I bought the Festival Fixers just like everyone else and then added them to my own products. My customers trust me."

"They trust you until they have a reason not to," Belle murmured.

Dot added, "Like my cousin, Larry. He grew a second nose right on top of the first one after a traveling salesman sold him some medicinal pimple popper."

Tilly gave a dignified sniff, which said everything one needed to know about alternative treatments.

Trip interceded with his palms open. "Let's not turn this into a witch trial. We're all on the same team here. Safety is our utmost priority at WishFest. It always has been."

"Then prove it," I said, gentler now. "Ask vendors to label their ingredients. No exceptions. Pull anything that can't be verified."

Doug seized on that like a lifeline. "Excellent suggestion. We'll add a requirement by—uh—close of business today." He looked at Laisira with raised brows.

She nodded. "How about the vendors must submit full ingredient lists to the festival committee. Will that work?"

I nodded.

He looked at me, grateful and harried. "Lyra, I'm sure the

Wellies would love to help you. And Laisira's at your disposal if you need her."

"Of course," she said to me and smiled. "Anything you need, Ms. Wells."

Three floral cardigans bobbed in simultaneous nods and clapped their hands.

"After Lyra warned us, we've been telling people not to drink anything that fizzes blue," Tilly said. "Blue is not a natural lemonade color."

"Unless it's blueberry," Belle said, always about anything with flair.

"Even then," Dot replied. "Blueberries are purple liars. They make you blue."

Brittany's smile thinned but she didn't break character. "Fine. I'll submit my list. But I'm telling you, this is an overreaction, and your fearmongering is going to hurt small businesses."

"Not as much as a lawsuit will," Holden said.

A hand lifted from the back. Evan Teller winced then rubbed his back, his cap tilted permanently toward skepticism. "What about the investigation?" he asked. "You said multiple leads. Does that include Lauren? People are talking."

The room held its breath, eager and cautious, like squirrels on a porch rail.

Holden measured his answer. "We have spoken with Lauren Glaub as part of our routine interviews. We are speaking with colleagues, patients, and the family. We do not name persons of interest unless there's concrete cause. I'll say this again, if you saw anything unusual in the woods the morning Mike disappeared, then call it in. We'd rather hear a hundred false leads than miss the one thing that matters."

LuLu's pen scratched again. I felt her watching me, too, weighing my words as if she were finally on the same page as me. The vial Kim tested could be the unknown ingredient in the Festival Fixer shots. She'd once told me journalism was putting puzzle pieces on a table, knowing some belonged to other puzzles entirely. Magic made those tables treacherous.

So did grief.

Beside me, Trip cleared his throat. "I know this isn't a general town hall meeting, but I feel it's a relevant update, given the situation. The parade route has shifted slightly to accommodate the ranger's cordon. The map's on the back table. Thank you, Dot, for re-lettering it after the—ah—coffee incident."

Dot smiled serenely. "I believe in baptism by espresso."

"Also," Trip went on, "tonight's fireworks are still scheduled for nine-thirty, weather permitting. We'll close Main Street to cars at seven—"

"Fireworks?" I blurted. I felt every head swivel again, but this time I didn't care. "I know we all want normalcy, but maybe we don't light up the sky over a town that's grieving and a forest that's under investigation."

Trip's expression pinched. "Well, now, Lyra. The town's already paid for them. People are expecting—"

"People expected Mike to be at his clinic on Monday," I said, softer than a whisper, which somehow carried anyway. In my mind's eye, I saw the crack beneath the trees. The way the ground had thrummed, alive and wrong. The way whispers—real ones— had slid through the leaves. "Expectations change. Yes, the festival still needs to go on as normally as possible, but I just think fireworks are a bit much right now, given the circumstances."

Tilly reached forward and squeezed my forearm.

"Let's table fireworks for now." Doug handed papers to Laisira and she made a note. "We'll confer with the family, with the rangers, and with, ah, Chief Thorn."

Willa lifted her hand. "Can we do something for the family?" she asked. "A fund, a meal train—something besides lighting up the sky?"

"The Wellies will organize it," Belle said promptly. "Tilly has a spreadsheet. Dot has a suspiciously large stockpile of foil pans."

"I buy in bulk," Dot said, unrepentant.

"We'll put sign-up sheets on the table next to the parade map," Belle added.

Already faces were brightening in that way that said people needed something to do. Wishville loved a casserole as much as it loved a rumor.

Brittany folded her arms. "And I'll donate a month of free classes to Mike's family. A distraction might help, given everything they're going through."

"That's generous," I said, meaning it.

The questions began to taper, replaced by the hum of side conversations starting up, papers being gathered, and chairs squeaking.

Doug banged the gavel like a man grateful for an exit. "Thank you, everyone. Vendors, please see Lyra and the Wellies regarding labeling. Parade volunteers, check in with Trip. If you have information related to the case, see Chief Thorn."

People stood in waves.

LuLu wove her way through bodies to reach me, her eyes keen. "Off the record?" she asked.

"When does that ever mean off the record with you?" I smiled so she'd know I wasn't scolding.

She smirked. "Never. I'll be in touch if anything more turns up. If Brittany stonewalls, I'll buy a sample and have it tested through my connections. People have a right to know what they're swallowing."

"Careful." Holden stepped into our conversation. "No vigilante testing. Chain of custody matters."

"Relax, Chief." LuLu patted his arm. "I can follow rules when it suits me."

Trip was already pinning maps with pushpins, talking about cross-streets and detours and the best vantage points for the marching band's drumline solo.

The Wellies corralled a line of vendors like kindergarten teachers during a fire drill, dispensing smiles and sternness in equal measure.

Brittany stood a moment longer where she'd been, as if calculating something. Then she flashed a trainer's grin, pivoted on her sleek sneaker, and joined the line with a sway of her ponytail that said, *Game on!*

I drifted toward the back, where the oversized corkboard displayed the month's meeting notices and a faded photograph of a ribbon-cutting from a summer twenty years gone. Holden joined me, remaining silent until we found a pocket of space by the exit.

"You did well," he said.

"Not sure about that," I replied. "I might have painted a target on my back by discouraging people from consuming their latest obsession."

"You already had a target," he said. "We both did. Comes with the job." He angled his body to block us from easy view. "Bellamy thinks some of the residues look…off. Not garden-variety supplements."

My pulse skipped. "Off how?" Holden knew about the Festival Fixers, but I hadn't had a chance to fill him in on what LuLu had found out about Kim testing the vial of tonic Mike had hidden in their garage.

"It's too early to tell." His words were a quiet warning to me as much as to himself. "But if that tonic's connected to anything in Elarion, we'll find out." Holden glanced toward the door where Brittany laughed with a vendor, her voice high and bright. "You'll get flak for calling her out," he said.

"I can take flak." I looked back at the chairs being folded, the maps re-pinned, and the casserole lists filling. The room had already begun turning grief into action, uncertainty into tasks. "What I can't take is this town swallowing something that might change the very core of who they are."

Holden's mouth tightened, like he was fighting a smile he didn't trust. "Then let's make sure they don't." He held the door open, the summer heat stumbling in over our shoes. "Ready, Wells?"

"As I'll ever be, Chief." Together we stepped out into the glare and noise of a festival that refused to stop, even when the heart beneath it faltered. "And Holden?"

"Yeah?" He looked down at me in question.

"I have something to tell you that might make a difference."

"I'm all ears."

CHAPTER
Thirteen

HOLDEN'S APARTMENT was on the fourth floor of the old brick building that faced the square—the one with the slate mansard roof and wrought-iron balconies that always seemed to collect a ruffle of leaves in every season. This was the first time he'd invited me up for a nightcap. We'd mostly spent time together at my place because it was away from prying eyes. My doing, not his, because I still didn't know what I wanted. But that would never change unless I started taking steps forward. I rode up the elevator with a paper bag of pastries I didn't really want with a stomach full of thoughts I couldn't digest.

When the doors parted, a runner in a herringbone pattern led to his place. He'd cracked the door and left the security chain on. Light spilled into the hallway in a warm amber trapezoid. At my knock, the chain slid back, and he opened to me with that steady, unstartled gaze that said I could have been the landlord or a hurricane, and he would have made room for both.

"Chair," he said, his voice pitched low.

"Chief," I replied, because we liked our jokes straightforward.

The industrial bones—brick wall, exposed beams, and metal window casements—were all softened by choices that were purely Holden: a dark leather sofa with throw pillows in salt-and-pepper wool, a low walnut coffee table with dovetail joints, a pair of framed black-and-white photos of a snowy patrol car and a Boylston Street finish line, and a shelf of carefully battered paperbacks arranged by the color of their spines. The kitchen, a line of matte black cabinets, held an orderly rank of glassware and a set of cast-iron pans that looked as if they had seen more omelets than he would admit.

Beyond the windows, the square glowed like a small stage set. The fountain whispered, birch trees tossed coin-shaped leaves, and the strings of festival lights threw soft halos onto the brick and asphalt. Through the open casement came the faint perfume of fried dough, espresso, and wet stone. Jazz hummed from a speaker somewhere, along with the brush of a snare and a tenor sax letting the late hour breathe between notes.

He'd already set two glasses on the sideboard. One with a single cube, and the other clear and sweating in solidarity. He handed me the water and took the bourbon for himself, but he didn't drink yet. He searched my face the way he always did, the way a weatherman scans for changes after a storm.

"Long day?" He raised an eyebrow in question as he reached for another glass and the bourbon bottle. At my nod, he poured me two fingers of something stronger.

"I lived five lives before lunch." I toed off my boots by habit, accepting the glass and taking a sip.

"Then let's make sense of one of them." He gestured toward the sofa. "Come on. Lay it out."

I put the pastry bag on the counter and claimed a corner of the couch. The leather was cool under my palm. He sat at the other end and turned a little toward me, the lamplight catching at the pale scar on his knuckle. We let the square's soundscape settle into the room. Soft voices, a distant door, and the chime of the clock over the courthouse filled the silence.

"LuLu and I cleared the air," I said. "She actually came over for a girls' night while you were gone to Burlington."

Holden lifted his brows. "You actually invited someone in? I'm glad," he said softly. "It's not good to be so isolated with no friends, other than me and your cat." He winked.

"And Calderis," I added softly.

His smile slipped a little. "Of course."

I steered the conversation back on track. "She told me something we needed to know." I pulled my notebook from my bag and found the flagged page, the one whose margin I'd darkened into a bruise with my pen. "Kim found a vial of liquid in their garage. It was Mike's, and she was suspicious, so she secured some lab time through a grad student at the university. Favor network, hush-hush."

His eyes sharpened, then narrowed in thought. "What were the test results?"

"The ingredients were not recognized by any standard panel," I said. "No common drugs, no flagged contaminants. Just…an unknown substance."

The words sat between us like shards of glass.

"Unknown substance," he repeated evenly, but his thumb flattened against the glass as if feeling for an edge. "You think…?"

"I think I was right to say something. It might be the Festival Fixer tonic," I said. "Or a relative. Something people are taking to run faster, heal quicker, and sleep like they did before life happened. Snake oil with teeth."

He blew air out through his nose, and the lights outside blinked on a gust as if the square took offense on his behalf. "And LuLu knows all of this because?"

"Because LuLu's good," I said. "She charmed Kim's grad student into spilling his guts and giving her the proof."

He huffed, half-snort and half-laugh. "I knew she was dangerous."

"Dangerously good, that is, but she agreed to keep quiet," I added. "For now."

"Good. We need to figure out who Mike was working with." Holden turned to the window and watched two teenagers loop the lip of the fountain, their laughter skittering across the square.

When he looked back, the iron in him had cooled. "Kim clearly loved Mike to risk her job like that."

"She always has." The old ache of lost love moved in my chest with a slow, familiar wingbeat. "Whatever she did, she did to try to keep him safe."

"Or to keep herself from knowing something she already suspected." He took a small sip of bourbon, winced as it went down, then set the glass beside the notebook. "Okay. My turn." He rubbed his beard as if in thought.

I nodded. "Burlington?"

"Rufus didn't go to an estate sale," he said flatly. "He met two men I'd describe as upright appliances."

"A stainless-steel set?" I fought a grin.

"More like a scratched fridge and older-model chest freezer." He let the humor pass so the facts could land. "They met at a diner off Maple and Pine. The scar on the bald one runs temple to jaw like a contour line, and the second one wears a ponytail he thinks softens his shoulders. Names are aliases, but habits are sticky."

"Habits like…?" I prompted.

"Moving product that sits outside the FDA's approval," he said. "They're part of a black-market ring, peddling 'alternative treatments' and 'adjunct therapies' to boutique gyms, private trainers, whisper-network healers, etc. Supplements that promise things doctors won't, like enhanced endurance, rapid recovery, remission, regrowth, and more. Some of them are just expensive vitamins with a marketing degree. Some of them are more."

I thought of the glassy hush inside the well, the careful seals, the warnings written in a script older than my great-grandmother's. "More," I echoed, tasting the old language of it on my tongue. "Rufus is their broker?"

"Middleman with a scarf and a pitch," Holden said. "My source heard him say 'limited batch' and 'proven results' and 'word-of-mouth only.' He name-dropped two out-of-town trainers and one local gym in a way that felt like bait." Holden flipped my notebook toward himself and wrote VOSS? then circled it. "Brittany's been chirping about 'boosters.' She's hungry. Hungry makes people useful to men like Rufus."

"Hungry makes people careless," I said softly.

"She claims she only used the Festival Fixer and mixed it with her private batch of holistic products. I'll be curious to see what she lists as her ingredients." He looked at me, and the carefulness of it made a small muscle jump in my throat. "You okay?"

"No," I said honestly. "But I'm steady."

He nodded once. "Makes me wonder if she is the blonde who met with Mike. The vial is either the Fixer or Fixer-adjacent, and Rufus is pushing it."

"I never did like a pusher," I said.

He smiled at that, quick and crooked, then reached toward the coffee table for his legal pad. The pad had the same pragmatic handsomeness as everything else in the room: clean-lined, uncomplaining, and ready to be useful. He ruled a vertical line down the center. "Left column you, right column me."

We worked in low voices, writing and talking, the lamplight low. On my side: LuLu ~ Kim ~ vial ~ lab says unknown; Fixer rumors (speed, strength, 'mending'), distribution whispers; Lauren hears clinic gossip—maybe access point. On his side: Rufus—Burlington diner; two associates; black market ring; gyms/trainers; limited batch; Voss Vitality; state health contacts off-the-record.

I glanced out the window, pondering what we both had written. Down in the square a couple crossed with linked fingers, a delivery truck backfired, and the courthouse chimed admitting it was later than we planned. I could smell yeast from the pizzeria on the corner and toasted sugar from the café on the breeze wafting in through the open window. My body cataloged it all because cataloging was what I did when I needed to make sense of things.

"This Fixer," Holden said after a moment, drawing my gaze back to him. His eyes were on my scrawl. "If it affects people the way we suspect—if it's not just a placebo with better packaging…"

"Then it's made from the enchanted herbs and healing stones from Elarion." I felt the old Guardian's caution in my bones. "We don't know the long-term effects on humans. We need to retrieve anything more we find and shut down the operation permanently."

A vibration in my bag thrummed against the sofa cushion.

I peeked inside and touched the orb phone, felt it wake against my fingertips, and a haze of cobalt began to coalesce into a sharp, winter-water gaze. Calderis' face hovered in miniature, the line of his mouth an unspoken admonition. I let the image dissolve back into opacity, then pushed the sphere deeper inside.

"Work?" Holden asked.

"It can wait," I answered.

Holden didn't push. "All right." He tapped the pad with his pen. "I'll float a quiet query to a buddy at the state health department: any upticks in flagged supplements, mystery compounds, and ER docs whispering about 'miracle tonics.' Off the record."

"I'll go over the vendor ingredient lists from the Wellies, paying close attention to the Voss products. If anyone is using more of the tonic, they won't be able to hide the effect it has on people."

Outside, two cyclists coasted past, drawing my attention, their freewheels ticking like a watch. A woman laughed near the café and then clapped a hand over her mouth as if apologizing to the night. The fountain sighed a gurgle of water. The square had a way of knitting itself into a lullaby just when you needed the world to hold still.

Holden stood and went to the kitchen. He lifted the pastry bag, inhaled in frank appreciation, and brought it back like an offering. "Bribe?" he asked, opening it to reveal a pair of sugar-dusted crullers and a bright, sticky twist that looked like it wanted to ruin his shirt.

"Insurance," I replied. "For telling you things you don't want to hear."

"Then you're underinsured." He tore a cruller in two and passed me the neater half, then grimaced when flakes dusted his dark T-shirt anyway. He cursed under his breath.

"You have other shirts."

"Not like this one. It's my favorite," he said lightly, then softer, "thanks."

I nodded, tearing my gaze away from the way the shirt, the same stormy color as his eyes, molded to his impressive muscles.

We ate and worked and let the scene be quieter than the stakes. The sugar gave me brief, ridiculous courage. I used it to look at him once more while he wasn't looking at me, to memorize the way the lamplight caught on his sleek beard, and to imagine the shape of a life where we didn't have to measure our words through duty.

He caught me anyway. "What?"

"Nothing," I said, which was the easiest lie in the world and the hardest to live with. I felt my face flush, so I added quickly, "You have sugar on your face."

He swiped at the wrong cheek.

I pointed.

He laughed and tried again, then gave up and used the back of his hand. It left a small, ridiculous constellation by the corner of his mouth. I let him keep it, a private star chart in a universe neither of us had dared to name.

"Text me when you get home," he said a little later, when the plan felt like a plan and the clock had turned the corner into tomorrow.

"I'll let you know I'm safe," I said, because I wasn't going home.

"Same thing." He walked me to the door.

The hallway smelled like wax and old wood. The elevator hummed its patient hum. He waited while I stepped in, one hand braced against the frame, his silhouette cut out of warm light and brick. Behind him, the room flickered in small ways I would remember—glass sweating a circle on walnut, his legal pad full of notes, and a city map folded open to Burlington with a coffee ring eclipsing the downtown area like a warning.

"Lock up," I said.

"Yes, ma'am." The corner of his mouth hitched. "Be careful with Brittany."

"Always." I shrugged. "And if that fails, I have an edge." I grinned.

"So I've witnessed firsthand." He winked, and the elevator doors finished their patient closing, sealing him on his side of the night.

On the ride down I watched my reflection knit and unknit in the brushed metal walls. The doors opened to the lobby. When I stepped out onto the brick apron along the square, the air felt charged and the fountain was still speaking to itself. From here, if I tilted my head, I could see Holden's balcony—the black rail, the tall fern, his reflection in the glow behind the glass—and it struck me that we were two people on either side of a window, fighting the same internal storm.

The well's breath moved up through the ground, old as a river, warning and wanting and wary. *I hear you,* I told it and tucked the vow tighter into my heart. I would not let a bottle of borrowed miracle tonic pry up the floorboards of this town and destroy the world beneath.

And I would not let romance sidetrack me, either.

I adjusted my dryfit t-shirt and crossed the square, my boots remembering each uneven brick the way a hand learns the face it loves…by repetition, care, and choosing not to look away.

Fourteen

THE NIGHT PRESSED cool against my cheeks. The square lay hushed beneath its web of festival lights. Halos caught in leaves; a glaze cast shadows on brick; the fountain murmured like a confidant who'd run out of advice.

My heart was too full and too split.

The tidy plan we'd just made with bourbon and index cards was still warm in my pocket. The unreadable look Holden gave me as the elevator doors closed still burned in my mind. And threaded through all of it, the cobalt echo of the message that had flashed across the orb in my purse while I sat on his couch still lingered.

Come at once. I need you. There is something you must hear.

Calderis' *I need you* still crackled under my ribs, the afterimage of his face remaining behind my eyes. I didn't tell Holden. It wasn't strategy; it was fatigue. Tonight, I could not manage being half of a triangle and all of a Guardian. So I walked, my boots whispering over the square's uneven brick, until the wishing well rose from the dark like a familiar mouth.

No time, and too weary to change into my ceremonial robes.

Dew beaded on the stone lip, each drop catching a pinprick of light. The runes carved around the rim pulsed when my palm hovered, recognizing my signature.

"Keep quiet for me." I whispered the incantation softly.

The well sighed.

Gravity slipped its leash.

The world tilted, and I fell into the well.

Elarion caught me like water turning to silk. I landed on a bank of bioluminescent moss that yielded under my boots with a pulse that traveled up my spine. The air here always tasted cool, green, and mineral-sweet.

Overhead, the cavern sky was a bowl of slow constellations, stars drifting like pale fish under glass. The crystalline city unfurled beyond the entry hollow: spires latticed with light, bridges braided from sound and starlight, and terraces draped in luminous vines whose bells chimed when no wind moved.

Calderis waited where the path met the first terrace. The realm's glow struck blue sparks along the runes etched in his armor. Ribbons the color of stormwater threaded from his vambraces and stirred in a breeze I couldn't feel. His mouth kept its straight line, but worry had stitched a finer seam there.

"You came," he said, glancing around. "Alone."

It should have sounded like a scolding. It didn't.

"You said it was urgent," I replied, letting the *alone* slide past. The distance between us vibrated like a plucked string.

"You should not travel unguarded. My security system is down again," he said. "Each crossing is dangerous with rebels on the loose."

"Then let's not waste time," I said. "Tell me what you know."

He studied me for a minute, sternness wrestling with something gentler. Then he inclined his head like a soldier ceding the field to triage.

"We traced the signature," he said quietly. "The Festival Fixer carries Dweller enchantments. Fractured. Diluted. Wrong."

Cold closed around the back of my neck. "From the forbidden area surrounding the Vault?"

"Yes, and from other places." His jaw hardened. "Stolen by the rebels."

"They're in Wishville," I stated. It wasn't a question.

"They move there and between realms," he said. "They're the distributors. In your world, they barter for coin and favor. Here, they trade what we value—time, memory, skill, and strength. They twist our balance into currency."

Energy bartering. Elarion's oldest economy.

I'd grown up learning how a healer might trade a day of vitality for a cloak that turned into a blade. How a memory-keeper could buy a night of safety with a song that sealed two quarrels shut. Humans measured worth with paper and numbers. Dwellers measured worth with their selves.

"How do you know for certain?" I asked.

"The Weaver Sisters saw them." He looked toward the lower terraces where the river of light curved through the city. "Come."

We took the starlit path down.

The city hummed, a thousand small enchantments breathing in rhythm. Lantern-fruit hung in clusters on silver-barked trees, their pulsing cores brightening as we passed. Waterfalls stepped down from the higher caverns: one a sheet of melted glass, one fine as thread, and one breaking into spheres mid-air before rejoining without a splash.

Dwellers lifted their faces when they saw Calderis. Respect shaped the angle of their heads, and their questions were tied neatly shut in their mouths. Their eyes skimmed me with the blend I knew all too well: the Guardian who belonged everywhere and therefore nowhere.

The *Starlit Loom* stood near the river, with walls woven from moon glass and silkstone in shifting patterns that caught the star-river's reflection and threw it back as constellations I didn't recognize. The façade itself was a garment in motion. Panels slid from translucent to opaque, while threads of light tightened and released as if the building breathed. The sign above the door spelled its name in animated script that changed color with each heartbeat.

The letters, **STARLIT LOOM,** gleamed like a weaver's shuttle caught midair.

Inside, the air vibrated. The place smelled of spun silver, heated stone, and star-anise ozone. Looms formed aisles and alcoves—ecosystems rather than machines—upright frames grown from polished bonewood, shuttle-arms like jointed wings, and pedals that hummed with sympathetic resonance. Threads hung in combed waterfalls from ceiling racks, each filament alive with tone and color like dawn shades and bruised plum, aurora greens, a black thread that ate light, and a clear thread like weaving with breath.

The Weaver Sisters moved as fish move in water. There were three of them. The eldest with hair like spun starlight, braided thick and coiled. The middle with twilight strands plaited through pearl. The youngest with braids that floated when she turned her head. Their eyes held glints, the practiced reflection of souls.

When their gazes landed on you, you felt seen.

If they liked you, they wove you gentler.

"Chief Calderis," said the eldest, her voice three notes woven into one. "Guardian Wells. We felt the well open."

Calderis bowed. "Tell her."

The middle sister dusted her fingers. The sprinkles that fell made the floor briefly starry. "A fortnight past, we received a commission for five cloaks of concealment. A rare and difficult task."

"They were performers. Pilgrims, maybe," the youngest said, though her mouth pinched as if the words tasted metallic.

"These were not performers," the eldest said. "They were masked. Cloaked in a glamour that would turn most eyes aside. But the Loom reads one's soul before it threads." She gestured to a basin by the nearest frame.

I crossed to it.

The bowl was carved from moon glass, its surface raised with runes. Inside lay a pale skein looping over itself like a sleeping creature. I reached out, and the air above it hummed. An image pricked under my sternum. My magic retreated a fraction, wary and curious.

"We begin with a soul-draft," the middle sister said, joining me. "Not theft. Just a sip to taste for a person's balance and intent."

She brushed the thread. It sang a note so pure that my throat hurt. The sound sketched a woman laughing and turning away. I tasted citrus and winter smoke. I remembered her walking into her first job with a coat too thin and a plan too big. The thread sang again, and the shape dissolved.

"The draft tells us what pattern to weave around," she finished. "Like measuring a body that has no flesh."

"What did you taste in them?" I asked.

"Envy," the eldest sister said. "A hunger sharpened to a point. An absence where regard should be." She glanced at Calderis. "And residue from a shadow-weave."

I clenched my jaw. Shadow-weaves were forbidden because they carried dangerous magic that ate through anything beneath them. "I told them we had a queue," the youngest said, guilt tightening her voice. "I hoped delay would send them away."

"It didn't. They bartered even more," the middle sister said. "They offered service energy—three days of protection runes laid across our Loom."

I looked up. Fine, translucent sigils were anchored along the ceiling spine, stitched down with light-nails that pulsed. Protection was just one form of currency in Elarion. Good work, but it felt wrong all the same.

"You accepted the barter." Calderis' words were dull with disappointment.

"We accepted the trade that kept our house from harm." The eldest lifted her chin. "They are customers under our law until unmasked. We felt their darkness, but we had no proof."

"You had a reading," he said.

"A reading is a weather report," she said evenly. "We do not imprison clouds."

I stepped between their iron and silk. "Tell us exactly what they requested."

The youngest sister drew a slate forward. Spidery runes assembled themselves line by line, chalk writing from the air. "Five cloaks, cut to human frames—one small, four large. They'll shift color from river-glass to shadow. The enchantments include hiding your energy signature, muffling the sounds you make, bending sight so others overlook you, and blocking any scrying attempts."

"So, invisible to human eyes," I said, "and to Dweller wards."

"They also asked for an anchor stitch," the middle sister added. "To hold a glamour steady in the presence of iron."

Calderis' attention sharpened. "They plan to move through human machinery."

"Cars," I said. "Hospitals. Labs."

"When they set their palms into the basin of truth, the water bubbled," the eldest sister said softly. "It slicked over like oil—that is the sign of a corrupted intention. We should have turned them away."

"And yet you did not." Calderis' tone filled with acceptance and fatigue, instead of accusation.

"We feared what refusal would bring," the youngest whispered. "They did not come as petitioners. They came as a force."

A loom behind us sighed, the warp loosened as if exhausted by the memory. Threads around the shop answered with a whisper like Vex's thoughts.

"How do you put the magic in?" I asked, partly to shift the air and partly because craft steadied me. "The concealment."

"Shielding works like a braid," the eldest sister said. "Three strands, each with a simple job. "The first strand is sight. It bends light so the eye slips past you—like teaching the world not to notice your shape. The second strand is sound. It catches the noises you make and softens them before they escape—footsteps, breathing, shifting clothes. The third strand is signature. It hides your magical energy by tucking it into a small fold outside normal space, so wards and sensors think you're not there. When all three strands are woven together, the wearer becomes very hard to find." She touched a half-finished length, and it vanished. Her fingers left indents in the air. She released the garment, and the fabric shimmered back to a river-surface where a wall had been.

"It's beautiful," I said and meant it. "Yet terrifying for the possibilities of how this could be used."

"Yes," she said simply. "There are positives and negatives to most good work."

Calderis stepped beneath the ceiling sigils. The runes flickered, recognizing his authority, then settled. "Call me if they return," he said.

"We will," they answered together. This time, it sounded like a promise.

"And if they press you for more?" he asked, and his voice gentled. "If they arrive as a force again?"

"We will refuse and summon you anyway," the youngest said. "Even if it brings danger inside our door."

The eldest sister fixed her needle-sharp gaze on me. "Guardian, you're caught between two duties. A thread stretched between two looms pulls the whole weaving out of shape." She tilted her head, eyes shimmering. "Choose which loom you're willing to snap."

It hit low, like a stitch popping in a dress I'd insisted still fit. "I serve balance, not one realm over the other," I said, hoping the words remembered their weight.

"Balance can be tricky," the middle sister murmured. "Your choices affect many."

I nodded once, feeling the weight of her words more than ever, and replied, "As do yours."

Calderis bowed just enough to honor their risk, but not enough to excuse *their* choice. We stepped back into Elarion's night, mercifully beautiful despite what we'd learned. The star-river ran dark and bright at once, constellations unspooling under bridges that sang when crossed. High above, glass-wing butterflies drifted—leaf-light bodies with bell-soft sound.

We walked until the Loom's glow thinned. My thoughts slid over each other: rebels in Wishville, invisibility cloaks, and enchanted tonics. Humans would panic if they learned the truth, and rebels would fight if we didn't stop them first.

"They will come again," Calderis said at last.

"They'll likely need repairs," I said, agreeing. "Possibly more cloaks for more hands."

He stopped at the river's edge. Reflections shattered along the runes of his armor like galaxies breaking and recombining on steel. "We cannot be delicate anymore. The treaty relies on the entity remaining in the Vault, staying out of each other's realms, and a festival wish being granted."

"I know." I folded my arms so my hands wouldn't reach for the sharp edge of his jaw. "If humans discover they've been ingesting Dweller essence, the veil keeping our worlds apart could tear from their panic alone. If Dwellers discover we allowed it, they could rip the veil wide open."

"You must not walk the seam unguarded," he said with authority and something more. "The rebel's deal in energy theft. They will see you as a prize. You are two currencies at once."

"Bait," I said.

He flinched. "I do not like that word near your name."

"I don't either." I watched the star-river slide by like beads on an invisible wire. "But I know how to make a hook taste like a prize."

He frowned. "Send word the moment you find more tonic, herbs, or stones. Even a rumor of it. I will work on securing the forbidden area once more. I suspect the rebels are moving to the surface using the invisibility cloaks."

I nodded.

He stared at the water, his jaw flexing. The air between us hummed, an unresolved chord. He looked at my mouth, then away with a soldier's discipline. Heat pulsed under my skin. I let the realm take the blame.

"May the stars guard your steps," he finally said.

"And yours," I whispered, swallowing hard.

The lightwell stood nearby, a pale column. Its surface rippled as I stepped in, warm as an embrace and weightless as a laugh. I glanced back. Calderis stood with his hands clasped behind him, all strong, sharp angles. Warrior. Enforcer. Keeper of lines not being crossed. A man with too many burdens and a conflicted heart.

The well took me, soundless and swift. The last thing I saw was the river's reflection across his armor. Up top, I stepped over the edge into Wishville.

I repeated my vow. I would not let a vial of borrowed miracle pry up the floorboards of this town, adding, I refused to let magical thread be traded for human fear.

I crossed my arms over the damp evening chill and followed the bricks down the hill toward home, each uneven stone a stitch on a string I'd learned by heart—counting promises and keeping the cloth from tearing beyond repair.

CHAPTER
Fifteen

MORNING CAME on like a clean page, crisp and a little too honest about everything written the night before. The town shook off its hush and put on its festival face with bunting snapping and vendors clattering crates. Coffee steamed from the cart on the corner, making my mouth water. I grabbed a cup, and we headed up the hill.

Vex trotted at my heels with the sly self-importance of someone who'd had an adventurous evening and intended to keep reminding me. *Humans should not attempt commerce before second breakfast*, he whispered in my mind.

"You shouldn't have stayed out so late with Fenrin," I murmured. "We'll schedule your nap between interrogations."

"I'll pencil it in." he bumped my calf.

LuLu was already at the clearing, dynamite in lipstick and a denim miniskirt with too many pockets to be legal. She waved a stack of printouts like she was flagging down a wayward parade. Her hair was twisted into a messy bun but already falling out as she ran toward me.

"Ingredient lists," she said, triumphantly. "Or the lies pretending to be them."

"Bless you," I responded. "Let's make some friends."

The Wellies had combined their booths into one, for this festival, under a canopy of crocheted garlands and optimism. Tilly had arranged mason jars of herb salts in a gradient, Belle was bedazzling a chalkboard with a warning about glitter ingestion, and Dot had a saucepan over a camp burner, stirring something amber that smelled like honey and something complicated. They were costumed for a future in which aprons counted as armor.

Ruffled, floral, and fearless.

"You're early," Tilly sang out. "Which means we can get you in before the rush and the unwashed masses of the wellness curious."

"Love the masses," Belle said, "not the unwashed."

Dot flicked her spoon in welcome. "We kept the vendors' binders like you asked, Lyra. Copies of ingredient lists, purchase orders, the whole paper trail. If there are papers to trail. Plenty of them are the 'family secret' sort."

LuLu plopped her stack beside Dot's burner and began sorting. "We're looking for anyone whose products contain tonic, boost blend, Festival Fixer, or words like proprietary, the kind of vocabulary that means 'don't ask questions.'"

Vex leapt to the table and immediately sat on the thickest stack. *I claim this pile by right of superior judgment.*

"Look at him trying to help. I swear his meows sound like words. Isn't he such a cute fuzzball?" Belle tried to scratch him, but he hopped out of the way muttering about this human in particular proving his point.

We got to work.

The Wellies, bless them, had made the kind of spreadsheet I dream about: vendor name, product category, ingredients, allergies, purchase sources, and certifications (real and decorative). I flipped pages, LuLu read aloud, and Vex provided colorful commentary for my ears only.

"Chamomile, lemon balm, oatstraw," Tilly recited. "Blessed be the nervous systems."

"Ginger, turmeric, black pepper," Belle said. "Inflammation, begone."

"Here's one. 'Festival Energy Elixir,'" LuLu read, "'contains adaptogenic herbs, proprietary essence, and a small miracle.'" She slid me the binder. "No milligrams. No breakdown. No miracle disclosure."

Dot set a small tray of cups in front of us. "Drink something before you pass out on our forms. Tea. Not a miracle. Or is it? Jury's still out."

Is this where I mention poison testing? Vex asked, his nose in a cup. *No? Just me? Fine.*

I held up my coffee cup. "I'm all set, but thanks, ladies." I shot Vex a warning glare.

We were fifteen minutes into the paper mountain, spotting a few different vendors with questionable ingredient lists, when Brittany breezed in from her booth with her ponytail high, leggings black, and tank top branded VOSS VITALITY in clean white print. She carried a duffel that could hide a small person or a very big secret, and her smile had the wattage of someone who knew precisely how good she looked in the morning.

"Ladies," she said, sunlight in human form. "And superstar." She waggled her fingers at LuLu, then, "Hi, fluff," to Vex.

Vex showed his teeth, then passed it off as a grin.

"Ingredient lists." I tapped the binder. "Yours say 'botanical base + proprietary festival tonic infusion.' Define proprietary."

Brittany rested a hip against the table, her eyes bright with performative candor. "Look, I'm not a pharmacist. I'm a coach." She popped open the duffel and took out three gleaming bottles with minimalist labels: RECOVER, REVIVE, RENEW. "I make holistic blends that people love. I wanted to offer something fun for WishFest, so I bought a tonic—same as everyone—and mixed it into my formulations. It's just marketing, Lyra. Branding."

LuLu's pen hovered. "Where did your tonic come from?"

"Pop-up sellers," Brittany said. "Random booths. They're everywhere."

"Have you seen any still in operation? Names?" I asked.

She tilted her head. "No idea. One had an owl on the sign? Or a moon? I really don't remember."

"Did you meet with Mike in the woods before his death and hand him a package?" I asked.

She blinked. "I have no idea what you're talking about. I swear, Lyra, I didn't meet anyone in the woods. I work out in the gym. I'm not much of a nature person."

Says the woman who is selling all natural *ingredients.* Vex hissed.

I glanced at Vex. He sneezed once and then blinked at me innocently.

Tilly folded her arms. "Britt, we love wellness with all our messy, glittering hearts. But if your product is just someone else's mystery tonic wearing your perfume, you're vending a question mark and that's just not safe."

"It's not a mystery," Brittany said, a shade too fast. "It works. My clients feel amazing."

"How fast?" I asked.

She shrugged, too casually. "Thirty minutes? An hour?" Her gaze slid toward the hill leading to the square. "Look, I didn't put anything unsafe in it." She lifted her hands. "I'm careful. I'm a professional."

"Professionals list *all* their ingredients," LuLu said. "Proprietary doesn't cut it when people's bodies are on the line."

Brittany's smile wavered, then shored up. "I'll update the sheet," she said with a nod. "I'll add 'festival tonics sourced from multiple vendors.' That's fair."

"It's vague," I said.

"It's all I've got," she shot back on a flash of irritation. "Besides, I'm not the only one doing it."

"True." Dot ladled her amber liquid into little jars with lethal precision. "But you're the one standing in front of us, sweetheart." She pushed her massive glasses up. "That's the price of good posture."

Brittany scooped the various sized bottles back into her bag, and for a heartbeat the ice behind her eyes showed. Then she snapped the zipper and stood. "I have a noon bootcamp and a line already forming. I'll bring you an updated list by two." She paused, softening. "I didn't meet Mike," she said to me alone, sounding genuine. "I wouldn't do that to Kim."

Something in me wanted to believe her, but the part of me trained by years on the seam between worlds wanted proof. "Two o'clock," I said, "or I'll have no choice but to confiscate your supply."

She nodded and was gone, a flash of ponytail and hustle.

"Well," LuLu said to the space she'd occupied, "that was the sound of a woman trying very hard to be both honest yet first to market."

Honesty doesn't have a rewards program, Vex said.

Tilly leaned in. "If you want a real lead, check Victoria's stand. She was doing...experiments just yesterday afternoon. We saw her dump a batch when it fizzed like a science fair volcano."

Belle widened her eyes. "A sticky pink geyser, everywhere. She cried. Then she sold the next batch anyway."

Dot pursed her lips. "We told her to list ingredients. She gave us a manifesto."

LuLu pocketed the top sheets and passed me the binder. "Let's go."

Victoria's stand squatted at the far end of Vendor Row under a banner that read *Vivi Vital* in a font that tried too hard. The tablecloth was lilac. The jars were pretty. The girl behind them looked like she hadn't slept, her freckles standing out stark against sallow skin, and her blonde hair stuffed into a bun that had given up.

She jumped when we arrived and pasted on a smile but couldn't make it stick. "Hi!" she chirped. "Samples?"

Vex hopped up and delicately knocked a sample cup off the tray with one paw. *Accident,* he thought when I shot him a look.

I put the cup back and offered my hand. "Hi, Victoria. This is LuLu. We're following up on ingredient lists."

Victoria's pulse stuttered in her throat. "I turned in my binder."

"You turned in a poem," LuLu said flatly. "'Made with good intentions and fairy light.'"

Victoria's laugh broke on the first note. "I…look, the recipe is…fluid. I did the best I could. I'm still perfecting it."

"With a festival tonic base?" I asked.

Her eyes flickered. "That's what everyone wants," she whispered. "The Fix—" She cut herself off, as if the word might summon something. "The vibe," she finished weakly. "They want the vibe."

"And you source this base from?" LuLu prompted.

"I bought a large bottle," Victoria said. "From a seller near the west gate. He said it was limited. I stretched it. You cut it with honey, lemon, and elderflower. People like elderflower." She swallowed. "The second day I found a different seller. It smelled the same." She blinked hard. "I can't afford more."

"Can't afford?" I asked gently.

Victoria stared at her hands. "Student loans," she said, and the words fell out like something unspooled. "The payments kicked in and teacher salaries don't cut it, not to mention my roommate moved out and this—" she gestured to the table like it might dissolve under her fingers, "—this was supposed to be my break. Everybody was talking about the tonic, and I thought…why not put my own spin on it? Why not get on board and profit?"

My voice softened. "Did you ever meet with Mike about this?"

"No," she said fiercely. "No. I knew him. He was kind." Her breath hitched. "He fixed my hip pain once. I wouldn't use him like that."

The muscle in my chest that had clenched loosened a fraction. "Tell us about the experiments," I said. "The Wellies saw fizzing."

Victoria's laugh cracked again. "Batch four. I added magnesium, but it foamed up like a toddler's bath and tasted like pennies. I dumped it. Batch five…settled. I sold that one." Her lips quivered. "People said they felt amazing. They came back and bought more."

Vex sniffed the nearest jar, his whiskers tense. *This smells like Dweller power*, he informed me privately. *And a little like burned marshmallow.*

"Victoria," I said, "do you have the bottles you bought the base in?"

She pulled a crate from under the table and set two empties on top. I turned one over. The label was unhelpful: a sigil that could've been an owl or a crown, and a phrase—**Limited Batch**—in elegant script that gave away nothing.

LuLu photographed both labels, then crouched to eye-level with Victoria. "We need the truth," she said. "You're selling to neighbors."

"I know," Victoria whispered, sounding miserable and resolute in the same breath. "I'll put a sign up. Full disclosure."

"Good," I said. "And for today…no more base stretching. If you can't verify what's in that tonic, you don't cut it into anything. I'll take any base you have left, herbs and stones as well. Also, let me know if you see any more popup sellers."

She flinched. "I'll make nothing. This will ruin me."

"Then make nothing," LuLu said flatly. "It's still better than harming someone. We all have problems. Find another way to solve yours."

Victoria's shoulders slumped. She swiped her eyes with the heel of her hand and nodded. "Okay. Okay."

A couple wandered up, drawn by the jars and the soft-pastel promise of renewal. Victoria straightened and met them with the truth on her tongue for once. "Full disclosure," she said, her voice shaky but clear. "I used a festival tonic base in earlier batches. I'm pulling those. Today's are tonic-free—just herbs and honey. If you want the other, I can't sell it."

The woman blinked.

The man looked disappointed.

Then the woman smiled, small and genuine. "We'll take two of the new ones," she said. "And a jar of that lemon balm syrup. I like knowing what's in it."

When they left, Victoria looked at me like I'd performed a magic trick. "Thank you," she said. "I thought honesty would get me eaten alive."

"It gets you fed slower," LuLu admitted, "but it tastes better." She winked.

After we confiscated any products we found that contained Elarion elements from Vendor Row, the clearing had fully woken with fiddles tuning, kids weaving between lampposts with ribbon wands, and the smell of cinnamon wafting through the area. Brittany waved from her booth, with two assistants in matching tanks filling bags at lightning speed. A whiteboard propped at the front read: **INGREDIENT UPDATE @ 2 PM** in block letters, underlined twice.

"Tentative points for effort," LuLu said.

Cats do not award tentative points, Vex said. *Only decisive naps.*

The Wellies had built a small fort out of our paperwork and were crowning a jar of lavender sugar with a ribbon. Tilly peered at us over the stack. "How did Victoria fare?"

"She told the truth." But we still weren't any closer to finding the distributors or the mastermind Mike had been working with.

Dot exhaled like she'd been holding her breath since yesterday. "Hallelujah."

Belle popped a lavender bud into her mouth like a celebratory mint. "If Brittany brings an update at two, we'll laminate it and hang it from her neck."

"Metaphorically," Tilly added, already reaching for the laminator.

"Metaphorically," Belle agreed, and then under her breath, "mostly."

LuLu tucked her camera away and gave me a concerned look. "You okay?"

"No," I said, "but I'll survive." I glanced at the empty bottles in my bag, the photos in LuLu's phone, and the cat who was now rearranging himself across the spreadsheets like an editor rejecting a subplot. "We have a label and a promise of an ingredient update from our last vendor. We have pulled vendor batches that were bad, along with more confiscated herbs and stones. That's something, but I fear there's still more out there."

Vex yawned, displaying an alarming number of opinions. *It is also time for second breakfast*, he announced.

"Soon," I told him, and scratched the soft spot behind his ear until his eyes went half-mast. To LuLu, I said, "I'll swing by Brittany's at two. If her list still says 'proprietary,' I'm pulling her supplies from Wellness Row."

LuLu's smile turned carnivorous. "I'll bring my camera."

The well hummed a slow warning that time was running out to permanently repair the seal on the Vault before the entity awoke fully, escaped for good, and broke the treaty beyond repair. I let the festival noise swell around us like a tide we'd learned to stand in without getting swept away.

CHAPTER
Sixteen

LATER THAT MORNING, after a much-needed break and snack for Vex, I was getting ready to head out again. The sky had turned gray, with a steady drizzle that would turn the square's brick into dragon skin. Vex refused to leave the windowsill and issued judgments from behind the glass like a magistrate in fur.

You're damp and under-caffeinated, he observed in my head. *A dangerous mix. Wear the blue raincoat. It makes you look like you know what you're doing.*

"That's the goal." I took the jacket. "Hold down the fort."

I'll hold down the fort, the sofa, and possibly that sunbeam if it returns. Do heroic things and take your time. He started purring and snoring a little too quickly. I had a sneaky feeling he wanted me gone so he could have Fenrin over.

Shaking my head on a grin, I tucked the orb phone and my notebook into my bag and headed for the *Zac in Motion* clinic. Lauren's text from earlier had been brief: **Come by soon before my afternoon patients. I found something. We need to talk.**

The waiting room lights were still on their lowest setting. A stack of laminated stretches fanned out on the entry table—hamstring, hip flexor, low-back relief—his handwriting on the diagrams precise and unshowy.

My chest pinched.

Lauren met me at the inner door, her performance pants the color of sea glass, and hair hanging in loose curls. She managed a smile, but it quivered. "Thanks for coming," she said. "I didn't sleep."

"Me either." I hung the blue raincoat on the coat rack and followed her down the hall past the treatment room and Mike's office. She kept moving like if she stopped, she might think better of whatever she was about to tell me.

We ended up in the supply room, full of floor-to-ceiling shelves, a rolling ladder, and labeled bins. Lauren shut the door and turned the lock with a soft click I felt in my bones.

She pulled a clear storage tub off the top shelf and set it on the counter. Inside lay a neat assortment of elastic bands—black, slate, and a few white ones printed with a simple wave pattern—each fitted with a small, inset stone no bigger than a pea. The stones varied. Some were smoky, others opal-like, and one a milky blue. The bands were various sizes, as if worn around the wrist, arm, or leg.

My stomach flipped with unease.

"I found them in Mike's office a while back," she said. "Bottom cabinet, under the sample gels. They were taped in the back. There were more in this tub."

"Why didn't you tell me or Chief Thorn?"

"At the time, I was trying to protect Mike, hoping to find some explanation I could live with. Now, I'm just trying to protect his memory."

I stared harder at the bands. The stones gave off a tickle of recognition against my skin, and it felt like touching a word in a language you don't speak but once heard sung. "What are they supposed to do?"

"He labeled them healing bands." Lauren made quote marks in the air. "I confronted him. He admitted he'd been experimenting. He called them adjuncts. Enhancement. He wanted to see if small, localized energy inputs would reduce pain perception or speed up tissue repair. I told him I wanted no part of it."

"You told him that?"

"Yes." Her mouth flattened. "He said he was being careful. He said he wasn't giving them to anyone without consent and that he was tracking the responses. He said—" She stopped, pivoted, and grabbed a manila folder from the shelf beside the tub. Inside were photocopied spreadsheets with patient initials, pain scales, and notes in Mike's tidy print. There was a column labeled *band used* with colored dots to correspond to the stones.

"He kept records." I was surprised and yet not. Mike kept records the way other men kept sports stats. It calmed him.

"He wasn't reckless," Lauren said. "Not like that. But he was…curious. And stubborn. And a little desperate to help." She rubbed her arms as if static were building. "I told him this wasn't evidence-based. He said evidence has to start somewhere. I told him it's supposed to start in a lab."

My gaze kept snagging on the milky blue stone. It gave me a headache the way a too-bright sky did. "What are they made of?"

"That's the thing…" She opened a smaller drawer to show me a single loose stone in a cotton-lined box. "He gave me one to look at. I didn't want to be complicit, but I also didn't want to be ignorant." She grimaced. "I asked Matt to help me test it. He's good with weird stuff, and he's also discreet."

I nodded, curious.

"He has a little field spectrometer, the kind you use for gem identification and other hobbies." She set the stone in my palm. It was cool and faintly throbbing, like an echo of a heartbeat at the earth's core. "He had no idea what it was. Said the signature was wrong for anything he knew: not quartz, not calcite, and not opal. No standard mineral profile. He said—and I quote—'This reads like a story pretending to be a rock.'"

I closed my fingers. The throb matched my pulse, then slid out of sync like two metronomes drumming on different songs. I knew instantly it was a healing stone from the Vault.

"Did you wear one?" I asked.

"No." She swallowed. "I tried to be the stopgap. The ethics committee of one, but I'm not Mike's wife. I don't get veto power. He used them with a few patients who were at the end of their rope. One in particular."

"Who?"

"Evan Teller, the one with a grudge against Mike." The name dropped in the room like a tool clattering off a bench, loud and inevitable. "Evan's back has been…" She searched for a word as if looking for one that wouldn't betray an oath. "Challenging. He was compliant in the first couple of weeks, then less so. He wanted a quick fix but didn't want to put in the work. He gave consent for the band. He said he'd wear anything if he could just move without that knife in his spine."

I thought of Evan. He was stubborn, big, and perpetually one splinter away from a full grievance. "Did the band help?"

"For a day," she said. "He came in grinning and said he'd slept for five hours straight. Then the next day he was short with the front desk. The day after that he swore. At everyone."

"Side effects?" I frowned. The stone in my hand pulsed a half-beat, and my stomach did a slow turn. "Or just Evan being Evan?"

"I don't know." She raked both hands through her hair, then flinched and put them down as if the motion hurt. "I asked Mike to stop. He said he'd already decided to. He said he didn't like how it felt to profit from success without understanding why."

"Did you ever meet him in the woods?"

Her gaze shot up. "What?"

"He met with a blonde woman who gave him a package," I revealed. "I've asked others. I have to ask you, too. Did you meet Mike in the woods?"

"No." The word came out sharp, clean, and immediate. She steadied it. "Lyra, I met him in the treatment room, hallways, and the stupid vending machine nook where he bought the terrible pretzels because he liked the salt. We didn't have time for woods. Or secrets like that."

I studied her face. It read true, if a little weary. "Okay," I said. "Then help me now. I need to take these."

"The bands?"

"Yes." I let the stone slide back into the box and reached for the tub. "They need to be tested to see if they're safe."

She nodded without argument, relief and guilt warring in her expression. "There are more," she said. "Two bands in his desk, one in the laundry room because the Velcro caught on a towel." She hesitated. "And one in my locker."

"Because you were…?"

"Because I wanted to know what they felt like in my hand, not on a patient." Shame and defiance twisted so tightly in her expression I couldn't pull them apart. "I needed to know if my body recognized the wrongness, or if it was all in my head."

"And?"

"It hummed." She looked at me like I might confirm she wasn't imagining things. "It hummed in a way I'd never heard before."

I thought of the Vault, of the threads I could pluck on the edge of my awareness, of the way a Dweller artifact sings when you bring it past the threshold of the ordinary. "You're not wrong," I said quietly, only admitting that much. "Bag it with the others."

She didn't ask questions as we gathered the stray bands and the locker one in silence, labeling evidence envelopes. When the tub was full, I closed the lid and slid the locking tabs into place. The plastic made a little click.

"Lauren." I put my hand over hers where it rested on the tub. "Thank you."

She nodded, her eyes shining. "Do you think this has anything to do with—" She didn't say Mike's death. It still felt like blasphemy to put the two words together.

"I think everything around him matters," I said. "We'll sort it all out. I promise."

She pressed her lips together. "If you talk to Evan—"

"I'm going now."

"Be careful," she said. "He's...not himself."

"Maybe he is," I said, and that was what I was afraid of. Permanent change.

Evan Teller lived above his sister's garage on the east side of town, a square, practical apartment with a porch that faced a tangle of pines. A sign for his handyman business—TELLER TINKERS—leaned against the steps. A truck idled in the drive as if he were getting ready to leave, the radio hissing the tail end of an angry sports show. As I pulled in behind it, Evan came out on the porch, squinting through the drizzle.

"Ah," he said, when he clocked me. "Historical Society's Chair of WishFest."

"Lyra is fine." I pulled up the hood to my raincoat. "Do you have a minute?"

"For what?" He leaned on the railing, his arms crossed, big and balled and unwelcoming. He looked worse than I remembered. His shoulders were hunched tight, there was a pallor under his tan, and his eyes were too bright.

"To talk about Mike Zaccaria," I said.

He snorted. "Pass."

I sighed. "Evan."

He rolled a shoulder, grimaced, and then pretended he hadn't as he walked over and shut the truck off. "What? You want me to cry? You want me to say he was a saint? He wasn't. He didn't fix me."

"That's not what he promised," I said evenly. "He promised treatment, not magic."

"Same difference when you're the one hurting," he said. "He told me if I did the work, I'd get my range of motion back. I did the work."

"Did you?"

He lifted his chin. "You calling me a liar?"

"I'm calling you…human," I said. "With a complicated relationship to foam rollers."

His mouth twitched, then hardened. "Those people with their stretches and their mindfulness and little rubber bands."

"About the bands," I said. "Did you wear one?"

He stared at me for two beats too long. "So, what if I did?"

"How did you feel?"

"Great," he said. "For a day." His jaw worked. "Then I felt like someone had swapped my blood out for hornets."

"Angry."

"Annoyed," he said. "Agitated. Like everything was too loud. Like my skin didn't fit and you were all talking under water." He rubbed the heel of his hand into his sternum like there was an itch under the bone. "And my back still hurts."

"So, you stopped using it."

"I stopped seeing him," he shot back. "I switched to Dr. Peelman. 'Snap, Crackle, Peel'—you know, the spine fairy." He grimaced at his own joke, then half-smiled because it was, objectively, a good line. "She never liked Mike. You know the whole Physical Therapist versus Chiropractor rivalry many of them have, plus all the holistic stuff he was getting into. She says chiropractic's better. Less woo-woo. More crack-crack."

I filed the *never liked Mike* part to look into later. "And does it help?"

"It helps when I go," he said. "I've been busy."

I eyed the truck, the ladder rack, and the tangle of extension cords coiled like snakes in the passenger seat. "Busy not doing the work?"

He flared. "You know what? You may be the Great and Powerful WishFest Chair to this town, but you don't know a damn thing about what it's like to have your body betray you."

You're not wrong, I thought but didn't say. Because if my body did betray me, I could heal myself through Sunfire Touch. I wasn't

Dorothy or the Wizard, I was the Great and Powerful Guardian of Elarion. "Evan, did you ever meet Mike in the woods?"

"In the woods?" He barked a laugh. "What, was he writing me love letters with pinecones? No. I met him at the clinic like a civilized person."

"Ah, but *you* wrote letters, didn't you? Not to him, but *about* him," I said. "To the medical board, several times." I'd done my research and added it to his file. I kept one on everyone in this town.

He paused. The pause was admission. "I wrote a letter," he muttered. Then, with the scowl of a man who knows that plural matters, "Okay—letters. He took my money, he didn't fix my back, and he gave me a mood bracelet that made me want to punch drywall. I have a right to complain."

"You do," I said. "You also have the right to be honest about whether you did the work."

He glared hard enough to dent steel, then his shoulders sagged one millimeter at a time until they slumped in exhaustion. "Maybe I didn't do *all* of the work," he said, like each word cost him a fortune. "It's hard. It hurts. It feels stupid when it doesn't work right away."

"I know," I said. "Mike knew too. Healing takes time and consistency. That's why he kept showing up. He never gave up on you."

Evan looked away, his jaw flexing. "Look, if you're here to absolve him, I'm not your guy. If you're here to check my alibi, I was fishing the morning he—" He cut himself off, swallowed, and snapped instead, "Ask anybody."

"Chief Thorn already did," I said. "I'm here because we aren't sure about the safety of the bands and would like to test yours. If you still have one, I need it."

He hesitated. The briefest flicker of the thought, *What if I want the hornet blood again*, passed across his eyes, making me wonder if the bands were addictive. Then he crouched, fetched a small plastic bag from under the doormat like he'd stashed contraband where the delivery packages go, and held it out between two fingers.

I took it carefully. The band inside had a smoky stone inset—the kind that hummed a little too close to my pulse. "Thank you."

"Whatever," he said, clearly sulking. "You going to Peelman next? Tell her I said she's better."

"Take care of your back, Evan."

He barked that not-quite laugh again. "I'll try." His words were innocent enough, but his tone sounded like he was picking a fight with a grizzly bear.

CHAPTER
Seventeen

SNAP, *Crackle, Peel* sat at the end of a strip mall between a frozen yogurt place and a boutique that sold motivational tea towels with quotes that made me want to lie down. The Peelman office window was wrapped in a vinyl mural of a stylized spine flowering into a tree, the slogan **Get Popped, Not Pilled** swirling underneath in cheerful script.

Inside, the waiting room was crisp white with fiddle-leaf figs and a diffuser pumping out a smell of blood oranges. A chalkboard listed weekly specials: *New Patient Posture Scan $39; Pelvic Reset Package $99; Teacher Tuesday—Show Your Badge, Get a Free Pop.*

The receptionist had lashes that deserved their own tax bracket and a name tag that read *Kara.* "Hi! Welcome to *Snap, Crackle, Peel*! Have you been popped with us before?"

"I have not," I said. "Lyra Wells here to see Dr. Peelman."

Kara checked the screen, brightened, and pointed me to a chair like a stewardess with a lovely emergency exit. "She'll be right with you. Love your jacket."

"Thank you," I said, and sat.

A video looped on a wall-mounted screen: slow-motion thoracic adjustment, satisfied sighs, captions like *Release!* and

Realign! and *Rejoice!* I watched three shoulders drop as if freed from metaphoric burdens.

Dr. Peelman ushered me back five minutes later exactly, on time like a train. She was mid-forties, compact, with a sharp bob and lipstick the exact red of a stop sign. Her hand was cool when we shook. Her office was a glassed-in cube with three diplomas, two foam spines, and a framed poster that read *Motion is Lotion* in a font that made my eye twitch.

"Chairwoman Wells." She smiled just enough to suggest she'd practiced it in a mirror. "What an honor."

"Lyra is fine," I said. "Thanks for seeing me on short notice."

"For the WishFest Chair, I always have a slot." She gestured to the chair. "What can I do for Wishville's favorite neighbor?"

"I'm here about Mike." I watched her mouth do a little sympathetic purse that would have read more sincere if the laugh lines near her eyes weren't so neatly managed.

"Tragic," she said. "Truly. Such a loss for the community."

"You knew him well?"

"We moved in the same wellness circles." The word *wellness* being emphasized. "We shared patients, occasionally. He was... well liked."

"But not by you," I said.

Her brows shot up the polite amount. "I beg your pardon?"

"You were tracking his unorthodox practices." I placed the bag with Evan's band on her desk where the fluorescent lights could make it look more sterile than it was. "Weren't you?"

She stared at the band, then sat back and smiled, wider now. "All right," she said. "Cards on the table. Yes. I paid attention to what Zaccaria was doing. If a competitor is dabbling in adjuncts that blur ethical lines, I want to know. And if a patient needs safer care, I want them in my hands."

"You mean you wanted to discredit him and poach his patients," I said. Sometimes truth landed better directly.

She didn't flinch. "Marketing is not a sin. Neither is believing

Chiropractic care can help people more than…physical therapy and mysticism."

"The bands," I said. "You knew?"

"I'd heard. Hearsay. We *all* heard. He kept it quiet, but quiet has a short commute in a small town." She tapped the plastic with a well-manicured nail. "If he was giving patients trinkets instead of protocols, that's malpractice adjacent."

"He kept records," I said, determined to get her to talk. "He monitored response. He wasn't tossing charms like confetti."

"And yet," she paused a beat, "he had people believing their pain would melt because of a rock. That's dangerous."

"So is telling people a 'pop' fixes everything," I said.

Her eyes flashed, then cooled. "If you want a sermon about placebo, I can send you links."

"I want to know if you reported him."

"To the board? Of course," she said crisply. "Repeatedly. Not because I hate him, but because standards matter. I also want to keep my doors open. Poaching"—she gave the word back to me without apology—"is a foul word for widening access. My care helps people. If I redirect them before some fairy tonic does harm? I sleep well at night."

"So, you tracked his practices to discredit him and steal his patients."

"I tracked his practices because they were unorthodox. And because I could serve those patients better." She folded her hands. "Evan Teller included."

"He says you're better."

"He says many things." There was a thread of disdain in her tone. "Mostly when he's in the room. Less so when he's due for home exercises."

"Do you know where the festival tonic is coming from?" I asked. "Who's selling it?"

"I know rumors. I know booths with owls and crowns and a sense of scarcity. I know Brittany is pouring it over her brand like syrup. I know Victoria cried in my office yesterday and gave a refund to a woman who said her heart raced after batch five." Her mouth pulled. "I know no one has an ingredient list that's truly honest."

"Did you ever meet Mike in the woods?" I asked, because the question belonged to everyone now. She didn't have blonde hair, but she could have worn a wig.

She laughed, unguarded and a little ugly. "Good Lord, no. I meet men in rooms with lighting I can control."

"Did you ever threaten him?"

"Professionally?" Her brow creased. "What are you getting at?"

"Threaten to report him. To ruin him."

"I told him I'd report him if he continued to blur the lines, and I did. I also told patients that chiropractic care would be safer and more effective for them than whatever he was dabbling in. That's called informed choice plus a little persuasion. It's legal, Lyra. If you'd like me to quote case law, I can."

"I'm good. Do you recognize this mark?" I slid the photo of the bottle label across the table—owl-or-crown logo, LIMITED BATCH in fancy script.

She narrowed her eyes. "I've seen that on two bottles in my lobby trash, half covered up by Brittany's labels. One of her customers swore it cured her plantar fasciitis overnight. The other said it made her feel like she'd swallowed a beehive. Neither stuck to a care plan long enough for me to decide who to believe."

"Do you have those bottles?" I asked.

"Trash day was yesterday. But Kara is a magpie. Check the back closet. She saves weird things in case they're useful for social media."

"I'll ask her."

Dr. Peelman's posture softened a fraction. "For what it's worth, I didn't want Mike dead. A little embarrassed, perhaps. A little less smug but not gone." She studied my face. "You're tired."

"I'm in a long conversation with the truth."

"You won't find it at a festival booth," she replied. "Or in a pebble on a bracelet."

"Sometimes you find parts in places you don't expect." I thought of the Loom and of the sisters' careful work, of cloaks that turned the wearer invisible.

She watched me. "If you decide you want an adjustment," she stated all businesslike, "say the word. First pop's on me."

"I'll keep that in mind." I stood.

"And Lyra?" she added as I reached the door. "If you're pulling those bands out of circulation, pull Brittany's little bottles too. If you need me to testify that I've seen adverse reactions, I will."

"Duly noted," I said. "And Dr. Peelman—"

"Yes?"

"Motion is lotion is terrible," I said kindly. "There must be something better."

She laughed, honestly this time. "You're not wrong," she said. "But it moves products."

I headed back to the front desk. Kara did, in fact, have the magpie box. In the back closet beside spare scrubs and a pyramid of branded water bottles lay a crate of "interesting trash"—two empty tonic bottles (owl-or-crown label intact), a handful of glittery flyers, and a bracelet that had snapped, its elastic snarled through an empty stone bezel like a mouth missing a tooth.

I bagged the lot, thanked Kara, and stepped back outside. The rain had stopped, finally.

The square had brightened by the time I reached it, the clouds thinning to gauze. People moved about as if nothing strange was happening in their town. The fountain tossed water droplets into the air again and again, like a promise of hope made to anyone who looked.

Under my feet, the well's energy came up through the cobblestones—old, patient, and wary.

"I hear you." I shifted the weight of the evidence tub from one hip to the other. "We keep securing the threads. We keep the cloth from tearing."

Vex's voice melted into my head like a warm spoon in honey. *And we eat lunch soon.*

My cat had a one-track mind. "Okay, okay. I'm on my way," I said out loud, knowing he would hear me even though he wasn't anywhere nearby.

I headed home to store the evidence tub, before climbing the hill to the festival clearing toward Wellness Row, toward Brittany's whiteboard promise of an ingredient update at two, and toward the bright slick booths where everything had a label listing all ingredients except the one that mattered most.

By two o'clock the festival had gone from quaint to loud. Fiddles were fully awake, the kettle corn drum was popping like hail on a tin roof, and Wellness Row shimmered with hopeful labels and the kind of smiles that promised you could be a new person by sunset.

Vex padded beside me with the smug bounce of a cat who had recently eaten a scone he swore he didn't steal...after I'd fed him lunch, of course.

Ingredients or bust, he reminded me in my head, more likely to take my mind off his naughty ways.

Brittany's booth was impossible to miss—clean white tent, citrus diffusers puffing out virtue, and assistants in matching **VOSS VITALITY** tanks ferrying little ice-bucket trays like cocktail servers at a very hydrated party.

She spotted me and lifted a hand. Her ponytail was perfect and her smile, practiced. "Lyra! Right on time." She snapped her fingers, and her left-hand assistant produced a printed sheet like a dove from a hat. "Here it is. Full transparency."

I took the page. It listed **base** (filtered water, glycerin, lemon, honey), **herbal infusion** (ashwagandha, rhodiola, ginger), **aroma** (natural citrus oils), and then the part I'd come for: **festival tonic additive (limited batch)**—0.5 oz per 16 oz bottle; sourced from multiple pop-up vendors.

"'Festival tonic additive' needs an ingredient list. Not just a name." I sighed. "I told you that."

"I thought the whole point of the update," she tilted her chin, "was to tell people I used it."

"Telling people you used it isn't the same as telling your customers what is *in* it."

"My product works." She lowered her voice as if the words themselves were a talisman. "My clients feel it. They're less sore and have better sleep."

"For how long?" I asked.

Her eyes skittered away. "Long enough to keep them coming back."

"And what about side effects?"

"There haven't been any." She couldn't quite meet my eyes. "My source assured me it was safe."

"And what source was that?"

She snapped her spine straight. "Mike Zaccaria."

My stomach turned over. "And look at what happened to him." I shook my head sadly. "Dr. Peelman assured me that there *were* side effects." I glanced at the logo stamped faintly at the bottom of the sheet—her brand watermark, clean lines, and a little wave for motion. "Brittany, if you can't verify what's in *that* additive"—I tapped the phrase—"you can't sell any bottle with it in it at the festival. You can sell your herbal base. Not the rest."

A small crack showed under the shellac in her expression. "You're pulling me?"

"I'm pulling your questionable products." I paused to let my words sink in. "Until you can tell people what they're drinking."

For a heartbeat she looked like she might dig her heels in and make a scene. Then she exhaled through her nose and nodded once, which was answer enough for me. She had no idea what was in that tonic.

"Fine. We'll pivot." She turned to her assistants. "Reroute. Herbal-only. Pull the 'revive' and 'renew' with the additive. Comp a base sample of the herbal to anyone who came for the tonic."

They moved fast—good soldiers in a war for a brand—sliding the suspect bottles into a storage tote and replacing them with iced mason jars of amber ginger tea. The sandwich board flipped. **TODAY: HERBAL-ONLY** in new block letters with an extra underline, and the smiley face less smiley.

Brittany handed me the tub and then rubbed her wrist. "Look, I'm not the villain you want." She didn't quite meet my eyes. "I didn't meet Mike in the woods, but I did talk with him. He was the one who told me about the tonic and that there would be pop-up vendors at the festival. I figured if Mike was on board, then the product must be safe. I bought what everyone else bought. I just packaged it better."

"Why did it take you so long to tell me?" I was disappointed that Mike was her source.

"I was afraid people would think I had something to do with Mike's death. I promise you, I didn't."

"I don't want a villain. I want people to stop getting hurt." And to prevent the entity from emerging and destroying us all.

She swallowed, then pasted the smile back on. "Herbal-only," she repeated to herself like it was a spell that might stick if she said it enough. "We'll be fine."

"We'll be by later," I said. "To make sure that sign is still true."

"Of course." For once the brightness didn't feel like an attack. "Good luck out there, Lyra."

Vex and I drifted back down the hill to the square. It was a painting in motion: dogs in bandanas drinking from tin bowls, toddlers asleep on shoulders, a busker coaxing a tune from a saw like the air itself had a memory it couldn't shake, and Mayor Doug Delaney alongside his assistant Laisira trying to keep the townsfolk calm.

Over by the community board, a lanky kid in a *Wishville Wags* T-shirt was handing out flyers with the zeal of a saint and the coordination of a new colt.

"Joey," I called.

He turned, his grin already lit. "Lyra! Vex!" He crouched to scratch Vex exactly once, then looked like he remembered that Vex only allowed scratches by written invitation.

Five demerits, Vex informed me privately, but he didn't swat Joey's hand away.

Joey stood, juggling his stack of flyers to hide the flush on his face. "Sorry, sir," he said as if he'd heard him, but that couldn't be possible.

"Tell me you've got puppies." I eyed the logo—a heart around a pawprint.

"We've got chaos," he said. "And a senior named Old Red who will only walk if you tell him the plot of the *Fast & Furious* movies." His smile flickered, then settled into something a little stranger. "Do you…have a second?"

"Always." I smiled. "What's going on?"

He darted a look left and right, then stepped closer, lowering his voice to that confidential register only teenagers and conspirators think is subtle. "So, um. I think I got a weird superpower? Which I'm definitely not keeping, so don't worry, but also I think my dog told me something about Dad."

Vex sat down like he'd paid for front-row seats.

I kept my face calm. "Start at the beginning."

Joey fished in his pocket and pulled out a small cloth pouch. He loosened the drawstring and tipped something into his palm. A stone no bigger than a pea, milky gray with a faint opalescent sheen.

"I found this in our garage in my dad's things," he said. "I showed it to a lady at a booth with an owl logo. She said it was for 'connection.' I thought—cool. Dogs. Connection. Maybe it helps with the anxious ones at Wags, right? And then…" He swallowed. "And then I put it in my pocket, and it was like someone turned a radio on in my head. But the station was animals."

"Voices?" I asked, stunned.

"Not words." He waved the flyers as if he could fan the memory away. "More like pictures and feelings. My dog, Tasker, looked at me and sent me this big, warm thing that felt like 'you' and 'pack' and 'meatball.' I knew he meant home and dinner and that he likes when I wear the red hoodie because it smells like the couch."

Flattering, Vex said dryly. *Dogs and their ridiculous taste.*

"More like funny," Joey went on, and Vex blinked. "Like a party trick. Then, last night, I took Tasker down the trail by the creek. You know, where the trees lean over? He got weird. He sent me the feeling of scared and an image of metal and a sharp picture of a big shape hitting a tree, like bam. He kept sending it. Bam. The feeling of a shove. And then he sent…Dad. Not a perfect picture, just the sense of him. Good. Soft pockets. Peanut treats. And he sent run and then shove again. Then a tree."

The square thinned around us for a second, like my body had dissected the scene.

"Tasker saw something the night Mike died?"

"I don't know if it was that night." Joey's eyes turned suddenly shiny. "He's a dog. Time is 'now' and 'food.' But he saw the bam against the tree. He felt the shove. He sent me a smell, too, but I can't translate it. Like burned marshmallows and something else I can't pinpoint." He made a face. "I think Tasker saw my dad's murder."

Victoria's batch had smelled like Dweller power and burned marshmallows, then again, so did half the bonfires with smores around the festival. "Joey," I said, gently, "how did you sleep?"

He winced. "I didn't. Every pigeon in town sent me their auto-biography. Also, three squirrels tried to sell me a timeshare in a pine tree."

Vex snorted.

"It's funny now," Joey said, his voice wobbling. "But last night it was…loud. And this morning Tasker got mad at a shadow and I *felt* mad in my bones. Then the feeling left, and it was just me again." He held out the stone like a kid offering a frog he regretted catching. "Can you take it? I don't want it anymore. And I don't want to hear things I can't fix."

I took the stone in my palm. It was cool and far away and then far too close, the hum sliding a half beat off my pulse the way the bands had. The well beneath us thrummed once, a faint warning rising through the cobblestone.

"Yes, I'll take it," I said. "Thank you."

"You think it's bad, right?" he asked. "Like—bad bad? It felt… borrowed. Like it belongs somewhere else."

"It *is* borrowed." I let him hear the certainty in my voice without giving any details away. "And it's not for us." I slipped the stone into an evidence envelope and sealed it. "You did the right thing."

He folded a *Wishville Wags* flyer into a tiny square and unfolded it again, his hands shaking just enough to make me want to feed him pancakes and let him sleep for twelve hours. "Don't tell my mom, please. She's already mad enough at Tony and me. Do I need to, like, sign something?"

"You need to drink water," I said. "And maybe a day off for both you and Tasker. If he wants to sniff the woods again, go with him in daylight. Let him lead. If he shows you the tree, or anything else, text me." I handed him my card. "And Joey…if the radio turns on again, even without the stone, you tell me, okay?"

His mouth fell open. "You think it could?"

"I think sometimes something keeps ringing after the bell," I said. "It usually fades. But if it doesn't, I'll teach you how to turn the volume down."

He didn't ask questions, just nodded so hard his hair fell into his eyes. The innocence of a kid, so willing to believe in the impossible without second guessing anything. I hoped he would stay that way as long as possible.

"You're…you're the best," he said, as if he'd been saving that sentence since middle school. "Tasker thinks so too."

Finally, a dog with good taste, Vex said.

Joey startled, as if finally realizing he had indeed been hearing my cat. "I don't normally hear words from animals. Vex is different. Am I going crazy?"

"Let's just say Vex isn't any normal animal," I said. "And you're not crazy. You're useful. A big help to solving your father's case."

He straightened under the words the way a plant does when you fix the light. "Okay. I'll text you if I find out anything more." He lifted the remaining flyers. "And I'll keep recruiting fosters. Because Old Red will only walk for Vin Diesel, and Vin won't return my emails."

"Rude of him," I said. "Tell Old Red I know a guy who knows a guy who can fake a good car noise."

"Cool." Joey jogged off, already pitching his next plea to a couple with stroller twins and an aura of soft yes.

I stood very still, letting the noise of the festival pour past me. Then I took out the envelope and looked at the little stone again. It lay there, innocent as a lie told for love. Burned marshmallow, shove and tree, run and bam.

A dog's truth.

Above the square, banners snapped like bright warnings. Under the square, the well breathed a slow, old caution.

"All right," I said to both worlds at once. "We're listening."

Vex head-butted my calf. *We're also hungry.*

"Second lunch," I agreed, and started toward the café, already thumbing a text to Holden: **Got another stone. Joey's dog 'saw' a shove + impact w/ tree on creek trail. No ID, but scent = burned marshmallow. Pulling Brittany's additive for now.** I paused before I hit send and added: **I'm fine.**

Because I knew he would ask, and I was.

Uncomfortable, angry, and heart-sore…but fine. The kind of steady that lets you take one more thread between your fingers, even when you know it's tied to something that doesn't want to be unknotted.

I tucked the envelope deeper into my bag and made for the smell of soup. Around us, the town kept singing its complicated song—hope in one key, fear in another, and love somewhere underneath trying to hold the melody.

Eighteen

THE LUNCH CROWD had thinned to a lazy hush by the time I pushed open the door to *The Wishing Lounge*, our local bar-and-grill that doubled as the town's unofficial meeting hall. It sat on the edge of Wishville like a cozy woodland tavern with crooked shingles and flickering stained-glass sconces. The clock above the dartboard read three-oh-five, that in-between hour when the fryers cooled and the sunlight poured in through the bay windows like warm honey.

Chief Holden Thorn and Detective Cal Deris were already at a corner booth. Holden nursed a cup of hot black coffee the size of his ego, while Cal sipped an espresso as he studied a folder of crime-scene photos with the kind of calm intensity that made mortals nervous. The sight of them together still made my stomach twist with nervous energy, but we were The Covenant Three.

There was no avoiding working together.

I slid into the seat across from them, fanning myself with a napkin and acting like they didn't affect me at all. "You boys start without me?"

Holden looked up, his gray eyes rimmed with fatigue but still sharp. "We're not exactly celebrating happy hour, Wells. Figured we'd get the grim updates out of the way before the dinner crowd piles in."

"The optimistic tone is always appreciated." I stole a fry from his plate.

He smirked. "Figured you'd show up hungry and underfed."

"Always." I grabbed my iced coffee from the waitress who seemed grateful to have *anyone* keeping her busy at this lull. "So? What's the latest?"

Holden leaned back, his chair creaking. "State Health Department says there's nothing new. No red flags, no alerts, no reports outside town limits. Looks like whatever's in those Festival Fixer tonics or healing stones is staying right here in Wishville."

"That's comforting," I said. Outside, I heard the sign carved from driftwood swinging gently in the afternoon breeze. Inside, it smelled like spiced whiskey and rosemary fries with folk music playing over the speakers. The booths were made of patched leather and twinkling lights hung from the ceiling. "At least the rest of Vermont isn't glowing in the dark yet."

"Don't jinx it," he muttered. "Last time you said something like that, we found frogs a neon green."

"That was one frog in Matt's biology class," I reminded him. "And it was paint." I rolled my eyes. "Teenagers."

Calderis finally looked up, his pale eyes catching the summer light like river glass. "Containment is good, but isolation makes the magic concentrate. Pressure builds."

I tilted my head. "Meaning?"

"Meaning," he said evenly, "whatever is brewing beneath this town is reaching a tipping point."

Holden sighed. "Here we go—Dweller physics."

Cal ignored him and flipped a photo onto the table. "My update. The invisibility cloaks that were ordered from the Weavers? They've been picked up, and the rebels themselves are gone."

"Gone how?" I asked.

"Vanished," he said. "No trace of any of them in Elarion. One cloak was tailored for a woman."

Holden's brows shot up. "A woman rebel?"

Calderis nodded once. "The signature was faint, fragmented. There are female Dweller rebels, but not many." He swallowed once, his eyes meeting mine. "Arisial is one."

I felt my gaze widen and I blinked. "Your ex-girlfriend?"

He nodded slowly. "There's a reason why we broke up. And she knew how to dismantle my security alert system."

Holden's gaze slid toward me. "You thinking this connects to Mike's death?"

I hesitated, then nodded. "Maybe. Joey's dog Tasker saw something that night. Well—'saw' is relative. Joey said Tasker told him someone shoved Mike into the tree."

"Interesting. Talking to animals. That's Dweller magic," Calderis said.

I nodded. "Side effects of the stones. Hopefully, it's not permanent. Poor kid is getting no sleep with all the chatter."

"Shoved?" Holden repeated, brushing off humans talking to animals as if this was his new normal. "So, there *was* a skirmish, just like the medical examiner said."

I nodded. "It sure looks that way. Mike was a tough guy. It had to be someone strong. Or *several* someones." I rubbed the condensation off my glass, watching it smear in the sunlight. "Tasker said there was a scent of burned marshmallows. Vex smelled that around the festival grounds."

"It's summer. There are bonfires and smores everywhere," Holden said.

Cal's expression hardened. "Personalities altered by unstable magic, most likely from those stones and herbs in the Vault."

I added, "Evan Teller fits that theory after wearing the band Mike gave him. He's an angry patient, with unstable behavior, who wrote letters to the medical board. Maybe he finally snapped."

"Maybe," Holden said. "But if the stones or the tonic can twist someone's energy, then the killer could be anyone."

The waitress returned with refills. Cal thanked her with one of those almost-smiles that should come with a warning label. She practically floated away.

Holden rolled his eyes. "Do you do that on purpose?"

"Do what?" Cal asked mildly.

"Turn women into puddles."

"I don't know what you mean. Women are solid creatures, not liquid, unless that's another side effect you haven't told me about." Calderis looked at me.

"No, that would be a one hundred percent *you* effect." I pulled at the collar of my t-shirt.

Holden frowned.

"Hmm. Perhaps it's the uniform," Cal said. His "uniform" was a fitted navy shirt, unbuttoned far too low, and rolled at the sleeves. The badge clipped to the belt of his too-tight jeans was just wrong enough to make people curious.

"Funny how I wear a uniform, and I don't seem to have the same effect," Holden grumbled.

I begged to differ as I tried not to stare at his muscles bulging beneath his tailored gray button down, which was all the more appealing because it wasn't unbuttoned at all.

I cleared my throat. "Behave, both of you. We've got bigger problems than your charm levels."

Before either could retort, the door banged open and LuLu swept in like a stick of dynamite ready to go off. Sequined tank top, white capris, and oversized sunglasses perched in her curls. The late-day sun followed her inside, scattering light across the table.

"Well, well," she drawled. "The Wishville Dream Team. Mind if I crash the after-lunch club?"

"Depends," Holden said. "You bringing gossip or paying for dessert?"

"Both." She plopped down beside me, tossing her purse on the booth. "And don't act like you don't love my intel."

"Love's a strong word," he muttered.

LuLu flagged the waitress. "I'll have my usual. Extra olives." Then she turned that bright smile on Cal. "Detective Deris. You've been scarce. Thought maybe you left us for good, back to your glamorous city beat."

"Wishville keeps me occupied." He inclined his head. "Kind of like you."

"Mmm." She leaned forward with her chin in hand and her grin wide. "Interesting."

"Definitely." His gaze stayed locked onto hers.

The spark between them was instant once again, like a struck match. I could practically *feel* the energy ripple across the table, Dweller and mortal currents brushing for half a second. If only she knew what he really was.

If only she knew what he meant to me.

Holden caught my eye, studying me curiously.

"So, LuLu." I avoided his gaze. "How's the gossip mill?"

"Grinding full speed," she said. "Half the town's talking about those healing bands Mike was making. And someone spotted a van. A woman and some men unloading boxes of more Festival Fixers behind a single tent on Wellness Row."

Holden sat up and met Calderis and my gazes, the unspoken thought of it might be the rebels passing between us. His gaze shifted to LuLu's as he asked, "When?"

"An hour ago." She shrugged.

He scribbled a note. "I'll check it out."

"See?" She grinned. "I do have value."

Calderis' tone softened. "You have more value than you real-ize, Ms. Morales."

She laughed, brushing his arm. "Careful, Detective. Compli-ments like that will get you in trouble…or a date." She winked.

"I'm aware," he murmured, and for a heartbeat, his eyes didn't look human at all.

I kicked him lightly under the table. *Dial it back*, I mouthed.

He blinked, and the spell was broken.

LuLu stirred her martini. "You three always look so serious. You need a hobby. Something besides corpse-talk and conspiracy boards. We should go out. All of us, together."

Holden's lips twitched. "This *is* my hobby. Job, hobby…life."

"Oh, honey, that explains so much." She squeezed his hand.

Outside, sunlight slanted across Main Street, gilding the flower boxes and a faded mural of the wishing well. Summer in Wishville lingered—long days that refused to end, and the air thick with the promise of more turbulent weather.

LuLu tilted her head, studying each of us. "You know, you've got that secret-society vibe again. Like you're planning something you shouldn't and leaving me out." She stuck her bottom lip out in a mock pout that brought a smile to Calderis' face.

I coughed.

"Just police work," Holden said too quickly.

"Right." She sounded unconvinced. "Well, whatever it is, I hope it doesn't ruin the rest of the Summer WishFest."

I flinched at her choice of words, but she didn't notice. My job meant everything to me, and lately, I felt like I was letting both realms down.

Cal spoke softly. "We're doing everything we can to keep everyone safe."

"I trust you guys." She winked. "Especially you, Detective."

When she turned to tease Holden about his tie, I caught the faintest shift in Cal's expression, like something almost wistful. I felt his struggle because it was my own. It hit me then how cruel the boundary between our worlds could be. He couldn't tell her who he was, what he'd seen, or what he'd sworn to protect. And she would never know why the air around him sometimes shimmered like heat over water.

By the time her friend called from the bar, the sun had dropped lower, brushing the treetops in gold. LuLu slid out of the booth, gathering her glittery bag. "Don't work too hard, boys.

And Lyra, text me later. You definitely owe me a night out. And… I've got a headline brewing."

When she left to meet her friend, the door swung shut behind her, the bell jangling once.

For a long moment, none of us spoke. The lounge had grown quiet again, caught between daylight and dusk.

Holden broke the silence first. "You okay?"

Calderis' gaze stayed fixed on the window where her reflection had been. "She reminds me of someone," he said softly. "Before Elarion became what it is."

"Someone who laughed like that?" I asked.

He nodded once. "Someone who made even the light stay longer."

A pang of jealousy hit me when I realized he was talking about his ex. If she had never become a rebel, they would probably still be together.

Holden cleared his throat, his gaze locking onto mine. "Well, speaking of staying longer—" he glanced at the time "—I'm going to check out that lead. You two can brood all you want." He tossed a few bills on the table and left, sunlight spilling across his retreating silhouette.

I felt jealousy over Calderis, along with guilt over Holden, and all-around confusion.

I turned back to Cal. "You know she's human, right? No magic. Just charm and chaos."

He smiled faintly. "Perhaps that is its own kind of magic. Unless you give me a reason why I shouldn't be interested in her." He stared intently into my eyes.

"Calderis," I said softly.

"No pressure," he said even softer. "I get it. Some loves only last a lifetime. I'm immortal and not going anywhere. Who's to say we both can't have it all?"

I laughed, shaking my head. "You're impossible." Then his words sank in. Why hadn't I thought of that? Did I really have to choose? Maybe, just maybe, I could have both.

"Not impossible." His gaze met mine and held. "Just learning and adapting, taking things one day at a time, Lyra."

One day at a time sounded pretty good right about now.

Outside, the sky deepened from gold to apricot, and the sound of children playing drifted in from the streets. Summer stretched on, bright and deceptive, like everything in Wishville lately.

Yet as I gathered my notes, I couldn't shake the feeling that our days might be numbered.

The sun still hung high when I stepped out of *The Wishing Lounge*, the kind of long, amber light that stretched summer afternoons far past their welcome. The air was warm, thick with the smell of fried onions and lilacs from the planters lining Main Street. I squinted against the brightness, still turning over Calderis' words in my mind.

He'd gone back to Elarion minutes ago, disappearing in that ripple of light that always made me ache a little. And with Holden gone as well, there was an emptiness inside of me. For once, I was alone. Something I needed right now, but that almost never lasted.

I'd barely taken ten steps when I heard my name.

"Lyra!"

I turned just in time to see Kim Zaccaria rushing toward me from across the street. She looked completely undone. Her hair was wild, her cheeks streaked, and her whole body was trembling.

"Kim?" I hurried to meet her halfway. "What's wrong?"

Her voice came out in ragged bursts. "It's Tony…he's missing! I can't find him anywhere!"

My stomach dropped. "Missing? When did you last see him?"

"Hours ago," she cried. "He said he was just going for a walk to clear his head and feel closer to his dad. He took his father's journal with him and said he wouldn't be long…but he never came back, Lyra. It's almost sunset!"

The fear in her voice tore at me. Mike had barely been gone. The grief was still raw.

"Did you call Holden?" I was already pulling my phone from my pocket.

"I tried the station, but they said he was out following a lead. I only trust Holden and you." She gripped my arm. "You're my last hope. Please, you have to find Tony before dark."

"I will." I stepped away for a moment and hit Holden's personal cell phone number. It rang twice before his low, gravelly voice answered. "Lyra? What's up?"

"I just ran into Kim Zaccaria," I said quickly. "Tony's missing."

A pause crackled through the line. "How long?"

"I'm not sure. She just said hours. He left the house with his father's journal and said he was taking a walk in the woods. She hasn't seen him since."

I heard him curse, and a car door closed in the background. "I'll alert the deputies to keep an eye out on the main road and river path. You stay put, Lyra…don't go into the woods alone."

"I wasn't planning to." I hesitated, lowering my voice. "Holden…she said Tony went to feel closer to his father. You know what that might mean?"

He sighed. "Yeah. Mike's old walking trail runs near the ridge, right near the path that led to where we found his body."

I stepped away for a moment and lowered my voice. "Exactly. Calderis went back to Elarion a few minutes ago for a meeting to update his father so he can't help." I inhaled a shaky breath. "If Tony wandered that way alone, he could run into the rebels."

"We'll find him," Holden said firmly, "before that happens."

I glanced back at Kim, who stood wringing her hands, her eyes darting between me and the phone and around the street. I could feel her panic like electricity in the air.

"Holden," I murmured. "She's falling apart. I can't just leave her here waiting."

"Then keep her with you," he said. "We'll regroup and figure out who can help us track him fastest."

A thought struck me, sharp and sudden. "Someone who knows the area. Someone who might *sense* him."

He caught on instantly. "Yeah. I was thinking the same thing."

"Then we call them first."

"On my way." He hung up.

I slipped the phone back into my pocket and joined Kim, trying to sound steady even though my pulse hadn't stopped racing. "Holden's on it. We're going to find Tony."

Her eyes filled again. "You promise?"

I nodded. "I promise. We already know someone who might be able to help."

"Who?"

"Someone who's good with finding things that don't want to be found," I said softly, not wanting to worry her by involving her other son.

She nodded.

"But for now, you need to go home in case Tony comes back on his own. Keep your phone close."

She looked like she wanted to argue, then just nodded weakly. "Thank you, Lyra."

As she hurried off down the street, I watched her figure blur into the golden haze of the early evening. The air shimmered with heat. The breeze carried the faintest whisper from the woods beyond the meadow, a low hum that brushed my senses like a warning.

Tony was missing.

Calderis was gone.

And the sun was sinking fast.

By the time Holden's cruiser rumbled up Main Street minutes later, the light was already shifting toward gold and violet.

"We need to find the kid before dark." He climbed out. "And if he's not in town, we call in the one person who can track him better than anyone else."

"Joey," I said.

He nodded grimly. "And Tasker."

I glanced toward the distant line of trees, the edges of the meadow glowing like fire. "Then let's move fast."

CHAPTER
Nineteen

THE WOODS GLOWED gold and green, every beam of sunlight spilling through the canopy like melted glass. Dust motes drifted in the air, catching the light as they moved, fragile and slow—a kind of suspended beauty that made the hour before dusk feel like it belonged to no one.

That was the thing about Wishville at twilight, it always looked too perfect. Too still. It was unsettling now because you never knew what could be hiding in that stillness.

I'd learned to heed its warning.

Holden led the way, his long strides steady, a flashlight already in his hand though the light hadn't yet faded completely. He'd called Joey as soon as Kim had left and asked him to meet us in town with Tasker before Kim could keep him home. After a quick search for Tony with no luck, we headed to the woods. Joey now trailed behind him, gripping Tasker's leash in both hands, while the dog's nose skimmed the ground in focused circles. Every now and then, the leash went taut as Tasker caught a scent, the leather creaking with strain.

I followed, the air prickling against my skin. Dweller energy brushed faintly beneath the surface. Not enough to see but enough to feel, like a charge rising from the earth. It pulsed from deep underground, faint and rhythmic, a low hum I now recognized all too well.

The Vault was stirring again.

"Let's start near the river path." Holden's voice cut through the quiet, low but certain, as she looked at Joey. "I have a hunch that might be the way Tony went if he was trying to be closer to your Dad."

Joey's reply came small but sure. "Tasker says he smells him. But...it's weird. He says the air smells like the same spot where the snakes used to hide."

Holden frowned, slowing his pace. "That supposed to mean something?"

Joey's head bobbed once. "Yeah. It means something bad's nearby."

Holden shot him a look but didn't argue. I didn't either. The boy was right, even if he didn't understand how right.

Because I could feel it too. That faint, dark energy under the ground, like the forest itself had hit pause. Every leaf felt too still, every sound too sharp, as if the world was listening for what came next.

"Keep going," Holden said finally. "If Tasker has the scent, don't lose it."

The trail narrowed as we walked, trees crowding closer, branches hanging low enough to brush our shoulders. The sun's light fractured into narrow bars, turning the leaves to copper and gold. My boots sank into damp earth, the smell of pine needles thick in the air. Somewhere ahead, a raven cawed, the sound slicing through the hush like a warning.

None of us spoke for a while. We didn't need to. The silence said everything.

If we didn't find Tony before dark, we might not find him at all.

Tasker barked once then darted off the path. Joey's eyes went wide. "He's got something!"

Holden took off first, his flashlight beam cutting through the trees, and I followed, branches whipping against my arms as we ran. The air grew cooler the deeper we went, the light dimming fast until we burst into a small clearing.

Papers littered the ground in a broken circle, fluttering slightly in the breeze.

I crouched, with my heart pounding, and picked one up. The edges were creased, smudged with dirt and sweat. I recognized the handwriting from the journal I'd glimpsed before Tony had hidden it that time in their garage. The writing was Mike's with his neat, careful, and deliberate style. But it wasn't sentences. It was a string of numbers.

Coordinates.

My pulse skipped.

"Holden." My stomach tightened. "He figured it out."

"Figured what out?"

"The cipher in his father's notebook." I scanned the page. "The spiral pattern wasn't random. It's a code, and he solved it. These numbers…they're the coordinates to the Vault."

Holden's jaw clenched. "You're telling me a teenager just cracked a cipher?"

I nodded grimly. "And now he's trying to find it."

The realization hung between us, heavy as the thunder rumbling in the distance. Before Holden could speak again, my phone buzzed in my pocket, the vibration startling against the silence. I fumbled it out, the screen lighting my hand in a cold glow.

Weylan.

"Weylan, please tell me you have good news?" I had sent both him and Sparks a text, asking for eyes in the sky and on the ground.

"We found him," came his steady voice. "I'm up in the balloon. He's off the ridge path, deep in the woods. Sparks is with him."

My heart thundered. That was the direction of the Veiled Vault entrance where Mike was found.

"Is he hurt?" I asked.

"No." Weylan paused. "Just confused. He says the coordinates led him here, but he can't see what he's supposed to find."

I exhaled a shaky sigh of relief. "The Vault's still cloaked," I told Holden. "He can't see it."

Holden rubbed a hand over his jaw. "Good. Let's keep it that way."

I turned to Joey, who stood nearby out of earshot petting Tasker, his face pale with worry. "We found him," I said gently. "Someone is with him."

Relief flooded his face, and he clutched Tasker's collar. "Can we go get him?"

Holden shook his head. "No, buddy. We'll bring him back. You and Tasker head home and tell your mom he's safe."

Joey opened his mouth to argue, but Tasker barked once and nudged his leg, already turning back down the path. The boy hesitated only a second before following.

As their footsteps faded, the air seemed to shift—heavier, denser, like the forest itself was closing in. The hum beneath the ground grew clearer, thrumming faintly in my bones.

"He knows too much," Holden said quietly.

"I know." I nodded. "I'll have to erase what he remembers about the Vault after his animal talking power wears off."

"Yeah. Before it tempts him again."

We started toward the path off the ridge. The trail sloped downward, the ground slippery. The trees thickened around us, trunks twisted and old, their bark patterned with strange symbols. Natural at first glance, but to me, unmistakably Dweller runes, faintly glowing where moonlight touched them.

The closer we got, the stronger the vibration grew. The Vault wasn't just beneath us. The entity inside was fully awake and listening.

By the time Sparks' electrically charged hands appeared through the trees, my pulse was a drumbeat in my throat.

Tony sat on a flat boulder, his knees pulled tight to his chest and the leather-bound journal clasped in his hands. His face was pale, with his eyes wide and glassy. He looked both terrified and entranced.

When he saw us, he didn't move. His voice, when it came, was small but certain. "I found it," he whispered. "I just can't see it, but it's here. I can feel it."

His words sank into the stillness, echoing faintly.

The Vault thrummed in answer.

A cold shiver ran through me. "Tony," I said softly, "you did what no one else could. But you need to come with us now, all right? It's not safe here."

Holden crouched beside him, his tone gentler than usual. "You did good, kid, but this isn't a place you should be. We need to get you home."

Tony nodded slowly, but his eyes stayed fixed on the ground that looked normal to the human eye, but I could see the faint spiral etched beneath its surface. I could feel the energy all around us, like heat waves over sand.

I gave his arm a tug and led him away from the hidden entrance.

As we led him away, I felt nothing beneath the ground anymore. And somehow, that silence felt worse than the sound.

By the time we reached the festival clearing, it was empty. Night had settled soft and full around Wishville. The sky was the color of ink diluted with moonlight, and the air smelled faintly of lilac and woodsmoke. The grass glowed in ribbons where the moonlight touched it.

Kim stood at the edge of the field, her phone pressed to her ear, pacing in tight circles with Joey and Tasker by her side. When she saw us, she dropped the phone and ran, her sobs breaking through the still night.

"Tony! Oh, thank God!"

He let the journal fall as she threw her arms around him, pulling him close. "I'm sorry, Mom," he whispered, his voice shaking. "I just wanted to be near Dad."

She rocked him against her, tears streaking her face. "It's okay," she murmured over and over. "It's okay now."

Holden hung back, giving them space. "We found him near the ridge," he said quietly. "He's shaken, but fine."

I stooped to pick up the journal, my fingers brushing the worn leather cover. This book had been a map to what Mike had been doing and where. In the wrong hands, it could be disastrous. It burned faintly against my skin, like touching a live wire through fabric. I frowned. "Tony," I said softly, "can I hold onto this for a while? I'll give it back, I promise."

He hesitated, glancing between me and the book. "I guess," he said slowly. "I just…I think Dad wanted me to find that place. The numbers, the way they spiraled, it meant something."

"I know." I forced a smile. "But some things are safer when they stay hidden."

He nodded, vulnerable and trusting, and my chest ached.

While Kim checked him over, I drew in a slow breath and reached out. My fingers brushed Tony's temple. A faint shimmer passed from me to him, amber light slipping beneath his skin delicate and precise. I felt the memory lift from him like a weight. The coordinates, the cipher, and the pull of the Vault…gone.

He blinked, and his eyes looked clearer. The fear in them softened into confusion, then calm.

I repeated the memory erase with Kim next, brushing her arm as she held him. Then with Joey, who'd run up behind us out of breath, and finally with Tasker, who whined softly as the wave of energy brushed through his mind.

Gentle work—the kind that required heart more than power. A memory lock, woven of light, warmth, and the promise of protection.

When it was done, I exhaled, exhaustion curling through me. "You should all go home," I said. "Get some rest."

Kim nodded, clutching Tony's hand. "Thank you, Lyra. I don't know what we would've done without you." She touched the journal fondly as if saying goodbye.

Her voice trembled, but her face had gone calm.

They turned and started toward their home, the moonlight spilling over them in silver bands. For a moment, everything looked peaceful again. Perfect. Almost enough to make me believe it.

Almost.

Because as they reached the bend in the path, something pricked at the edge of my senses, faint and sharp like a pin pushed beneath the skin of the world. A whisper slid through the air, low and ancient.

I froze.

Holden glanced at me. "What is it?"

I shook my head, confused. "The Vault."

He frowned, scanning the tree line. "I don't hear anything."

"Exactly," I said quietly. "That's the problem." The woods behind us weren't silent. They were empty. The difference was worse. I had promised Calderis I wouldn't investigate these things alone anymore. Even I could sense the danger. But that didn't mean I would forget about it.

"I'm locking the notebook in the safehouse tonight," I said. "No one can see it."

Holden nodded. "Good. Keep it that way. We'll tell Calderis in the morning."

As we walked back toward town, the wind rose and died again, soft and hollow. When I looked back one last time, I felt like someone or something was following me. Like there were eyes on me. The lampposts flickered ahead. It was probably nothing, I told myself. Wishville wiring was older than most of its residents.

Picking up the pace, I headed home.

Twenty

BY MORNING the clearing felt like a memory of itself—same trees, same ribboned lanterns winking between birch branches—but the light was too bright, and everyone's voices were a shade too careful, like they were speaking around a bruise. The wishing well stood strong, catching the rays of sun as if nothing bad ever happened here. If you didn't look closely, you could almost believe it.

But I always looked closely in Wishville.

Victoria's booth looked like a fox den after a storm. Canvas flaps were ripped, tables were overturned, and crushed glass glittered like frost over trampled grass. Perfume hung in the air—her floral oil blend—twisted with the smell of something burned. People drifted past pretending not to stare.

"Don't you so much as let even your shadow touch the rope, young man!" Mr. Finch scolded a teenager who'd leaned too close to the yellow line he'd strung around the wreckage. He planted his boots wide, his straw hat teetering and mustache bristling with righteous purpose. "Evidence is delicate. Even shadow smears count, you know."

"Do they?" I asked, easing up beside him.

"In my heart they do." He cocked his head at me. "Chief Thorn coming?"

"Any minute." I squinted at the dirt just outside the rope. Faint tracks, the kind nervous feet make. And deeper prints under the booth frame, too long between steps to be a child. The wood of the collapsed display table bore four gouges like a rake dragged backward.

A burst of delighted screaming drew my eyes to the green.

The Wellies had set up an impromptu stage on a picnic table. Tilly, in a velvet shawl, whirled a bundle of sage so aggressively it smoldered like a comet. Belle shook a tin of salt with the gravitas of a priest. Dot clutched a copper pot like a holy relic.

"Hark!" Tilly cried. "A malevolent whiff attempts to breach the sanctified barrier of commerce! We rebuke it in the name of… retail!"

There was polite clapping.

Belle dumped salt in a curlicue that sprinkled a toddler's sandals. "Purity for your footsies," she told the child solemnly.

"Oh, for heaven's sake," Finch muttered, though his mouth twitched.

Mayor Doug Delaney hustled up the path, Laisira gliding along at his side with her clipboard hugged like a shield. Doug's tie was already askew, and his sleeves rolled high. He wore the look of a man trying to hold a parade and a funeral simultaneously.

"Lyra, good," he said, switching to his public smile for the circle of vendors hovering nearby. "Everything's under control."

"Is it?" a glassblower asked, his thumb cutting toward Victoria's booth.

"It will be," Laisira soothed, her voice sounding more confident than she looked. "We are pausing the wish token wishes in the well for one hour while we tidy things up a bit. Please direct guests down the hill to the fountain readings and the kids' scavenger hunt. We'll make announcements. Thank you for your patience." She gave me a tiny nod that pleaded, *Help me keep everything from falling apart.*

I nodded once and gave her a reassuring smile I didn't actually feel.

I focused on the booth. It radiated the kind of wrong energy. I let my hand hover a breath over the soil, not quite touching the surface, just feeling the way a palm feels for heat.

Something had crouched here in the night. "I don't think this was the work of raccoons," I said to Finch as I straightened.

"Blessed be." Finch crossed himself with two fingers and a nail set.

"Let's not panic the spectators," Laisira whispered, then spoke louder for the crowd. "Please enjoy free mini-donuts courtesy of the festival!" The word free scattered the gawkers like migratory birds.

The Wellies redoubled their efforts.

"Behold the triple ring of protection!" Tilly chalked a wobbly circle, while Belle sprinkled more salt, and Dot held the copper pot upside down like a bell. The chalk snapped, the pot dropped, the salt flew, and Tilly drew the last segment with a broken nub and a prayer. "Body, soul, and—"

"Wi-Fi," Belle whispered.

"Wi-Fi," Tilly agreed solemnly.

"You'll gum up my grass with that," Finch warned. "Salt kills root systems."

"It kills evil, too," Dot pointed out.

A murmur rolled through the clearing like wind in dry leaves. Heads turned as Holden Thorn shouldered through the shade at the path's mouth, his sunglasses in place, jaw square, and badge catching a shard of sun. He moved the way shadows lengthen— quietly, steadily, and without question.

"Morning," he said, lifting the rope and ducking under. He went still the way he always does when a scene starts speaking to him. He tilted his head and listened with his eyes. "Finch, thanks. Keep the line tight."

"Yessir."

Holden squatted. His fingertips traced the gouges in the wood, hovered over the glitter field, and pointed at a smear of pearly dust near the back table. He rubbed a pinch of it and sniffed. "Quartz?"

"Quartz with something," I said. "Part Victoria's chemical dust, but I'm getting ozone as well. Like a spell blew sideways."

He frowned. "There's no broken lock, no smashed cash box, and no bites taken out of the funnel cakes next door. If someone came to steal or snack, they forgot how."

"They came clearly looking for something they didn't find. And possibly to announce themselves," I said softly.

"Whoever *they* are." His eyes cut toward the well.

Doug inched up to the rope with a fixed smile. "Chief? The media's sniffing around." He gave him a pointed look. "I could use a statement that includes words like 'isolated' and 'handled.'"

"I'll give you 'isolated,'" Holden said dryly. "I'll get you 'handled' when I have it."

"Good enough." Doug was already turning to distribute optimism to the crowd.

Laisira pasted on a smile and shepherded people toward the music tent as if moving a flock across a narrow bridge.

A little girl approached the rope with a wish token and the solemn rank of a tiny judge. "Is the wish place closed?"

"Just for a bit," I said, crouching to her level. "We're giving it a nap."

"Everyone's cranky without snacks." She pouted.

"Truer than you know," Holden muttered.

The girl giggled and scampered off toward the free donuts sign.

The Wellies moved closer, forming an eccentric wall between the crowd and the rope. Tilly swanned her shawl with such authority that three college boys backed up. Belle flipped a sign that read, **Purification Tea $4 to $3 and business improved**. Dot ambushed any rubberneckers with samples of lemon balm cookies. "Eat peace," she told them. "Goes down better than panic."

Amid the chatter and music and the well's quiet glitter, a needle of unease stitched along my ribs. I swept my gaze beyond the booth to the fringe of the woods. The trees had that listening posture, each leaf a cupped palm.

"Anything?" Holden asked without looking up.

"Feeling, not seeing." I swallowed. "Same hum as last night."

He worked in silence, photographing angles, measuring heel spreads with a worn metal ruler that always looked too small in his hands. He bagged a shard of crystal, bagged a curl of fiber torn from the tent seam. He found a pendant half-buried at the back, a spiral cut into its center. He held it toward me on the tip of his pen.

"It matches Tony's notebook cipher."

"You think Victoria knew?" he asked.

"I'm not sure," I replied.

He pocketed the pendant like you pocket a live coal. "We'll dust it."

The music tent kicked up a happy jig as if the fiddler was determined to bend the day toward joy. It almost worked. People started dancing. A toddler toddled. Someone shouted about cider slushies. Normal beat louder than the weird…for now.

Holden's phone buzzed.

He checked the screen, and what little ease he'd worn tightened like a pulled thread. "Thorn." He stepped away to hear better. "Slow down." He listened, the set of his shoulders stiffened.

I knew before he said it.

He came back under the rope and didn't meet my eyes until he had to. "Mike's clinic," he said. "Smashed up overnight."

My mouth went dry. "Anything taken?"

"Nothing." He let the single word hang.

"Same as here," I said. "The booth wrecked, the clinic wrecked, yet nothing missing from either."

"Matt took the day off from summer school to be with Lauren," he added. "She's pretty shaken up."

"What now?" I asked.

"We investigate." He jerked a nod to Finch. "No one crosses the rope. Laisira's in charge. Mayor might not get 'isolated' after all, but you can bet he'll get 'handled.'"

Finch saluted with his nail set. "Aye."

Dot pressed a cookie into Holden's hand as we passed. "Eat peace," she ordered.

"Doctor's orders?" he asked as he ate it.

"Grandmother's," she corrected, and for the first time that morning, I believed we might make it to noon without the sky cracking open because of our strong community. At least I hoped so.

We walked out of the clearing together, with sunlight shining on our backs like a blessing...yet I couldn't shake the feeling that it might be more like a warning.

Twenty~One

THE CLINIC'S smashed glass still rang in my head as we cut across the back field toward the woods. The air had gone from cinnamon sugar to sap and damp bark, and the festival sounds thinned behind us until the fiddler's tune was only a suggestion. Lauren had been all trembling hands and white knuckles, Matt a quiet wall beside her. Drawers were dumped, cabinets overturned, and files weirdly untouched.

"I'm glad Matt was able to be there with her," I said. "She shouldn't be alone."

"Matt's her glue. He's got her." Holden shortened his stride for two steps so I could catch up. "You sure you're good?"

"I'm okay," I said honestly, and then blinked at the sight before me.

A figure emerged from the band of shadow where the woods met field. Detective Cal Deris stepped into a spear of sun and carried it with him. That's what it always looked like when Calderis wore his human glamour. He'd just surprised me because I didn't know he was coming.

He pulled us into the hush under the trees with a look. "The entity," he said without preamble, his voice low. "It's gone."

The word clanged like the final plate on a bad tower. So that was why the woods had felt quiet last night.

"Gone how?" Holden asked.

Cal's eyes were winter clear. "The outer stitches on the seal show lift at three nodes. The energy signature inside is missing." His jaw ticked.

My phone buzzed.

"Sparks, what's wrong?" I asked.

"I'm on the north loop with Alden. Weylan's up top," he said. "Alden let us know he saw Victoria. She's walking with someone in a hooded jacket. They were headed toward the spiral entrance to the Vault. We tried to circle, but they cut low along the ridge."

"We're close," I said. "Do not engage. Tell Alden to stand down."

"Do I look like someone who shouts 'surprise'?" Alden asked dryly in the background, clearly having overheard me. "I've done my part. I'll leave the rest to you."

A twig cracked on their end. "You've got maybe three minutes if you cut in by the birches," Sparks said.

"We're moving." I hung up.

"Who?" Holden asked as we started to jog.

"Victoria and an unknown hooded person," I said.

"Maybe our blonde rebel," Holden said grimly. "Maybe she's the host for the entity."

Cal's eyes shuttered briefly, an acknowledgement of both truth and fury. "We separate the host from the captive. Lyra, use your Magma Ward heat barrier and obsidian shards to isolate her. Sparks flanks. Holden—"

"Cuffs and tackles," Holden said.

We slipped into the woods, letting it swallow us whole. The light broke into rays under the canopy. The ground pitched down toward the ravine and energy pulsed in my bones like the ocean you can hear but not see.

Sparks appeared alone. He pointed—two fingers, two bodies —down the slope. Through a splice of beech and maple, I saw

Victoria stumbling, her hands bound in front with a strip of torn fabric. The woman at her elbow moved in a stealth-like manner—balanced, anticipatory, a predator inhabiting a puppet's skin. The hood snagged, and a head appeared. I gasped. It wasn't the blonde rebel…

It was Kim Zaccaria!

"Knife," Sparks blurted , snapping me out of my shock.

The glint at Kim's right hand caught my eye.

He didn't look away from the target to speak. "You've got one clean shot."

"Two," I said, and lifted my hands.

The Magma Ward in me hummed awake like a choir's throat-clearing. I built a heat barrier across the path, invisible until you leaned on it—heat at a frequency that pushed back. The air in front of us went tight and sizzling.

Kim stopped. Her chin lifted, and the smile she gave us was almost Kim's, just turned five degrees too sharp. "Lyra," the thing wearing her like a coat said warmly. "You impress me. Although, I knew you would."

Victoria blinked at the sound of my name and tried to bolt. Kim's knife twitched. I angled the ward. "Don't," I said softly. "You'll cut yourself on the edge of the knife."

Holden stepped out with his badge visible, his commanding voice steady. "Kim Zaccaria, drop the knife."

Kim's pupils fixed on him with a terrible, bright curiosity. "Sorry," she cooed, though her voice was no longer hers. "Kim isn't home at the moment. But I *am* an excellent hostess." Her gaze slid back to me—hungry, sensing something only she could feel. "Come now. Trade places with the poor woman. You're the one I want. You need to finish the job your ancestor failed to all those centuries ago. You're the only one who can."

My breath hitched. The human sacrifice the Elder had used was my ancestor.

Of course. The Elder hadn't been able to combine both human and Dweller souls, and I was one of a kind. The only half-breed and exactly what the entity needed to finish the job, but I was too strong for it to take my soul without my consent.

It must have slithered free in the woods, drawn first to Tony's panic like a beacon, then jumping into Mike's journal, full of his written emotions. And when we'd returned Tony to Kim—and she'd touched the journal—it had simply followed the stronger pulse. Kim. Mike's widow. Grief, devotion, dread…all of it radiating from her like a feast. She was the perfect temporary host, and the one most likely to lead it back to me. Victoria was a bonus with her skills.

Which is what the entity craved most.

Calderis moved with the kind of stillness that preceded an attack, placing his body between Victoria and the blade's angle. "Sparks," he said.

Sparks ghosted right.

I sent the ward's second curve low, a hooked pressure that would sweep legs. Kim jumped clean, landing catlike on a flat stone, and slashing the hot air with her empty hand. The counterstrike hit my ward like a thrown door. Sparks—violet, blue—spat where our workings met. The smell of ozone bit my nose.

"Cute," the entity purred. "Did you teach her that, Enforcer?"

Cal didn't answer. He blurred left, and when the knife flashed toward Victoria, it struck a pane of nothing and skittered away into leaves.

"Now!" I snapped.

Holden charged low the way they teach you in marine drills. I lifted the ward just in time for him to hook Kim's knees and yank. She fell hard, her breath blasting out of her lungs with very human shock. The entity surged to haul her up. I manipulated the air around her with pressure and prayed I wasn't pinning Kim too hard to crush her.

Sparks stepped in and absorbed the entity's next shove. He turned the life force in his palm the way you turn water in a cup and spilled it across the ground behind her. The energy slicked along root and rock and reared up as a wall.

"I boxed," Sparks said with a shrug.

Kim writhed, her wrists twisting. Holden wrestled the cuffs on and they clicked. She went very still.

Then she laughed. Kim's voice, but the entity's delight. "You put jewelry on a weak being."

"I put jewelry on a lady," Holden said, his jaw muscle jumping, "and she's coming home."

"Lyra," Cal said without looking, and I moved.

I knelt at Kim's shoulder and let amber light flow through my palm into her skin. It wasn't a cleanse, this time, it was a lane. A corridor opening between host and hitchhiker. The thing inside her arched like a cat as its claws lost purchase.

Cal pressed his palm to Kim's brow and murmured an old Dweller cadence—a litany that named the "rooms" of a self and asked the self to remember its shape. The air thickened with each line, shifting from sharp glass to solid stone. On the third line, Kim's body shuddered as something inside her came unhooked.

"Hold," Cal murmured.

Sparks touched Kim's sternum with two charged fingers and pulled. You never see the extraction. What you see is the air rippling. But I felt it slide, slippery and furious, through the corridor I'd made: a cold current that tried to reverse and couldn't. It came out like smoke veined with broken light.

It lunged for me, then Calderis, and finally any throat.

Cal lifted his other hand and pressed it to a small obsidian capsule engraved with sigils that woke like embers. The smoke hit the vessel's mouth with a soundless scream that we felt in our molars. It collapsed inward, condensed by the geometry of the thing it never meant to touch, and was gone. The capsule sealed. The sigils breathed once, twice, and went dark.

Everything settled like a dropped curtain.

Kim sagged in Holden's grip. He softened around her without letting go. "Hey," he said, his voice a tone I'd heard maybe five times ever. "Kim, are you with me?"

Her eyes fluttered. The blue behind them was hers again.

Panic followed on its heels. "Chief? What—did I—Tony—where's —" She saw the cuffs and flinched. "Why—?"

"You're safe," I said quickly. "I got a text update from Joey. Tony's with Joey at home. When you disappeared, he called Matt and Lauren to come stay with them."

"I don't—" Her breath hitched. "How did I get here?"

Holden looked at me over her head. I nodded. He popped the cuffs with the world's gentlest clack and slid them away, his palms open so she could see they were no longer there.

Behind us, Victoria pressed shaky palms to the ward I had set around her. "Lyra?" Her voice was like a paper cut, thin and stinging. "You're…glowing."

"Occupational hazard." I dispelled the ward with a touch. The invisible heat shield fell away, and the air cooled again. She swayed, and Calderis' hand appeared at her elbow as if he'd meant to be there all along.

"Rescue," he told her, a word like a blanket. "That was all."

She stared at the capsule in his hand. "Am I hallucinating? That…was that…"

"Nothing for you to worry about." He looked at me. "You know what to do."

I turned back to Kim and took her hands. "Kim, look at me," I said. When her eyes found mine, I set the weave. "Listen. There were five thieves. They hit Victoria's booth and Mike's clinic overnight. Smashed things and scared people. They grabbed you and Victoria to make it dramatic. You escaped into the woods. Weylan spotted you on one of his balloon rides and called Chief Thorn, Detective Deris, and me. That's what happened." I let the story gel. "You're safe."

"Five thieves," she repeated, the words catching and then knitting. She hiccupped a laugh-sob. "Weylan found us."

"That's right." I turned to Victoria. "Same story. You escaped. We got to you in time."

Victoria's pupils were blown wide. The human brain is a powerful shapeshifter, you just have to give it a scaffolding it wants to live on. She swallowed, nodded, and brushed dirt from her sleeve with trembling fastidiousness. "Five thieves," she whispered, and her mouth tried on a shaky smile it could keep. "I can tell customers that. They'll buy tea."

"Of course they will." I was inspired by the simple heroism of people trying to survive a day.

Holden stepped aside to call dispatch, his voice pitched low to weave our lie into the cloth of the town. "Two burglaries, coordinated," he said. "Two victims escaped. Suspects at large. No ongoing threat. EMT sweep, low priority. Extra patrol in the North Loop and Market Lane." When he hung up, he tipped the phone at me as if to say, *It's done.*

Sparks kicked the knife over to me, and I bagged it. He shot a glance toward the ridge and then said for my ears only. "You think he can lock it with that thing angry in the container?"

"He'll lock it," I said with conviction, glancing at the women whose minds were still fuzzy. They wouldn't register most of what we were saying.

Calderis listened to the capsule in his palm, the way you listen to a seashell for an ocean you met once and can't forget. "The inner rite will hold if the breach was opened with intention, not forced apart," he said, more to the trees than to us. Then, to Victoria, his tone filled with something like kindness. "You will feel tired. Eat. Sleep. Do not go near the water today."

He was softening towards humans. I could see it.

She nodded like he'd told her to take two aspirin and call in the morning, obviously still in shock.

He looked at Kim, worried but unwilling to say so. "You will remember nothing," he told her, and the gentleness there made me melt. Then he tipped his head to me, grateful and brief, before slipping into the trees.

The woods accepted him, closing without a sound. A minute later the air settled as a door far underground rotated. The pressure eased, birds remembered their songs, and Kim shivered. I put my jacket around her shoulders and Victoria took one sleeve like they were tethering to each other.

Holden stood very still for a heartbeat, like prayer in a man who doesn't pray. Then he grimaced at me in a way that meant *we go tell a story now* and *I hate it* and *thank you* all at once.

"EMTs will meet us at the road." He shifted into command mode. "Sparks, walk point. Lyra, keep your…ward thing handy."

"Technical term," I said.

It wrung a ghost of a smile out of him.

We climbed toward the edge of the trees in a knot of four. At the break in the brush, the festival sounds rolled back in. A band was tuning up, kids were shrieking near the ring toss, and someone was hawking kettle corn like it was salvation.

We stepped out into the sunlight. The lie we'd concocted took its first breath and learned how to walk.

Behind us, under a hill stitched with roots, the Vault shifted in its sleep and pressed its wound to the stitches Calderis would lay. Maybe it would hold. Maybe it wouldn't. Wishville has always been a town that lives with maybe.

But for that one long minute, with Kim's fingers cold in mine and Holden's jaw set and Sparks's eyes on the trees, things felt more normal. Little white salt flecks the Wellies had spilled like a dotted line along the path led the way back to ordinary. It felt like we'd given the town a full breath again.

Sometimes a breath was all you got.

Sometimes it was enough to finish the day.

"Five thieves," Victoria murmured, practicing the old human magic of repetition. "We escaped."

"Exactly right." I guided us toward the noise, the donuts, the music, and the work of keeping a town whole.

BY MIDDAY, Wishville was pretending to be fine.

The final day of WishFest had resumed in full swing—music drifting from the main stage, children running through the craft tents with sticky hands, and the smell of caramel corn fighting for dominance over kettle corn.

Holden was everywhere and nowhere, orchestrating the official version of events which Kim and Victoria's memories now included. Lauren's clinic was now "an unfortunate act of vandalism," and Victoria's booth "a late-night prank." The mayor had spun it all into a tidy speech about resilience and community spirit, and people were trying their best to clap at the right places, hoping the vandalism and pranks didn't happen again.

Me? I needed air.

I was walking the narrow lane behind the food booths, sipping what might have been coffee at one time, when someone whispered, "Psst! Lyra!"

LuLu popped out from behind a lemonade stand, her sunglasses sliding down her nose and wild hair pulled into a messy bun that looked like it was holding on by faith alone. She carried a paper cup and an expression that meant she'd found trouble and couldn't wait to share it.

"Tell me that's lemonade," I said. "Actual lemonade and not one of your experimental concoctions."

She grinned. "Both, but don't worry. I'm not into tonics. It's lemon-berry-balm with a shot of good ole' caffeine. Keeps me alert and slightly unhinged."

"That's your baseline."

She looped her arm through mine. "Walk with me before I explode. You're going to want to hear this."

We cut between tents, weaving past festivalgoers and the clatter of games, until the noise faded into the hum of the back lanes. The alley behind the yarn shop was quieter, half sunlight and half shadow with summer heat heavy in the air.

LuLu leaned close. "Okay, don't freak out. Remember Rufus, the artifact collector who was pushing that Festival Fixers stuff?"

"The tonic I *banned* from the vendors' list? Vividly."

"Well," she lowered her voice, "I saw him this morning. He wasn't making deliveries. He was meeting someone. A woman with long blonde hair. I couldn't see her face because she had a hood up, but they were talking near the old loading docks."

I stopped walking. "That's where the delivery van was last seen."

"Bingo. I heard her say something about a meeting in the business district. The old warehouse near the rail line."

The one with the boarded windows and the sign eaten by rust. "You sure?"

"Positive. And get this—Rufus looked a little spooked. He kept glancing over his shoulder like he expected someone to jump him."

"Or arrest him," I murmured.

"Exactly. So, I figured, since you're already knee-deep in weirdness, why not check it out myself?"

"Let me guess," I said. "You came to fetch backup before you broke in."

"Technically, I came for moral support," she said. "Breaking in was going to be a solo act."

"Not anymore."

Her grin widened. "I knew you'd say that."

The business district was nearly empty. During WishFest, most of the shops closed for the afternoon so the owners could join the celebration. The brick storefronts sat quiet under the weight of summer light, and the only sound was the drone of bees in the planters along the curb.

We took the long way, cutting through a narrow alley that smelled faintly of paint thinner and herbs. Pigeons scattered as we turned the corner.

The warehouse loomed at the end of the block, a hulking shape of red brick and broken glass. A faded sign above the rusted door still read *Coastal Imports*, the letters half erased by time.

LuLu crouched behind a stack of wooden crates and waved me down beside her. "Look."

A side door creaked open. A woman stepped out with her cloak's hood pulled up and a spill of golden hair glinting beneath it. The sunlight caught on the edge of something metallic at her wrist—a bracelet or a charm. Four tall men followed her, each wearing long dark coats despite the heat. They moved in precise rhythm, like soldiers or shadows.

The hair on my arms lifted.

Something about the air around them felt wrong—denser and tuned to a frequency that brushed against the part of me that didn't belong entirely to this world. It was like hearing a chord that only Dwellers could hear.

Don't react, I told myself. Not here in front of LuLu.

"What do you think they're doing?" she whispered.

"Trading something." I squinted, pretending it was out of human curiosity.

Down by the door, Rufus was talking with the blonde woman,

his posture tense. One of the men handed him a small crate. He peeked inside, nodded, then snapped the lid shut.

He wasn't in charge. He was taking orders.

I felt the faintest ripple of power shimmer along the edges of the men's cloaks. Light bent too subtly for LuLu to notice, but it was unmistakable to me. It wasn't fabric. It was energy.

Cloaking magic.

Calderis' words from last night returned, *The invisibility cloaks that were ordered from the Weavers? They've been picked up, and the rebels themselves are gone.*

My pulse quickened. *The rebels.* The so-called "Rebel Five." I was staring right at them.

"Lyra?" LuLu whispered. "You're doing that far-away look again. The one where you see ghosts."

"I'm just…thinking."

"Well think quieter," she said, "because I think Rufus just looked this way."

He had. His gaze swept the alley, then his brow furrowed. For a second, his eyes met mine…and then LuLu's elbow bumped a stack of empty boxes.

They toppled in a spectacular crash.

The sound tore through the stillness like a starter pistol.

The blonde woman's head jerked up. The four men moved instantly. One jumped onto the loading dock, another melted into the shadow of the doorway, and the rest blurred around the corner.

Blurred. Not ran. *Blurred.*

"Run," I hissed.

LuLu didn't argue.

We sprinted down the alley as Rufus shouted behind us. When I risked a glance back, the door slammed and the rest of the figures were gone. Vanished. We ducked behind another stack of crates, panting.

LuLu grimaced. "Subtle as ever. I guess spy work isn't my destiny."

"I don't know," I said between breaths. "We lasted a whole minute before detection."

"Should I put that on my résumé?"

Before I could answer, Rufus appeared at the corner, his face red and furious. "Are you insane?" he shouted. "Do you have any idea what you've just done?"

LuLu straightened, brushing dust off her knees. "Hi, Rufus. Fancy seeing you here. Lovely weather for criminal activity."

He threw up his hands. "Unbelievable."

I stepped forward, calm but firm. "Maybe start with why you're meeting hooded strangers behind abandoned warehouses."

He looked around, checking the street, then lowered his voice. "Because I'm *working*, that's why. I'm FBI." He flashed a badge. "Undercover. Been at this operation for a year."

LuLu's mouth fell open. "Wait…you're a fed?"

"Congratulations on ruining my sting," he snapped. "I've been tracking those people for months. They're running a black-market ring, importing illegal questionable *holistic* goods through festival circuits."

"Like the Fixers tonic," I said.

"Exactly. And just when I had enough to make an arrest…" He gestured wildly at the alley. "Crash! Bang! You two pop out like comic relief."

"Hey," LuLu said, indignantly, "we're *heroic* comic relief."

He glared. "You're lucky I don't haul you in for obstruction."

I kept my expression neutral even as my mind spun, trying to process it all. A federal sting, enchanted contraband, and a team of smugglers who could vanish on command.

Rufus rubbed his temples. "They always slip away," he muttered. "Every single time. I've chased them all around this area, and somehow they just disappear. It's like they can turn invisible."

I forced a polite laugh. "Maybe they're magicians."

He didn't find it funny. "If I didn't know better, I'd say they were ghosts."

Not ghosts. Dwellers from Elarion wearing invisibility capes, but he couldn't know that.

"Well," I said carefully, "at least you know you're on the right trail. We'll keep our distance from now on."

"Good." He jabbed a finger at us. "If you see them again, you call me. No hero stuff. Got it?"

"Got it."

He stomped toward his van, muttering about civilians and paperwork, leaving the alley echoing with the sound of his boots.

LuLu snorted. "Wow. He's cranky when he's saving the world."

"Occupational hazard." I still watched the place where the men had vanished. The sunlight was normal again, but the air shimmered faintly, just enough for me to feel it under my skin. A trace of power, old and cold.

They had cloaked, not run.

Whatever Rufus thought he was chasing, it wasn't human smugglers. It was the Rebel Five.

But again, I couldn't tell Rufus that.

"Come on." LuLu tugged my sleeve. "Let's get out of here before Agent Sunshine changes his mind."

"Yeah." I forced my voice to steady.

We walked back toward the main road, our footsteps echoing between the brick walls. The afternoon light had gone hazy, gold bleeding toward amber, and the air was thick with the smell of oil and wildflowers.

LuLu talked—something about how we needed smoothies and an alibi—but I wasn't listening. My thoughts were with the shimmering air I'd glimpsed before it faded, the exact same ripple I'd seen near the spiral entrance to the Vault.

The rebels weren't finished, but they were too dangerous for me to handle alone. If they were still trading through Wishville, hiding in plain sight under human faces and festival banners, then the thin line between our worlds was about to tear beyond repair.

I'd have to tell Holden and Calderis.

Soon.

For now, I forced a smile for LuLu and the passing festivalgoers, pretending I wasn't carrying the weight of two worlds on my shoulders.

"Smoothies, huh?" I said.

"Triple-berry." She winked. "With extra serenity."

"I'll take a double shot." I laughed.

And together we disappeared back into the crowd, just two ordinary women at a summer festival—while somewhere behind us the shimmer in the alley faded, leaving the faint echo of laughter that wasn't human at all.

Twenty~Three

BY AFTERNOON, Wishville had settled into that lazy rhythm of the festival's end. The crowds were smaller now, sunburned and happy, trailing ribbons and laughter as they drifted toward food stalls and last-minute raffles. The air simmered with roasted sugar and the faint metallic ring of the carousel glistened.

The wishing well stood quiet in its clearing, the sunlight dancing over its surface as the wind blew through the trees. Everyone had made their final wishes. The tokens had been dropped, and the chants whispered. The last of the tokens rested at the bottom, catching light like tiny stars.

No one lingered anymore.

I stood at the edge of the clearing beside Holden, pretending to study the booth map in my hands while the final cluster of festivalgoers disappeared down the main path.

When the air fell still, I whispered, "Now."

He glanced once around the empty field, then nodded. "Let's go."

We crossed the rope barrier and approached the well. The moss-covered stones gleamed faintly. The energy felt different now, balanced and peaceful. Whatever darkness had seeped out when the Vault cracked had been contained. The seal was whole again.

"Calderis did it," I said softly.

"Guess we owe him a thank-you card," Holden murmured.

I set my hand on the rim of the well. The water rippled beneath my touch, cool and shimmering with threads of silver. "Hold on," I said.

"Always."

Whispering the words, I held his hand as we stepped over the edge, and the world folded. Colors stretched, light bent, and the sound of the human world vanished into a single, sustained hum. My stomach dropped, then the ground rose to meet me in a soft, glowing rush of air and scent.

We landed on our feet in Elarion.

The sky above glowed in bands of violet and pearl, streaked with ribbons of gold light that pulsed with the rhythm of the realm's core. The trees glistened faintly, their leaves translucent and humming with energy. Streams of light wound through the forest like living veins, and the air smelled of dew on crystal.

Holden steadied himself and blinked. "Still not used to that."

"You'll get there," I said, though I wasn't sure any mortal truly could.

A tall figure stood waiting by a cluster of luminous stones, his cloak rippling with a deep blue sheen.

Calderis.

"Greetings," he said, his voice clipped but his eyes warm. "The barrier between realms weakens when the seal resets. We must move quickly."

Holden frowned. "Where to?"

Calderis gestured toward the slope beyond the glowing trees. "An ancient Dweller laboratory. It was sealed centuries ago after the Shadow Wars, hidden in the forbidden area. No one has entered since…until now."

The look in his eyes told me *why* we were here before he said it. "The rebels?"

He nodded. "I found traces of their work inside." Calderis' gaze hardened. "And whoever directed them."

We followed him through the forest, the ground soft beneath our boots. The hum of Elarion grew stronger the deeper we went, like a thousand crystal chimes vibrating in harmony. Ahead, carved into the side of a glistening cliff, was a massive door of stone and silver, etched with ancient Dweller runes.

It parted at Calderis's touch, revealing a cavernous hall.

The air inside was colder. Luminous tubes lined the walls, flickering with residual energy. Tables of strange metal stood covered in shards of glass and crystal, their surfaces scarred from recent use.

"Someone's been here." Holden swept his flashlight across the room, and his eyes followed suit. "Recently."

Calderis crouched near a broken vial. "Alchemy residue. Human chemicals merged with Dweller essence." His gaze hardened. "This is where the Festival Fixers were made."

I swallowed. "Then this is where Mike's scientist worked."

He nodded. "It seems so."

A soft scrape echoed through the hall.

"Did you hear that?" I whispered.

Before either man could answer, shadows peeled away from the walls, five tall figures in dark cloaks with their faces hidden.

The Rebel Five.

"Scatter!" Calderis shouted.

They struck first.

A wave of pressure slammed into the floor, throwing sparks of energy through the air. Holden rolled behind a table, drawing his gun, while Calderis drew his blade—a length of silver that burned with blue flame. I called upon Magma Ward, feeling the obsidian shards flare bright.

One rebel lunged. I ducked, sweeping my hand through the air to twist the energy around him. Light coiled like a ribbon, catching his cloak and tearing the enchantment. His form flickered, and infernal glow lit his eyes with a molten gold.

"Where'd he go?" Holden fired a warning shot that ricocheted off a metal beam.

"They're using invisibility cloaks." I deflected another burst of dark energy with a flash of my own. "Same ones that were commissioned."

Calderis parried two attackers at once, his blade singing through the air. "They're trying to reclaim their power source."

We pushed them back, driving them toward the far wall. Two fell under Calderis' strikes, their cloaks disintegrating into ash. The others retreated until a voice cut through the chaos, smooth and cold.

"Enough."

We froze.

From the shadows behind the remaining rebels, a female voice rang out—familiar, confident, and laced with silk and venom.

"I think we've all made enough noise for one day," she said.

I turned, and my blood went cold.

Standing at the edge of the light was Laisira, the mayor's quiet, capable assistant. The Clipboard Queen of Wishville. Her cloak was darker than the others, embroidered with pearls, and her long blonde hair hung loose. In her hand she held a small, curved blade. And with her other arm, she gripped… I gasped.

LuLu with a dagger pressed just under her chin.

LuLu's eyes were wide and terrified but defiant. "Don't you dare hurt me! I haven't even published the exposé yet!"

"LuLu!" I cried, stunned to see her. She must have followed Holden and me into the well. Either I had been distracted, or she was very good at her job, because I hadn't heard a thing.

Holden stepped forward. "Let her go."

Laisira smiled. "You shouldn't be here, Detective. Neither of you should."

Calderis' voice dropped to a low growl. "Arisial." The name hit the air like thunder.

I blinked. "What did you just call her?"

"Arisial," he repeated, his voice breaking on the edge of fury. "Her Dweller name."

And then it hit me—Laisira spelled backward. "You," I whispered. "You're his—"

"Former," she said with a sneer, her human glamour fading away to her iridescent opal hair and lavender eyes. "*Very* former." She was stunning. I hadn't seen her in forever.

Calderis' expression hardened. "You disappeared after the uprising. You helped the other side."

She laughed, the sound like breaking glass, and suddenly she didn't look so beautiful. "Helped? I *led* them, darling, and I'm not the only woman. There's one far more powerful than me. You just didn't notice. Your job was always more important than me. While you were sealing away power, I was learning how to use it. And then I found a way to bring it here through the humans' greed." She glanced at Holden. "They'll sell anything if you call it wellness."

Holden's jaw tightened. "You murdered Mike Zaccaria."

Arisial tilted her head. "Murder? If you call murdering his plans to stop our expansion of selling to outsiders, then I suppose I'm guilty as charged. Mike created an opportunity when he caused the cave-in. That opened another doorway to Elarion, which allowed a few of us rebels to slip through. He didn't know that, of course. He simply kept mining the entrance before the cave-in, too afraid to venture beyond because it was dangerous and he had a family." She sneered in disgust. "He had no idea an entire world lay beneath. He thought I was a brilliant scientist but never knew my lab was an ancient magical one. Our work was too important to stop. It needed a strong leader. Mike was weak. When he found out our product could be dangerous, he wanted out...so I let him. Simple as that."

"Our work?" Calderis spat. "You desecrated sacred tools to poison mortals!"

"I evolved them." She pressed the blade closer to LuLu's neck. "Don't make me waste a pet. I like this one. She's brave."

LuLu's voice trembled. "I'm also not afraid to bite."

That earned a chuckle from her captor. "You're delightful, and I have the perfect cage for you."

Calderis stepped forward with his blade raised. "Let her go."

Arisial's smile faltered, just slightly. "Oh, my poor sentimental warrior. I see you're fond of this one, but you've forgotten how to fight without rules." She flicked her wrist. A wave of dark light shot across the floor as her blade slammed into Calderis' chest.

He staggered back, gasping, the blue light of his blade sputtering.

LuLu screamed.

"Calderis!" I shouted, catching him as he fell to one knee. His skin had gone ashen. The veins along his neck glowed faintly black.

Arisial smirked. "Torn between two women, and still vulnerable to shardstone, I see."

Shardstone. That must be the one element that was Calderis' own form of kryptonite.

All Dwellers had their own weakness but usually kept it a secret. The fact that she knew his was a testament to how much he must have loved her at one time. She never could have loved him in return since she struck him with a blade laced with it.

I rose as fury flooded through me. "You shouldn't have done that."

"Oh, I think I should."

I reached inward, summoning Lumen Wells, pulling energy from the underground crystals until it filled the room. The light from the walls pulsed in answer, the ancient lab trembling under the surge.

Arisial raised her hand, calling her own power to strike, but I was faster.

I flung the energy outward, spinning it into a cage of golden light. It wrapped around her like liquid glass, freezing her mid-motion. The dagger clattered to the floor, and LuLu scrambled free, panting.

Arisial strained against the cage, her eyes flashing. "You think this will hold me, Half-blood?"

"Long enough," I said.

I dropped beside Calderis. His breathing was shallow, but his hand still clutched his blade. "Don't talk," I said, resting my hand on his chest.

"Too…late," he rasped, forcing a faint smile. "You did well, Lyra."

"Don't you dare make this sound final," LuLu said from his other side, taking his free hand in her own.

Holden cleared his voice but didn't speak.

Light flared at the far end of the chamber.

Three regal figures stepped through, blinding the room with their beauty. Vaerion, Calderis' father, was cloaked in obsidian; Elanith, his mother, was silver-haired and ageless; and Lumira, his sister, her hands glowing faintly with healing light.

Vaerion's gaze swept the room, cold and commanding. "Take him."

LuLu and I got to our feet and stepped back. Elanith and Lumira knelt beside Calderis, touching his chest, removing the blade, their energy fusing into his as they lifted him. He shuddered, then went still, unconscious but alive.

Vaerion turned to me. "The human must be erased." His voice was absolute. "She cannot leave with memory of this realm." His gaze settled on LuLu then hardened as it returned to me. "Do it, or I will end her myself."

LuLu froze, her eyes darting to me. "Whoa now, wait just a minute. You're not really gonna—"

"I'll do it," I said quickly.

He studied me for a tense moment, then nodded once before signaling his guards. "Bring the prisoners."

The rebels—what was left of them—were rounded up, Arisial still thrashing inside the golden cage. As they vanished through the portal with Calderis and his family, Vaerion's command echoed, "Erase her, Guardian, it is your duty."

When they were gone, the silence was heavy.

I turned to LuLu.

Her face was pale, but she managed a shaky laugh. "Guess this is where you tell me it was all a hallucination, huh?"

"Something like that." I lifted my hand, reaching for the amber light that would blur her memories and twist the truth into something survivable. "I won't hurt you. You won't feel anything, I promise."

She flinched, then straightened. "I trust you. If it helps, then do it." She squeezed her eyes shut tight.

We weren't out of the well yet, but I knew her brain would remain fuzzy for a while after I erased her, and she wouldn't remember a thing by the time we got back to Wishville. Inhaling a deep breath, I focused, letting the amber light bloom between my fingers and pressing it to her temple.

Nothing happened.

The magic sparked once, then died.

I tried again.

Still nothing.

LuLu blinked and cracked one eye open. "Um…is it supposed to tickle?"

I stepped back, my heart hammering. "I don't understand. It's not working." I glanced at Holden.

He shrugged, looking helpless.

"Maybe I'm too stubborn to forget." She laughed nervously.

"No." I shook my head. "This shouldn't be possible."

A sound like distant footsteps reached us. More Enforcers coming.

I grabbed her arm. "We have to go."

"Lyra—"

"There's no time!" Holden snapped and ushered us both along.

We sprinted toward the far end of the hall, the portal humming faintly. The air bent around us, the glow of Elarion fading as we leapt through.

The last thing I heard before the light swallowed us was LuLu whispering, awed and terrified, "I'll never forget this."

And that, more than anything, scared me...because I believed her.

Twenty~Four

THE THREE OF us tumbled out of the wishing well in a burst of light and air, landing hard on the damp grass.

The shift from Elarion to Wishville was always jarring, like stepping out of a dream mid-sentence. The air was thicker here, tinged with the scent of sugar and woodsmoke from the festival, the sounds of laughter and carousel music cutting through the dizzy quiet in my ears. It had been risky to go during daylight again. Last time, Holden had fallen into the well, trying to save me from drowning. This time, LuLu had followed us, her sneaky journalist drive keeping her stealth-like. I'd almost lost them both.

There wouldn't be a third time, I vowed.

Holden sat up first, rubbing his temples. "Every time we do that, I swear my bones rearrange themselves."

"Be grateful you still have bones." LuLu groaned, sprawled on her back beside the rope fence. "Because I'm ninety percent sure mine melted halfway through that…vortex thing."

I pushed hair from my face, breathing in the earthy scent of clover and summer. "You'll live."

She squinted at me. "Ahh, but what will my *quality* of life be?"

Holden offered her a hand. "C'mon, journalist. Up you go."

LuLu took it, wobbling as she stood. Her sunglasses hung

crooked on her nose, and there was a streak of dirt across her cheek. Somehow, she still managed to look like she'd walked off the front page of a glossy magazine.

"Tell me we didn't just fall through another dimension," she said. "Because if we did, I'm charging hazard pay."

Holden arched a brow. "How about we call it classified instead?"

"Fine." She brushed herself off. "Classified trauma, but you owe me an explanation." Her eyes met mine.

I nodded once. "Fair enough, but not now."

We all looked around. The clearing was empty except for the glowing well and a few drifting flower petals from the earlier wishes. The rest of Wishville was alive with sound—a guitar somewhere, the shriek of kids chasing each other, and laughter rising with the scent of kettle corn.

Life had gone back to normal. Or at least, the illusion of it had.

No one had noticed the three of us climb out of the heart of the earth.

"Looks like your cover story worked," I said to Holden.

He nodded. "Festival's winding down. Mayor Delaney's already spinning the vandalism as a prank gone wrong."

LuLu gave a dry laugh. "If that's a prank, I'd hate to see a felony."

"Speaking of which," Holden lowered his voice, "we need to debrief at the station after dark. I'll tell Delaney we're doing evidence inventory." His eyes flicked to me. "How's Calderis… really?"

"He'll be okay," I said quietly. "His family will heal him…I hope," I trailed off. The memory of his blood, his hand tightening around mine before he faded into unconsciousness, burned behind my eyelids.

Holden's jaw flexed. "He'll make it."

I nodded, hoping he was right. I'd seen Dwellers die after being exposed to their weakness, but his mother's gift of healing was strong. I just hoped it was strong enough.

LuLu looked between us, then sighed. "You two talk like you're carrying secrets for the CIA. Which, by the way, I'm *not* writing about, even though it could be the story to redeem myself. But I give you my word I won't write about anything I saw today. Not until I figure out what that place even was."

"Good," Holden scanned the field, "and for what it's worth, thanks for not panicking."

She grinned weakly. "Oh, I panicked, just on the inside. It's called journalistic composure."

That drew the smallest smile from him.

The sunlight shifted, pouring gold through the trees. The crowd sounds faded to a hum. For a moment, it almost felt peaceful.

Then LuLu frowned and rubbed her arms. "Do you guys feel that?"

Holden's brows formed a V. "Feel what?"

"The air—it's…humming." She lifted her hand, brushing it through the space above the grass. "Like static before lightning."

I went still. My Dweller senses flared faintly, responding to her the same way they did near energy currents.

"It's just the wind," I said quickly, wondering how she had sensed that. Holden never had after transporting. And why didn't my memory seal work on her?

She gave me a skeptical look. "Pretty sure wind doesn't buzz, sweetheart."

Holden studied her. "You probably picked up some kind of residual charge. Happens after adrenaline spikes."

LuLu nodded slowly, though her brow stayed creased. "Yeah…maybe. It's just weird. I've always had this thing—gut feelings, hunches. My mom used to call it my sixth sense."

"Maybe trust it less around ancient glowing portals," Holden said.

"Noted," she said dryly. "Still, I can't shake it. That place—it felt…familiar somehow. Like déjà vu in a language I don't speak."

I forced a laugh. "Maybe you're just more intuitive than you realize."

Her gaze lingered on me a moment too long, then she shrugged it off. "Or more insane."

We walked back toward town together, the last of the festival winding down. Banners fluttered lazily in the breeze, and the smell of fried dough hung thick in the air. Holden's hand brushed mine occasionally as we walked—accidental or not, I didn't dare ask.

When we reached Main Street, the crowd swallowed us. Mayor Doug Delaney was on stage announcing raffle winners. The Wellies danced in front of the fountain, tossing salt and chanting about "blessing the raffle tickets."

Ordinary chaos, all of it beautiful to me.

Holden leaned close. "Go home, both of you. We'll regroup after the cleanup tonight."

LuLu saluted. "Gladly, Chief. See you soon."

"Not you, LuLu," he said with mock sternness. "No more jumping into wells, following mysterious women, or investigating after dark."

"Okay," she said innocently. "What about during daylight if I bring snacks?"

He sighed. "You're impossible."

She held up her hands. "That's my charm." Then she turned to me, her expression softening. "I think I need a break, Lyra. A real one. Maybe I'll go home for a while and visit family. I've been talking about it for years."

"You mean Miami?" I asked.

She hesitated. "Maybe farther. My parents are there, yeah, but my grandmother's from Mexico. There's a little town in the Yucatán she always talks about—where the river glows at night. I've never been."

"That sounds beautiful," I said.

"Yeah," she murmured, half-smiling. "Maybe after I turn in

my WishFest article. Sun, fun, and food, but no glowing wells. Just normal people with normal festival fare."

Holden smirked. "Sounds safer. And yes, I think it's probably wise for you to go home for a bit."

She tilted her head at him. "Oh, you'll miss me, and you know it."

"I'll enjoy the peace." His tone was softer than his words.

She laughed, the sound bright against the backdrop of the fading music.

We lingered a few minutes longer as the sun dipped toward the horizon. The sky turned honey-gold, the horizon glittering through the trees. It should have felt like an ending, but the air was still charged—restless.

LuLu felt it too. I could see it in the way her hand brushed her necklace, in the way her eyes flicked toward the well again. "I promise you I will write the boring stuff for a while," she paused a beat, "I could use some peace."

"Thank you," I said.

"But I still want that explanation." Then she hugged me—a quick, fierce squeeze that smelled of citrus and flowers. "Whatever's going on with your glowing friends, fix it before I get back."

"I'll try."

When she walked away, the faint trace of energy trailed behind her, invisible to everyone but me.

Holden stood beside me, watching her go. "You think she'll keep quiet?"

"Yes," I said. "But something's changed in her. It's like transporting through the well awakened something inside of her. She's...connected now. The realm brushed her. It's still humming through her."

He frowned. "You mean she's dangerous?"

"No," I said. "She's different. I'm not sure how, but I intend to find out."

The first firework burst overhead, scattering gold light across the square. Holden's reflection flickered in the shop windows, tired but steady.

"We'll keep an eye on her," he said.

I nodded, my eyes drifting back toward the well. Its surface shimmered faintly, reflecting the fireworks—and deeper beneath, the faint glow of Elarion pulsed like a heartbeat. I wondered if Calderis could feel it too, wherever he was. And as the crowd cheered and music swelled, I told myself to enjoy this fragile, borrowed peace…

Because deep down, I knew it wouldn't last.

Morning sunlight spilled over Wishville like a blessing. The festival booths were gone, the streets swept clean, and the well's clearing looked freshly washed by dew. The townsfolk wandered in slowly, drawn by curiosity and the promise of "official closure," as Mayor Doug Delaney called it.

Every season after WishFest, the well granted a single wish—a symbolic one, chosen by the well from the wish tokens dropped in all week. It was tradition for the mayor to announce the end of the festival so the wish could be chosen. No one really expected it to *work*, but somehow, every season, it did.

I stood near the rope barrier, sipping lukewarm coffee while Holden spoke quietly with Doug by the platform. The crowd buzzed with cautious excitement, eager for something normal again.

The mayor took the microphone first. "Good morning, Wishville! We made it through another beautiful WishFest!"

Applause rippled through the square. For once, it didn't sound forced.

"And," Doug continued, "I'm pleased to report that the investigation into the terrible incidents this week has come to a close. The culprits are in custody."

Holden stepped forward, crisp in his uniform, his voice steady. "Thanks to local cooperation and federal assistance, the suspects responsible for the vandalism, the clinic break-in, and the death of Michael Zaccaria have been apprehended."

A hush fell. Even the wind seemed to still.

Holden continued, careful and deliberate. "The individual known to many as Laisira was in fact Dr. Ari Sial, a former biochemical researcher. Evidence shows she was operating under false credentials, developing and distributing the so-called Festival Fixers tonic through an illegal network. Mr. Zaccaria unfortunately got involved with her, believing she could truly help his patients. When he uncovered her deception and threatened to expose it, she silenced him instead."

Gasps swept through the crowd. I spotted Victoria near the fountain, clutching a friend's arm with her eyes wide.

Doug took the mic again. "The distributors who worked under her have also been detained and transferred to federal custody. The FBI will handle the remainder of the case. Wishville is safe again."

It was as close to the truth as anyone would ever know.

The applause came slowly, a ripple of relief rather than celebration. Holden caught my gaze across the crowd and gave a small nod. Truth wrapped in enough lies to keep Elarion hidden —that was our victory.

After the announcement, a sudden squeal broke through the chatter.

"Oh my gosh!" Brittany Voss practically bounced in place, waving her hands. "My wish came true!" She stared at her phone. "I wished for *new beginnings*, and guess what? Our new fitness studio got final approval just now!"

Cheers and laughter rippled through the crowd as the sunlight caught the ripples of the well, scattering gold light over everyone's faces.

I felt the faint hum beneath the earth—the seal whole again, the magic responding—but to the townsfolk, it was just a pretty shimmer.

Some things were better that way.

Later, the square emptied. Vendors had loaded their trucks, and children had chased the last bits of confetti away. Now, the air smelled of sugar and popcorn. LuLu stood by her car with her trunk open and boxes piled neatly inside.

She looked like summer itself with her big sunglasses, denim jacket, and a travel mug in hand. "Well," she said, "guess this is goodbye, at least for now."

"I'm going to miss you," I said, trying to sound casual. I always knew our friendship was short term, but I was sad to see her go so soon.

She smiled faintly. "I'll be back. I still need a story to redeem myself, remember?"

Holden joined us with his arms folded. "I'm glad you're taking that break. You've been through a lot. But if you remember *anything* else useful about this case, call me before you talk to anyone else."

"Relax, Chief," she said. "I'm off duty. I Promise." She hugged me tight, smelling faintly of vanilla and cookies. "Try not to fall into any more portals," she whispered.

"I'll do my best. And we'll talk later. I haven't forgotten."

She nodded, then she slid into her car and drove off, the tires crunching over gravel. For a moment, the road shimmered in the heat haze, and then she was gone.

I had just turned toward the station with Holden when my phone buzzed.

LuLu.

"Change your mind already?" I smiled.

"Nope." Her engine hummed in the background. "Just thought I'd do one last good-deed detour before hitting the highway. Lauren's place is on my way out of town. I figured she'd want to know the good news. You know that the thieves and the creepy scientist lady are caught."

My stomach tightened. "LuLu, maybe don't…Lauren's still shaken. Let me tell her."

"It'll take two minutes," she said. "I'm practically there."

I glanced at Holden. "She's going to Lauren's."

He frowned. "Of course she is," he muttered. "This isn't the kind of information that can just be dropped like a bomb. It takes finesse."

I heard LuLu's laugh through the phone. "Relax, Chief. I know how to finesse. Besides, I just pulled into their driveway. Don't worry, I'll keep my phone on so you can hear how smooth I can be." It sounded like she slid her phone into her pocket.

I heard a doorbell chime through the line.

Then Lauren's warm, lilting voice, "LuLu! What a surprise!"

"Hey! I just wanted to say the case is over," LuLu said. "You can finally relax."

Lauren laughed. "That's wonderful! Come in, come in. Oh, ignore the smell—Matt burned another batch of marshmallows."

There was a pause. "Smells more like smoke than sugar," LuLu said lightly.

"Matt's baking again," Lauren said, her voice moving farther inside. "Told you he's not very good."

I stopped dead.

Holden had already started the car and looked over at me sharply. "Put her on speaker," he said.

I did.

Holden gunned the engine. "She's on Lauren's property?"

"Yes. The house on the outskirts of town by the woods."

He took the turn hard, his tires spitting gravel. I put the phone between us, the open line filling the car with every muffled sound.

Through the rustle of fabric and footsteps, I heard LuLu's

voice—lower and more cautious. "Matt, right? You're baking this early?"

Matt's voice came sharp and strained. "Trying to keep busy."

"Smells…strong," LuLu said. "You okay?"

Lauren laughed softly. "He gets restless. We've been through so much with the clinic getting trashed and what happened to Mike."

The sound of a pan hitting the counter clattered. "Don't," Matt snapped. "Don't say his name."

Silence.

"Why?" LuLu's voice sounded confused and then it lifted an octave. "Oh, my gosh, the burned marshmallows! You killed Mike!"

"What?" Lauren gasped. "LuLu, that's not—"

Matt's breath hitched audibly. "I didn't mean to."

"Matt, what are you saying?" Lauren cried out.

Holden's grip tightened on the wheel. "He's confessing," he muttered.

"I'm recording," I responded.

LuLu spoke gently. "Then what happened, Matt?"

He sounded wild, cornered, and far too unstable. "He was going to sell the clinic. After everything Lauren did for him— every late night, every patient—he was cutting her out. She was getting her PT license to become his partner, and he was just going to take it all away. It wasn't right."

Lauren's voice cracked. "Matt—stop."

He ignored her. "I tried to find a way to buy him out, but when that fell through, I went to talk to him."

"You did?" Lauren asked, sounding near tears. "When?"

"That morning, near the woods. I thought you were walking Sully on our property. When I heard you by the lake, I couldn't believe it. So, I blew the dog whistle only he can hear to lure him away from you and left a trail of treats to keep him running in the other direction." He shrugged. "You know I always keep that whistle and dog treats in my pack, and I always take my pack when I'm in the woods. Once you were far enough away, I circled back to Mike." His words came faster now, tumbling. "I just wanted him to listen, but he wouldn't. He said he was in too deep and had his own mess to clean up. I saw where he was digging and asked him about it. He said I wasn't part of it, and he couldn't worry about me or Lauren."

"Oh, Matthew…" Lauren whispered.

A choked breath sounded through the phone. "Lauren meant nothing to him after all the years she gave to him and his clinic. I couldn't stand for that. I saw red and shoved him hard. He fell back and hit the tree with an awful crack. That snapped me out of my haze. It was an accident. I panicked and didn't know what to do, so I left."

Lauren's voice broke. "Matt, oh God."

LuLu said carefully, "You need to turn yourself in."

He shouted, "No! She'll lose everything! She's the love of my life. Everything I've ever done is for her. I can't let her down now."

The sound of a struggle erupted—a chair scraping, something crashing to the floor, and Lauren screaming. The dogs barked wildly.

"Hang on," Holden said, stomping on the gas and flooring his cruiser. The car shot down the winding road that led to Lauren and Matt's house.

Through the phone, LuLu gasped. "Matt, stop! Please!"

"Don't ruin this for us!" he shouted.

A crash sounded—more glass shattering. The call was distorted with noise.

"LuLu!" I shouted. "We're coming!"

Holden's siren cut through the silence of the forest road. The cabin appeared ahead, sunlight glinting off the front windows. Smoke curled faintly from the chimney…or maybe from the burned marshmallows.

I leapt out before the car even stopped. The front door was ajar.

Inside, chaos ensued. A shattered mixing bowl, flour across the counter, and LuLu backed against the island with her hands up. Matt stood in front of her, wild-eyed, with one arm restraining Lauren, who was sobbing and begging him to stop, and the other holding a butcher knife. The dogs barked and danced around as if they didn't know what to do.

Holden crossed the space in three strides with his gun raised. "Matt Glaub, you're under arrest for the murder of Mike Zaccaria and the attempted murder of Lourdes Morales! Drop the knife!"

Matt froze. Then, with a sound halfway between a sob and a roar, he lunged.

Holden caught his arm mid-swing and twisted until the knife dropped. I darted forward, pulling Lauren clear as the two men crashed into the counter. The scent of smoke thickened with the pan still on the burner, blackening.

"Matt, stop!" Lauren cried. "Please, it's over!"

He slumped suddenly, his energy depleted. The fight drained out of him as fast as it had come.

Holden cuffed him, breathing hard, and read him his rights.

Matt's voice cracked. "I didn't mean to. I just wanted him to understand. Lauren is a goddess who deserves the world."

Lauren covered her face and sobbed. "Oh, Matthew, I never wanted the world. All I ever wanted was you."

I pulled her into my arms, feeling her shake. "It's over," I said softly. "It'll be okay in time."

Holden led Matt to the car, reading him his rights, while I stayed with Lauren and LuLu. Sunlight streamed through the broken window, catching the dust in the air and the faint curl of smoke from the forgotten pan. The dogs lay panting and whining on the floor.

LuLu leaned against the counter, pale but steady. "Guess I found a headline for Ernie," she said weakly.

I managed a sad smile. "You also found trouble. Again."

She shrugged. "Story of my life."

When the patrol car pulled away with Matt in the back seat,

the woods fell quiet. Lauren sat at the table, staring at nothing, whispering her husband's name and petting her distressed dogs.

Outside, the wind stirred through the trees. It carried the faintest shimmer of Dweller energy—peaceful and balanced at last.

For the first time in weeks, I let myself breathe.

Epilogue

A FEW WEEKS LATER, the house smelled like cedar and coffee.

Afternoon sunlight filtered through the lace curtains, catching dust motes that sparkled in lazy swirls. The place was too quiet after everything that had happened, almost unsettlingly normal. The only sounds were the soft ticking of the clock, Vex's rhythmic purr from the armchair, and Holden's low voice as he flipped through the case notes one last time.

"Matt Glaub was officially sentenced this morning." He closed the folder. "Manslaughter, not murder. He confessed. The DA said Lauren's testimony and the accidental nature of it saved him from a harsher sentence."

I nodded, staring into my coffee. "He'll have time to think and hopefully heal."

"She's doing the same," Holden said. "Lauren started therapy last week. Kim's helping her. They're rebuilding that clinic together."

That brought a small smile. "Kim could rebuild the whole town if she wanted to. She's got that stubborn light in her."

"Her kids are doing better, too," Holden added. "Joey's back at the animal shelter, and Tasker's his shadow again."

"He told me the dogs listen to him more now that he doesn't have the stone" I smiled fondly.

Holden nodded. "And Tony's looking at colleges for engineering."

"Good. I'm glad," I said, adding, "Evan Teller's doing better, too. He came by the Historical Society yesterday. Apologized for being, quote, 'a raging jerk with delusions of grandeur.'"

Holden's mouth twitched. "We'll call that progress."

Outside, the wind stirred through the maples, carrying the scent of pine. The world felt softer again. Balanced.

"Brittany and Victoria are making a killing with their new all-natural product line," I added. "Apparently, 'Cleanse Without Consequence' is flying off the shelves."

Holden groaned. "Of course it is."

"And the Wellies." I laughed under my breath. "They've appointed themselves the town's moral support committee. Tilly's planning 'weekly cleansing circles,' Belle's trying to start a yoga group, and Dot's blessing every pastry at the bakery."

"She tried to bless my coffee," Holden said dryly. "I told her caffeine was already holy."

That earned a laugh from me. "And Rufus?"

"Gone," he said. "FBI reassigned him to another case."

"So, where does that leave *us*?" I asked softly, remembering Calderis' words about being able to have it all. With Holden's shorter lifespan, my time with him would have to come first.

"Where do you want that to leave *us*? The choice has always been yours, Lyra," he said just as softly.

"Maybe it's time we found out." I reached out and held his hand, looking up into his stormy gray eyes, letting all of my feelings for him show.

A tender smile tipped up the corners of his lips seconds before he lowered his head and pressed his lips to mine.

The doorbell rang, and we both jumped apart, laughing.

Get a room. Vex's tail twitched irritably from the chair.

"Expecting anyone?" Holden asked.

I shook my head and went to the door.

When I opened it, LuLu stood on the porch, sun-kissed, wind-blown, and very much alive. Behind her, leaning on the railing like he'd never left, was Calderis. He looked healthy again, color back in his face and that faint Dweller glow humming beneath his skin. His eyes glanced at Holden and then met mine with understanding, and something in my chest unclenched in relief.

"Hope you don't mind me crashing the reunion." LuLu smiled. "We kind of ran into each other on the road, I asked where you lived, and he led the way since we were headed to the same place."

Holden stepped up behind me, his eyebrows raised. "That must've been an interesting walk."

"You have no idea," LuLu said, her eyes teasing as she stared at Calderis. "Your boy here doesn't talk much, but he can glare in at least five dialects."

"I prefer silence to small talk." Calderis smirked faintly, staring right back at her, and I was okay with that…for now.

"Well," I smiled despite myself, "welcome, both of you."

They stepped inside, and the house suddenly felt alive again. Calderis moved with his usual quiet grace, but LuLu filled the air like sunshine with her talking, laughing, and taking in every detail.

"So," Holden said, crossing his arms. "You still remember?"

"Every glowing tree and dramatic sword swing," she said easily. "Don't worry, I'm not publishing a thing."

"That's a pretty big promise from a journalist whose career depends on a story to redeem herself." Holden eyed her warily. "Why keep the biggest one of your life a secret?"

LuLu's smile turned mysterious. "Because I've got my own story now." She glanced at me, then at Calderis. "After I left, I drove home for a bit. Then I took a vacation and spent a few days with my family back in Mexico. My grandmother kept saying I had 'the shine'—that I was like her mother's mother."

Holden frowned. "The shine?"

LuLu shrugged. "Guess it runs in the family. We're not…creatures or anything like that. But there's old magic in our blood. Earth magic, moonlight, intuition…whatever you want to call it. I always thought I was just good at reading people. Turns out I was reading *energy*."

I exchanged a glance with Calderis.

He nodded slightly, understanding flickering in his eyes.

"So," Holden said, "you're saying you're one of them now?"

LuLu laughed. "Nope. Just *aware* of them. And maybe a little bit useful, if the town ever decides to host another supernatural meltdown."

"Which means we have leverage," Holden said with mock seriousness. "You talk, we talk."

"Exactly." She winked. "Mutually assured exposure."

Vex hopped down from the chair, stretching. "Great. Another one. Just what this house needed," he muttered out loud, his tail flicking.

LuLu gasped, clutching her chest theatrically. "He talks!"

"He lectures," Holden grumbled.

"He's brilliant." Vex sniffed.

Calderis chuckled low in his throat. The sound wrapped around the room like warmth.

"So," LuLu clapped her hands together, "about that 'staying useful' part. I'm thinking of sticking around permanently. I like it here. The festivals, the food, the mild chance of mystical doom… and all of you."

I smiled, feeling my heart warm. "You're serious?"

She nodded. "Completely. But there's one problem." She bit her bottom lip. "I don't have a place to stay yet. Every inn's booked solid with post-festival tourists, and the rental cottages are all booked, and literally no one ever leaves so there's no houses to buy."

Holden arched an eyebrow. "You expect the Chair of WishFest and Guardian of the Well to run a boarding house?"

"Only if she has room," LuLu said sweetly, fluttering her eyelashes at me.

I laughed. "I have plenty of room."

"See? She likes me."

Vex huffed, curling his tail around his paws. "We'll see how long that lasts."

"Relax, furball," LuLu said. "You'll love my new roommate."

"Roommate?" Holden asked.

Right on cue, there was a tiny chirrup at the door. LuLu bent down, scooped something from the porch, and turned around holding a fluffy ginger cat with tufted ears and bright amber eyes.

"This," she announced proudly, "is Fenrin. Her name was on her collar with a note taped to it that said, *Please adopt me*. Isn't she precious?"

Collar? Sneaky, Fenrin. Vex's eyes narrowed. "Absolutely not. I refuse to be tied down."

Fenrin purred happily and wriggled free, darting straight to Vex and curling up beside him. He put up a mild protest and then purred as he settled down beside her. I was pretty sure with a smile on his face.

Holden sighed, arching a brow at me. "We just restored peace to the realm. Now you're adding another pet."

Calderis smirked. "Balance is overrated."

LuLu laughed, dropping her bag by the door. "Guess we're all stuck with each other now, huh?"

I looked around the room—the detective, the Dweller, the journalist, the talking half-blood Whispen cat, and the full Whispen trying to climb the curtains—and felt something I hadn't in a long time.

Hope.

For the first time since the Vault cracked, the world felt whole.

Calderis moved closer, his voice soft enough for only me to hear. "The realms are quiet again. For now."

"For now," I echoed.

He hesitated. "But there's something else."

My smile faded. "What?"

He reached into his coat and handed me a folded scrap of parchment—aged, fragile, and glowing faintly around the edges. My pulse stumbled when I saw the handwriting.

Flowing, familiar, elegant.

Serenna…my mother.

The note was brief, written in Elarion script but pulsing with unmistakable energy. I translated automatically, whispering the words aloud.

The balance must break to be rebuilt. Do not seek me. I am where you cannot follow.

Holden came over, having overheard, and frowned. "What does that mean?"

Calderis's jaw tightened. "It means she's alive."

LuLu followed, looking between us. "Alive is good, right?"

"I'm not sure," I said quietly, remembering Arisial's comment about not being the only female rebel. Could my mother have switched to the other side?

My thoughts hung in the air, heavy.

Vex stopped fawning over Fenrin long enough to mutter, "Here we go again."

Outside, the wind shifted, carrying the faint scent of rain…and something waiting.

I folded the note and tucked it into my pocket. "I thought everything I was doing was for her…because of her. What if she betrayed me? What if she flipped to the other side?"

"Are you okay," LuLu asked?

"No, I'm not okay." I looked them all in their eyes.

"What do you want to do?" Holden asked me softly.

I pushed down the tears that threatened to spill over as I said with firm conviction, "I want to find her. I need to know the truth."

"And what if the truth is something you don't want to hear?" Calderis asked.

I swallowed past the lump in my throat, then took a deep breath and said with conviction, "Then you can be sure I'll be the one who brings her to justice."

253

Dweller Powers Linked to Water, Lava, and the Core

Because Dwellers live beneath the well and near the Earth's hidden layers, their powers tie into subterranean elements—water tables, magma flows, and the planet's inner energy.

Water Affinity

1. **Aquifer Calling** – ability to summon fresh water from underground springs.
2. **Mists and Veils** – conjuring fog or vapor to obscure vision.
3. **Current Shaping** – manipulating underground rivers and directing them to flood or recede.
4. **Memory Pools** – reflections in water that reveal truths, memories, or wishes.

Lava and Magma Affinity

1. **Ember Pulse** – channeling molten heat into bursts of energy or fiery weaponry.

2. **Obsidian Crafting** – forming weapons, keys, or charms instantly from cooled lava.
3. **Seismic Heat** – creating pockets of intense heat to deter intruders or destroy evidence.
4. **Infernal Glow** – eyes or markings flare with inner magma-light when power is used.

Core/Earth Affinity

1. **Seismic Whisper** – sensing tremors or distant footsteps through the ground.
2. **Stone Weaving** – reshaping rock, tunnels, or caverns for defense or concealment.
3. **Core Binding** – drawing strength from geothermal energy, boosting speed or stamina.
4. **Gravity Veil** – slightly altering pull of gravity around them (leaping, pulling objects down).

Hybrid Powers (Water + Fire/Core)

1. **Steam Veil** – merging water and magma to create blinding, scalding mist.
2. **Healing Springs** – heated water with mineral-rich, magical properties for mending wounds.
3. **Crystalline Growth** – forming luminous crystal clusters where water meets lava under pressure.
4. **Pressure Command** – controlling deep-earth pressure, causing geysers or controlled quakes.

Lyra's Hybrid Powers

As the only half-human, half-Dweller, Lyra bridges above-ground elements (air, light, celestial forces) with subterranean ones (water, magma, core). Her uniqueness gives her some Dweller powers and other ones that no full Dweller can access.

Celestial Affinity

1. **Sunfire Touch** – channeling warmth and light to heal or inspire courage.
2. **Moonveil** – manipulating moonlight for illusions, cloaking, or calming emotions.
3. **Star Echo** – heightened intuition or visions tied to constellations and night sky patterns.
4. **Skycall** – Influence over breezes, gusts, or even guiding birds.

Core Affinity

1. **Seismic Sense** – feeling vibrations through earth, sensing danger or hidden chambers.
2. **Lumen Wells** – pulling luminous energy from underground crystals.
3. **Magma Ward** – summoning protective heat barriers or obsidian shards.
4. **Aqua Vein** – drawing water from beneath the ground in times of need.

Hybrid/Balance Powers

1. **Eclipse State** – when sun and moon energies align, she can blend surface light with core fire for immense bursts of power.
2. **Breath of Worlds** – exhaling mist that merges steam, air, and memory-infused water.
3. **Harmony Pulse** – ability to temporarily stabilize cracks between worlds.
4. **Dual Sight** – seeing both surface illusions and subterranean truths simultaneously.
5. **Illusory Manipulation** – The ability to shift their surroundings, making structures disappear or entire

landscapes transform.

Vex (half-cat, half-Whispen)

**Whisper Magic
Abilities:**

1. **Shadow Phase** – slip between shadows in both realms.
2. **Mist Purr** – calming veil of vapor.
3. **Mind Whisper** – can communicate with others through their mind.

<u>SUNNY MEADOWS & KALLIE BALLAS CROSSOVER</u>

Cruising into Danger

Road Trip to Ruin

Bachelors, Badeges & Bad Luck

My Big Fat Fatal Wedding

<u>DIGITAL DIVA</u>

Talk to the Hand

Rise of the Phenoteens

Books By Kari Lee Harmon

COLDWATER COVE

Dark Seas

Frozen Waters

Dangerous Thaw

Deadly Frost

STANDALONE NOVELS

Valley of Secrets

Until Tomorrow

Project Produce

Love Lessons

LAKEHOUSE TREASURES NOVELLAS

James

Amber

Meghan

Brook

MERRY SCROOG-MAS NOVELLAS

Naughty or Nice

Sleigh Bells Ring

Jingle all the Way

TRIPLE R RANCH

Destiny Wears Spurs

Spurred by Fate

<u>PORTRAIT OF A WOMAN</u>

Resilient

Resourceful

Rebellious

Reclusive

About the Author

National Bestselling Author, Agatha, RT Reviewer's Choice & Golden Duck Award Nominee. Kari lives in Central New York with her husband & Samoyeds. She's a lover of wine & travel (especially cruising), obsessed with reality TV, and loves a good book with at least some mystery, romance & humor. She writes cozy mysteries & upper middle grade as Kari Lee Townsend, as well as suspense, romance, romantic comedy & women's fiction as Kari Lee Harmon. To keep up with all of Kari Lee's books, check out her website, join her newsletter, and follow her on Amazon, Goodreads, and Bookbub! All links are on her website.

https://www.karileetownsend.com

A small press bound by the belief that every voice matters.

Sign up for our newsletter to learn about new releases and more.
https://oliver-heberbooks.com/subscribe/

Follow us on social media:

facebook.com/oliverheberbooks
instagram.com/oliverheberbooks
amazon.com/oliverheberbooks
youtube.com/@OliverHeberBooksPublisher